"Forkner's writing shines with wit and wisdom in this beautiful story of love and family that will have you laughing one minute and crying the next. *The Real Thing* is guaranteed to steal your heart."

~Kim Boykin, Author of *A Peach of a Pair*

"An endearing, modern tale about Cowboys, Rodeo Queens, and above all – the simple truth that love is both messy and healing – and worth coming back for again and again. One of my favorite reads of the year!"

~Amy Impellizzeri, Author of *Lemongrass Hope*

"Brimming with genuine honesty, *The Real Thing* takes a heartfelt look at second marriages and blended families. You'll cheer for Forkner's characters, who are poignantly sincere and refreshingly determined, as they confront a series of challenges that test their resolve and redefine the meaning of family. A story filled with warmth and empathy – once you begin reading, you won't want to put it down!"

~Marin Thomas, Author of *The Promise of Forgiveness*

"An emotional and heart-rending story filled with humor, humanity, and hope. Tina Ann Forkner's writing is as hard to resist as an ice cream cone on a hot summer day!"

~Susan Sands, Author of *Again Alabama*

"Brimming with vibrant, lovable characters, Forkner makes magic with her powerful story of a new bride challenged with finding her place in a family saddled with a difficult past. Amanda is everything I look for in a narrator: feisty, irreverent, and all heart—and Forkner's rich descriptions and flawless dialog will have you cheering through your tears, and sure you have rodeo dirt to dust off your feet. Poignant and tender, *The Real Thing* is above all a deeply-felt novel of hope and faith, and the undisputed power of love to unite hearts when life gets messy."

~Erika Marks, Author of *The Guest House*

"With *The Real Thing*, Tina Ann Forkner gives us loving families with troubled histories and an imperfect, adorable heroine who can handle it all. This book teaches profound truths: love, parenthood, and marriage aren't supposed to be perfect, and it's the imperfections in life that can bring us the most joy. An enchanting, heartfelt book."

~Katie Rose Guest Pryal, Author of *Entanglement*

"A heartwarming—and heart wrenching—story of moving on, *The Real Thing* deftly explores stepfamilies and Alzheimer's disease with plenty of intrigue and a healthy helping of romance. Tina Ann Forkner weaves a tale of love, loss, overcoming fears and, best of all, discovering what it really means to be a cowgirl."

~Kristy Woodson Harvey, Author of *Dear Carolina* and *Lies and Other Acts of Love*

"*The Real Thing* rings true to its name. Tina Ann Forkner delivers with her latest beautifully nuanced rodeo-enlivened read. Unexpected twists lassoed me and pulled me deep into the plot. I had to know if Keith and Manda's love would endure the secrets that threatened to sever their bond. Forkner is skilled with creating realistic characters you can't help but root for. *The Real Thing* is a powerful, thought-provoking not-to-be-missed story!"

~Wendy Paine Miller, Author of *The Short & Sincere Life of Ellory James*

The Real Thing

The Real Thing

A Novel

Tina Ann Forkner

TULE
PUBLISHING

The Real Thing
Copyright © 2016 Tina Ann Forkner
Print Edition

The Tule Publishing Group, LLC

ALL RIGHTS RESERVED

No part of this book may be used or reproduced in any manner whatsoever without written permission except in the case of brief quotations embodied in critical articles and reviews.

This is a work of fiction. Names, characters, places, and incidents are products of the author's imagination or are used fictitiously. Any resemblance to actual events, locales, organizations, or persons, living or dead, is entirely coincidental.

ISBN: 978-1-944925-05-5

For Jake, Hannah, and Dawson

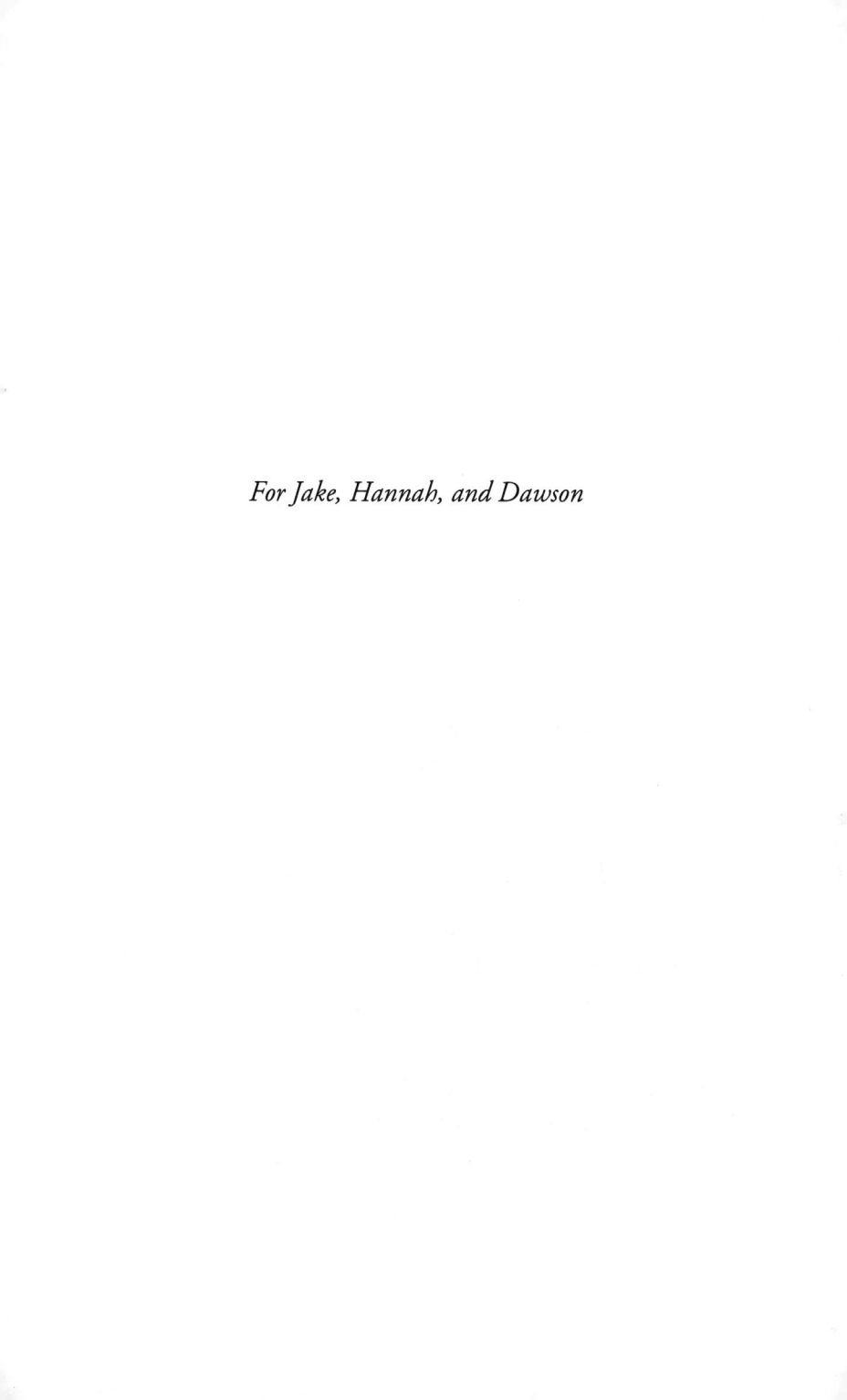

Acknowledgments

First and foremost I want to thank my readers for sharing your kind thoughts and for being so enthusiastic about my stories. I couldn't be an author without you.

Albert Forkner, I love you. I couldn't do this without your support. To our amazing children Jake Forkner, Hannah Linde, and Dawson Forkner: the love we have for each of you is boundless and never limited by the word "step." Thanks to my parents Dennis and Barbara Gray, who in their 50th year of marriage, are modeling for our children that love can still be done the old-fashioned way.

My gratitude goes to the Tall Poppy Writers for welcoming me into your fold. Your friendship, support, and wisdom have become invaluable to me. I am humbled to be among such talented and accomplished writers. Also, thank you to WF Connections. I appreciate the support and creative energy our wonderful group provides.

Special thanks to real cowgirl Georgeann Wearin, cowgirl poet, former rodeo queen, and the wife of a champion saddle bronc rider. Your advice about horses, fashion, and rodeo details proved invaluable. Thank you to Dakota and Joce Forkner for inviting us to their real western wedding where I borrowed a few of the wedding decorations. And thanks to 2011 Miss Southern New Mexico State Fair Rodeo Queen Caitlynn Roy for inspiring Queen Adri, and to Dardi

Roy for her friendship, faith, and teaching me how to ride Lizzie, who became Peyton's horse in the novel.

Many thanks to Troy Rumpf, Dameione Cameron, and Morris House Bistro, an exceptional restaurant serving mouth-watering Southern food located in Cheyenne, Wyoming, for giving me permission to create a sister restaurant in one of my fictional Tennessee towns. You know you are my favorite.

Thank you to author Lisa Samson. It is a great honor that you left your fingerprints on this novel in its early stages. Other book people to thank are Meghan Farrell, Lindsey Stover, Lee Hyat, Danielle Rayner, Jane Porter, Wendy Paine Miller, Amy Sue Nathan, and editor Sinclair Sawhney.

Thank you to my sister Cheri Kaufman who believed in this story from day one when it was a completely different book and for welcoming me into her home many times for more than a decade, enabling me to fall in love with Tennessee. Thanks for believing in me.

Thanks to friends & fam who remind me that I have a life outside of fiction: Dardi Roy, Anne Berry, Rene Hinkle, Jennifer Rife, Laura Whitmore, Dana McIlvane, Jessica Will, Kim Giffin, Denise Garcia, Troy and Laura Gray, Marjie Smith, and the ladies and veracious readers of P.E.O.Chapter AD Cheyenne. Thank you to Lori Townsend and Barbara Gray for giving up their personal time to provide such a close read of the manuscript. I appreciate you both!

I'm sure I have missed someone, so many thanks to all of my friends and family. You bless me. All glory goes to Him.

*"Then we began to ride. My soul
Smooth'd itself out, a long cramp'd scroll
Freshening and fluttering in the wind."*

Robert Browning,
The Last Ride Together

Chapter One

I STOPPED RIGHT in the middle of the wedding march, just as the rich tones of a string quartet arched into the magnolia trees. The cellist, whose black western hat sat lopsided on her head, stretched a note so long and low it beckoned me forward through the sea of expectant faces, but I didn't budge. A smarter bride might have ignored a problem with a drooping slip peeking below her hem and simply thrown herself into the waiting arms of her cowboy groom and considered herself lucky, but not me. Nope, I was as frozen as Alaska despite the warm Tennessee breeze playing with the wedding veil attached to my white cowgirl hat with the pearl band.

Around me, a sea of cowboy hats swiveled in my direction. I hoped nobody would get a good look at my face beneath the sepia lace and tulle, or at the bit of ratty lace hanging from my slip. They would've seen regret, which I'm sure would've been taken the wrong way. Marrying Keith Black, I assure you, was not a regret, but he might regret a bride who wore an intimate garment from a previous marriage at her wedding, if he knew.

Of course, he didn't know about the slip, but I did, and the weight of the slippery silk was beginning to feel like heavy, scratchy wool beneath my lightweight dress. As the music played, I tried to think what to do. My dress was thin and I didn't have a replacement slip handy, of course. Why would I? Plus, I couldn't very well take it off right then and there – could I?

Maybe I could. The cellist drew her bow across the strings, but I stood still, watching the treetops swirl and wave, goodbye it seemed, near the roof of Daddy's big old plantation-style farmhouse. Even the trees thought the slip should go. A sense of nostalgia for my childhood home filled me and for a moment I wondered how I could ever leave this place that had healed me more than once. And to live on a horse ranch where the ne'er-do-well ex-wife's memory is still papered on the walls in an array of lavender and purple patterns.

My groom cleared his throat, jostling me back into the moment. I took a baby step. Maybe the slip didn't matter. Keith had been part of my healing, too, and all I ever wanted since I'd laid eyes on him was to know him, to love him, and, yes, to marry him. I'd known right away, and he had, too, even though I still had doubts about his children accepting me. I know it's natural for them to push me away, but every time I'd tried to remove something of their runaway mother's from the ranch house that was now mine, too, they'd complained. Especially Peyton, my beautiful, brooding, about-to-be stepdaughter.

That's the problem with second marriages. Just like with the reclaimed objects and furniture my sister and I sell down at The Southern Pair, there are always memories attached that don't let go, even when the objects shift to a new person. I've seen it time and time again when a person thinks they're done with a certain bad memory, only to have it creep back up when they look at an object they once thought they had no attachment to – or realize they're getting married for the second time and wearing the slip from their first wedding day. Thank goodness I was at least wearing a dress made from my mother's, and she'd been my daddy's only love.

Memories can easily fool you into thinking things aren't really over, and when the memories are good, like with my dress, it's nice. Nostalgia is the best feeling because it brings to mind a memory of what we used to enjoy, perhaps making bread with our grandmother if it's a pan, or hunting with a father if it's a pair of trophy antlers, or the hug of a mother who left you too soon, like mine did. But, sometimes, I'll spy someone walking among the shelves of The Southern Pair and they'll spot something, maybe an old doll or coffee cup, pick it up, and their face crumples a little from the pain of finding it. Sometimes, I wonder about the tears that well in their eyes. I never ask about the memories dancing, or tramping, through their minds, although sometimes people tell me.

I didn't have to ask Keith, my groom, why he always frowned when he walked along the papered walls of his ranch house and why he avoided looking inside the gilded frames that hung heavy on either side, or why, conversely, those same halls made Peyton, my soon-to-be stepdaughter, smile. Of course, Keith couldn't take down the pictures even if he wanted to, since Peyton insisted they stay up. And, trust me, he tried. It turned out badly. With a frustrated apology, he had told me the pictures of his ex-wife had to stay. And just like that, the thought of those pictures made me step backward instead of toward Keith. He cast me a worried look and even the musicians held their bravado a few beats longer, probably giving me time to find my brain. Too bad it didn't work.

Call me crazy, but I couldn't do it, not yet. I had to get rid of that slip and the clinging memory of my first wedding and subsequent failed marriage. Keith deserved my whole heart. He might not have known it, but a piece of my broken heart was attached to that darn slip.

So, being the kind of woman who knows what happens when sad memories become attached to an object, I did what I had to do. I smiled an apology at my worried groom who stood handsome in his western tuxedo beside the preacher. He knew me already, so what I did next shocked everyone, except him. I blamed it on the past, and knew he would, too, but he would think it was because of his.

Don't we all blame our pasts?

The past gets a bad rap, but if we can think more about the good times, they make us better. I blinked away an unfortunate memory of my ex-husband standing beside a different preacher at a different wedding several years earlier. Sadly, at the moment, the clingy slip was out of place on a day that should be all about good times. So you see, it wasn't just Keith's past slinking into our wedding day. It was mine, too.

One thing I've learned from years of buying and reselling items at The Southern Pair, or even finding a new happier nail color for a broken-hearted woman, no matter how much we want to get rid of our ex-lovers, ex-troubles, and ex-hurts, they find ways to creep back into our lives. How could I wear that cursed slip in our moment of joy? I looked up at the trees, wishing I could float up into their branches to hide like I had when I was a girl.

The black leather-vested violinists intoned a fiddler's melody that once again forced me back into the moment. It teased the toes of my ivory stitched cowgirl boots, ruffling the lacy garter I'd slipped over one ankle, and I swayed forward a step and back again. Keith's smile faltered.

Oh, Lordy, help me.

It was all up to the viola now. It had one more chance, but its sweet accompaniment failed. Unable to look at my groom, I let go of Daddy's arm, gently extracting myself even as he drew me closer to his side.

"Mandy?"

"Daddy, I—" I couldn't even whisper the words.

I tried avoiding his eyes, but their wrinkle-framed worry snagged on my conscience. Turning away, I locked eyes with my groom.

Oh, heavens to Betsy. How did I ever get lucky enough to have a man who looked like a rodeo cowboy who'd just strutted out of a rodeo arena? And he more than looked the part—that's exactly what he was. Sounds like a good movie doesn't it? But it's true. I was about to marry a famous bronco rider, the only man I'd ever met who could handle me, and well, let's just say a personality that some people call colorful. Not that I could help it one bit.

Keith wrinkled his brows as I turned in my wedding march, gave me a warning look. By then, he was already used to my flare for the dramatic, but I am who I am. When I sense a problem, I need to fix it right away, and I had to fix something before this wedding could go on. I think that's why I opened The Southern Pair with my sister. Plenty of problems could be fixed immediately, even if only temporarily, with the selling or the purchasing of a discarded object.

"Manda," Keith whispered, his voice inviting, but his eyes somewhat aggravated.

After that, I didn't dare look at my twin sister, Marta, who'd be worried about the little frozen bride and groom still holding hands back in the barn. Only a half hour ago, she'd had the bakers set the sculpture on top of our western wedding cake right in the center of a white and burlap draped table. Rows of tables bedecked with matching cloths and turquoise-dyed Mason jars lined the barn, along with burlap napkin rings and floating candles. Marta had warned the preacher that the wedding must end at a certain time, or else the sculpture would be dripping down the sides of the cake.

The preacher glanced at me, then sent a frightened look toward Marta.

I'll just explain it to them later.

I smiled an apology, handed my bouquet to a surprised guest with a mumbled excuse even I couldn't understand, and fled in the midst of the processional. A warm breeze picked up, as if to spur me on my way. I headed toward the orchard and couldn't disappear fast enough through the rows of leafy fruit trees that showered their carmine-colored petals all over my lacy veil. I just knew they were cheering my quick retreat, and, in response, I yanked the skirt of my dress all the way up to my hips and ran full-on, high-heeled cowgirl boots and all. I wondered if this was what it was like to be one of the Quarter horses Keith raised at his ranch. Some days I sat on the back deck and watched them gallop across the pasture, their flanks shining, sinewy muscles flexing, their heads reaching for that invisible point ahead. I didn't like riding them, though. I was an orchard farmer's daughter, not a horsewoman. I'd always been afraid of horses.

Heaven only knows what my bronco-riding fiancé saw in

me. He liked to tease that it was because I was his pretty, young thing, my being six years younger than his thirty-seven, and I teased that I liked older men, but sometimes I felt like I was the one who'd snagged the bigger prize, hardly believing such a great-looking, talented, and smart man would want to marry me. And did I mention famous? Not that it mattered when it came to my falling in love with him, but he did just happen to be a *famous* saddle-bronc riding cowboy.

Keith Black probably could've married any horse-loving woman he wanted after his ex-wife ran off without so much as a good-bye, but, instead, he picked up his broken heart and chose me, a farmer's daughter who likes fancy things and is afraid of horses. Keith says I look pretty cute in a cowgirl hat and my favorite fringe suede vest, but despite a closet full of denim that he says hugs me in all the right places, I don't have a cowgirl bone in this body. Now, Keith, on the other hand, is the real thing, trophy belt buckle and all, and there I was, leaving him standing back at the altar with a bunch of eligible cowgirls in the audience while I ran away like a filly.

I couldn't help but ask myself if I was doing the right thing. While it's true, I could've given all those former rodeo queens in the crowd a lesson in hairspray and makeup, I didn't know the first thing about being a rodeo cowboy's wife. Even the way all those capable cow people sitting on hay bales trying so hard to make me feel like I belonged with them made me doubt myself. They had no idea who I really was inside, or what I was running from when Keith found me. What I was still running from, I reminded myself, pumping my legs faster.

Watery silk rode up my thighs as I stretched my legs into a sprint, but no matter how fast I ran, I couldn't shed the slithering at my knees. I ran faster, farther away from the wedding party, yanked off my hat-veil, and, for a moment, I dismissed the wedding altogether. I was a sun-kissed, fourteen-year-old girl, slipping through the orchard so fast that Marta couldn't keep up. I have always been fast. Even now, as I sped further away from the wedding, blossoms blurred past in pink streaks on either side. I didn't even bother to tuck in the strawberry-blonde curls that had slipped out of their pins. Marta would fix them when I got back, and I did plan to go back. They all realized that, right?

Hopefully, my groom, who I assumed still stood with that puzzled, but not truly surprised expression on his tanned, cowboy face, framed by a black Stetson atop that thick, peppery blond hair would wait as long as it took, but I couldn't be sure of a lot of things anymore. Nobody could. This fact occurred to me as I rounded the end of the row, stopped abruptly, and leaned with my hands on my knees. My chest heaved. I have to admit, it'd been a long time since I ran like that. In fact, it would have been easy for Marta to catch me if she'd wanted to follow, and considering that she might have, I peeked around the end of the row.

No Marta. They'd sent Peyton after me instead. She was

headed my way, the purple-jeweled cell phone she would never part with pressed so close to her face, I worried she might trip. That phone never ceased to annoy me. It had an old voicemail from her mother that Peyton played every night. Peyton had only been a little girl when she received that voicemail, but she checked that old phone several times a day, just in case her mother called—a hope she liked to cling to, but that was about as likely to happen as me getting on a horse. At least I hoped so. It gave me chills just to look at that phone, but getting her to accept a new one, or to put it away on my wedding day, was obviously too much to ask.

Ignoring the anger, or was it jealousy, the phone provoked in me, I reached under the hem of my dress and caught the edge of lace clinging to my skin. I was a grown woman and I wasn't going to give a woman who'd run off and abandoned her family another moment of thought on my wedding day.

"Oh, heavens to Betsy," I called to Peyton. "You should have stayed back with your dad!"

My soon-to-be stepdaughter paused to stuff the phone inside her pretty turquoise boots and then dragged the toes, scraping them through the orchard toward me and I caught my breath. Not because I was mad about the boots, but because that child had no idea how gorgeous she was with her short, breezy peach-colored sun dress against her olive complexion. 'Course, if I told her, she just would've argued in that fourteen-year-old girl way and there was certainly no time for that. The closer she got, the more I could make out the pout on her pretty mouth. Was the flush in her cheeks from the unusually warm, spring day or from being singled out in front of everyone at the wedding to go find her stepmother? I'd bet on the latter for sure.

And who thought that would be a good idea?

My dad. It had to be Daddy.

I wished I could meet her halfway and place my arm about her shoulders, but she wouldn't have liked that. Instead, I focused on working my dress up over my hips while I waited for her to catch up. When she came around the corner, she gaped as if I'd just chomped into a rotten apple I picked up off the ground and offered her a wormy bite. She even gagged a little bit for effect. I was obviously the most appalling person on her planet that day.

"*What* are you doing?"

I just ignored the snotty tone that'd been saturating her speech for the past few months. It was my wedding day. Nothing, except for that stupid slip, could steal my joy. Besides, she had a reason.

"I just can't bear to wear this old, ratty slip," I said, shimmying right out of the flimsy yellowing piece of silk I'd put on that morning without even considering its history.

"People actually wear those?" she asked. "I thought they were for old ladies."

I chose to ignore that comment and how it pointed out that I wasn't a spring chick anymore. But I was no old lady either!

"I'll be rid of it in a second."

"What on earth are you thinking?" she asked. "Dad's waiting for you." She jabbed her palms out for affect, shook her head back and forth, and abruptly crossed her silver bracelet adorned arms across her chest. What a little drama queen. All I can say is that she'd be fantastic in the local theater if she weren't so shy. But the kid had a point.

What in the world *am* I thinking? What would Keith think of me? I'm over thirty. I shouldn't be running away from my own wedding. I should be over this. A slip was just a piece of flimsy fabric.

Only it wasn't. I would explain it to Keith later.

I'm not the least bit superstitious –well, okay, just a bit, but even I know something like a little slip can't bring a person bad luck. It was more the sadness attached to it that bothered me. Not to mention, it was on the tattered side. I couldn't believe I'd let it get that way.

That very morning, I'd sat at the breakfast table in the same old slip and camisole I'd always worn with dresses without even thinking about it. And when Marta slipped the antique lace and silk shift we'd made from our late momma's wedding dress over my head, she'd not even noticed the slip and only told me how beautiful the dress was. And it was. I loved how it stopped below the knee, but was still short enough to set off the rhinestone-studded boots Keith's mother had given me.

"You look like the bride of a bronco rider, sis." Marta's hot pink lipstick grin made me believe it, too, at least for a few minutes. They'd gone to so much trouble making my wedding day to Keith different than the first one, and boy was it different with all that western wear. It wasn't until later, walking through the sea of cowboys and cowgirls toward Keith, who looked dapper in his black Stetson and western cut tuxedo, that I remembered my slip's origins.

"Holy cow," I muttered, the slip's thin fabric suddenly heavy, scratchy at first, and then catching like plastic wrap around my hips.

I can't wear this.

How could Marta not have noticed? How could *I* have even put it on? Habit, I guessed, but I didn't want it on my body now—not minutes before marrying Keith.

I'd had that dumb slip forever, long before Keith was in my life. I distinctly recalled receiving it as a gift at my first wedding shower, a drab event with pink and green mints and tart red punch. That slip had stretched with me through all of my failed pregnancies, remarkably snapping back to hang on my hips during the empty months that followed, and later still to the private funeral of my daughter, Sarah, who survived for a few minutes as if God had breathed into her tiny lungs and then sucked her life right back up to heaven. But it wasn't only those memories that bothered me about the slip. I'd also worn it when I married Sarah's dad, the same man who divorced me for someone skinnier, more beautiful, and more fertile. And did I mention skinnier?

I held the slip out between my finger and thumb, studying it as if it were a piece of somebody else's random clothing plucked off the ground. In a way, it was. I wasn't that girl anymore. Heck no, I hoped I wasn't that girl anymore. I doubted Keith would have liked that girl either, and I doubted he'd like this slip on my body.

"So, I take it you're not wearing that? You might have thought about that this morning." Peyton raised her pretty eyebrows and I couldn't keep from smiling. She was suddenly mothering *me*?

"No. I am not wearing this old thing. No way, no how, young lady."

"But, I thought you liked *vintage* things." She narrowed her gaze. "You said they have good feelings attached to them."

"Okay," I said. "I don't know what that has to do with the price of tea in China or with my wedding day."

She huffed and looked at me like I was the only one being difficult. "You're always getting rid of my mother's stuff and replacing it with all your *vintage* stuff. Is that her slip, too? Where'd you get it?"

I flinched, careful not to lose my omelet on her pretty cowgirl boots as I imagined wearing her deadbeat mother's slip. *Gross.*

I was about to say something about her attitude when I recalled a particularly intense argument that resulted from my trying to remove a certain lavender velveteen couch of her mother's from the ranch house. It had made no difference to Peyton that her mother abandoned her along with the couch, or that the sofa was the ugliest thing this side of the Mississippi. She'd kicked the shabby chic piece I'd replaced it with and told me how much she hated all of my *old junk*. Never mind how all that discarded *junk* was made new by my own hand, so that it could bring happy memories to new owners who don't mind paying a pretty penny at The Southern Pair. Still, understanding how an object can have so much meaning to a person, particularly a little girl who has lost her momma, I promptly removed the couch from my project room and put it in Peyton's already crowded bedroom.

"Of course this is not your mother's slip, Peyton. And I do love old things, but this slip—it doesn't have any good feelings attached to it. Trust me." I couldn't bring myself to explain why.

She rolled her eyes to the tops of the trees, looking every bit like a brat, but I didn't have the heart to fight with her. Granted, Peyton was a bit spoiled by her father. But let's be honest. Truly spoiled little girls have mothers who dote on their daughters and who don't run off and leave them to care for their little brothers and cry themselves to sleep at night. It's as if Violet Black – oh! I dislike sharing a last name with her – just vanished, and left Keith to pick up the pieces of Peyton's heart. Who does that?

At first, everyone had thought Violet was a missing person, but when the divorce papers came from the lawyer, her family and friends were devastated in another way. She'd rejected them all, choosing anonymity, baffling those who'd believed her to be a loving mother and wife. Only heaven knew why she really ran away and gave Keith everything, including full custody of the children. Sometimes I wondered…did she take anything at all? A photo of the kids? Some trinket to remember them by?

My heart broke a little more for Peyton as she took a great breath and let me have it.

"I figured it was just one more thing of my mother's that you needed to toss," she said, jabbing her finger at the slip.

I felt like she was jabbing me, but it was okay. The slip was gone and I was me again.

"Dad already told me we have to get rid of mom's stuff so you can feel at home." She stared me down and I noted tears gathering in her eyes. "But it's our house."

Whoa. I placed my hand gently on her arm and she shrugged it away. Peyton was about to have a meltdown. Thank goodness she didn't know I'd heard that conversation between her and her dad about my getting rid of their old stuff. I'll never forget how hurt I was when I rounded the corner just as Peyton was raising her voice to a very frustrated Keith. His glance had passed through the kitchen when I peeked in from the hallway and our eyes locked. Understanding the warning in them, I'd backed away, but not so far that I couldn't hear the rest of the conversation.

"You can't get rid of Mommy's stuff!" Peyton cried. "It's special!"

I remember thinking Peyton didn't understand that not everything in the house was associated with good feelings, at least not for Keith, and not for me.

Peyton was breathing like she was hyperventilating, something I noticed she did when trying to get her way with her dad, and when she got her way, she became perfectly normal again. If I'd ever tried that with Daddy, well, I never would have. Kids know what they can get away with.

"Yes, we can," Keith said, despite her gulping inhalations. "Like these dishes." He'd walked to the cabinet and removed a plate of her mother's sacred china ringed in a wide circle of purple. "Maybe Manda would like to have her own plates, and not your mother's." His voice, tinged with that cowboy drawl, had deepened to a warning tone.

I'd cringed, my frustration with Violet's old things notwithstanding. Keith was saying the absolute worst thing, even though it had been true that I was tired of having Violet's stuff everywhere in my new house. Everywhere! I *was* tired of her rodeo queen crowns, photos of her atop thoroughbred horses, and her trademark purple and violet decorations all over the house. I hated walking past trophy cases and feeling pops of anger that rang in my ears, and every time I picked up a lilac colored coffee cup, I swear the coffee tasted bitter. But now, seeing the pain on Peyton's face, I regretted my complaining. All of Violet's things reminded Peyton of her mother, and she was afraid of forgetting.

I'd decided I could probably keep her mother's tacky china if it made the kids happy, but before I could intervene, Peyton had rushed forward. She wrenched the plate from his hands, and in her clumsiness knocked it to the floor. It clattered and rolled at first, looking like it might simply rattle safely to a stop. I sucked in a breath and held it, pleading for it not to break, but a dull thud and a crack splitting the air as the plate broke in two was the only answer to my fervent prayer for Peyton's mother's plate.

I slowly exhaled, allowing muted images of ultrasound photos I kept hidden in an old family Bible, a flash of blue pen scraping my name across the bottom of divorce papers, a vision of Daddy on his knees in the hospital chapel when Momma was dying whispered through my mind, all reminders that maybe God likes to break things more than put them together. I added the image of Peyton's crumpling face as she lunged for the broken plate.

A BREEZE SWEPT through the orchard and lifted the hems of our wedding day dresses. Peyton looked like she might laugh as she pressed her skirt back down. Warming at the sudden change in her disposition, I wanted to reach out to her, brush her hair from her cheek and adjust her cowgirl hat, but my dad strode toward us. Wise-looking and slightly wrinkled in his bolo tie and western hat, he let Peyton clasp his arm.

"Grandpa Marshall!"

Cue the sweet, old man come to rescue the princess from the evil stepmother.

"What's going on?"

Peyton held her palms out in a grand gesture. "Manda's trying to get rid of her slip."

He eyed the slip, me, and Peyton. I was ready to rush into his arms myself, tell him what a big mistake I might be making, how the kids were never going to accept me as a stepmom, and how I was never going to fit into Keith's adventurous rodeo life. I couldn't do that, of course, not in front of Peyton. But he knew. He held up a finger with a slow wink while he placed an arm around Peyton and ushered her a few paces away.

I leaned over to dust off my boots while he whispered something in her ear. She beamed, then saluted as if he were the chief who just bestowed some great honor on her before she ran back to the wedding party. Only then did he take my hand.

"She loves you, Daddy."

"She loves you, too."

I bugged my eyes at him, doubting the truth in his words.

"Just like you love her," he said, placing his arm around me.

"That much is the truth," I said. "But I'm pretty sure Peyton won't ever believe it. She thinks I'm going to be the wicked stepmother from H-E-double hockey sticks." Daddy looked like he was going to disagree with me, but a squawking bird drew our eyes.

"Dratted crows," he said. The oily-looking black birds were always a problem.

"What did you say to get that smile from Peyton?"

Dad put his hand on my shoulder. "That's between me and Peyton."

"Fine." I swiped at a stupid tear.

"Now, Amanda," he said, using my full name the way he had when I was a teenager looking for advice – or getting grounded which was often the case, and justified, too. "It's not that she doesn't want you. She just doesn't want to forget her mom."

My chest ached. I couldn't help it. Why did that woman have to keep coming up in the middle of my wedding day?

"Now that's just the truth, Manda. We can't get around her missing her momma on a day like this. Her life is about to change again."

And this day was proof that her dad was never going to be with her mom again. Not that it could've ever happened anyway, since nobody knew where in Tennessee, or anywhere else, that no good woman was.

I waved my hands to keep my eyelashes from dripping. "Do you think she'll ever get over her mom and accept that

I'm in her life now?"

"Depends," he said, giving me a knowing look. "Do kids ever get over losing their momma?"

"Never," I said, almost erupting into tears, but there was no way I was going to ruin all that mascara. I sniffled. "So, at least tell me what you said to make her smile like that."

"I promised her a date with grandpa while you and Keith are on your honeymoon, just me, her, and Nashville. I'm sure Marta can keep Stevie."

"Daddy." I squeezed his hand. "I wish you wouldn't drive that far by yourself."

"Now, don't even start that. I changed your diaper, girl. I can drive forty-five minutes to Nashville. And I can walk my girl down the aisle. Are you ready? Your soon-to-be husband is waiting for you."

Emotion rose up, pressing against the back of my nose. The burning started, and I had to breathe deep to stop the tears. He'd done more than change our diapers. He didn't even blink when one of the church ladies offered to take me and Marta to buy our first bras. He would take us himself, he told her. And when we started our periods, he drove to the store and bought every brand of pad he could find since he wasn't sure what exactly we needed. He was there when pimpled boys picked us up for dates, making us stay seated on the couch until the boys got out of their honking trucks and knocked on the door. He made us change out of our denim miniskirts and into more appropriate clothing. He raised us all by himself, never shirking from things that moms usually took care of for daughters, and now he stood holding out his wrinkled hand to take my old yellow slip from me.

I handed it over. "I can't wear it."

He was confused, but smiled reassuringly. He'd done that a lot, too, when we were teenagers.

"This will sound ridiculous, but I was standing there, ready to get married and all of a sudden I realized: the slip!—it's the same one I wore at my first wedding." I swiped at a tear, and there went my mascara. Marta would have her hands full touching up the muddy trails I was sure traced my cheeks. Isn't there some saying that cowgirls don't cry? Well, like I said, I'm not one.

"It would be like wearing a hand-me-down from my last wedding, Daddy. Keith doesn't deserve that, and it's probably even bad luck."

He nodded, and my heart expanded to fill the far reaches of my chest. I loved this about him. I don't know if he really understood all of the emotional dramas Marta and I went through, but he always tried.

"You're right not to wear it." He tossed it into the closest apple tree where it snagged on a branch. I laughed, despite my tears, as he reached out to smooth a curl behind my ear. "This wedding, it's a whole new first. This is a new day." I hugged him for his goodness. If only everyone could see the world the way Daddy does.

I spotted Marta's leopard print cowgirl hat before I saw Marta herself behind Peyton, wobbling like a toddler to keep her matching high-heeled cowgirl boots from sinking into the loamy earth. She was a fancy farm girl if ever there was one. For about two seconds I wished I was wearing the leopard hat and boots, and I honestly preferred her shorter dress over mine, but dad had sworn he wouldn't be walking me down the aisle if I insisted on showing off more leg than was decent for a bride in front of the church ladies.

"Aunt Marta here to save the day," Peyton proclaimed, as if all would have been lost had Marta not arrived at just that moment.

And maybe it would have been, since I must have looked like a bird had nested in my hair after running a sprint through the orchard in my wedding outfit, not to mention that I really hoped she had some deodorant and perfume since I was starting to glow, and it wasn't from bridal happiness, either.

"What is it, cupcake?"

"My makeup."

"And your hair," she said, and I knew it was a travesty. Thank goodness Marta knew just how to salvage it, since she had the exact same hair. Our strawberry-blonde manes were not the only interchangeable thing about us, much to the exasperation of our teachers and friends when we were growing up, not to mention Daddy.

In fact, we'd switched places so many times that, at that

very moment, I couldn't help but notice how fresh Marta looked compared to me after my sprint through the orchard. My wedding pictures could turn out so much better!

"You are a bad, bad girl," she exclaimed when I asked if she wanted to trade places right now. "You'd better be joking."

"Well, of course I am, mostly. Nobody's kissing Keith, except me today, but you have to admit it's tempting. You look a ton better than I do. Look at me. All sweaty."

"You do look awful, but let's not resort to drastic measures. I happen to be an expert when it comes to you." Marta reached into her bottomless gold sequined purse and began touching up my face, spraying things on my hair to make the frizz go away, and handing me her vanilla-scented deodorant before I could even blink.

"Thank heavens you're here, sissy." There were many things I loved about having a twin, and one of them was that she knew exactly how to make me look good.

I let Daddy and Peyton tell Marta about the slip.

"Tell me you didn't really do that!" Marta grimaced. "Oh, sissy. You're so funny. But you're right. You can't wear that old thing." A beauty pick fluffed up a curl, and I held back a sneeze as a brush swept powder across my cheeks.

"I guess it's silly, but I'm glad to be rid of that slip just the same."

"It was a sad slip," Marta sympathized. Her four-inch hoop earrings, dangling back and forth, seemed to giggle along with her laughter. Peyton gazed at Marta like she was the queen of England, and I didn't blame her. I idolized Marta, too. She was a breath of spring, of sparkling daring. Just having Marta there making me over made things right.

"I wish we hadn't done all this cowgirl stuff for the wedding," I complained.

"You told me you loved it," she said.

"I do," I admitted.

"And you're about to marry a famous cowboy at that. It's perfect."

"But don't you think I look kind of fake?" The silver Concho bracelets jingled around my wrists.

"Since when have you ever worried about fake?"

I shrugged. "I guess never."

"Now let me check your nails. You haven't popped one off, have you?" She'd done them herself, complete with jeweled flowers in the center of each pretty nail.

"But all those people sitting on his side," I said. "They're the real thing. Did you see some of the outfits those rodeo queens have on?"

"Former queens, most of them." Marta pointed out.

"They aren't all queens," Peyton assured. "Some of them are barrel racers, and a bunch of them are just normal ladies who can't even ride a horse."

"Unlike you," I said, reaching for her hand. "You're a real cowgirl, Peyton. I showed your barrel racing trophies to Grandpa Marshall."

She blushed. Once, when I suggested she should enter the rodeo queen pageant, she was mortified. Not all horse-women—so cute how she said that—want to be rodeo queens, she told me. I have to admit I was disappointed. She would make a darn cute rodeo queen.

"Manda, you have to hurry. My dad is going to think you jilted him at the altar."

Marta giggled as she took the veiled hat from me. I watched the worry temporarily fall from Peyton's face as she watched Marta carefully adjust the hat over my curly hair. Dad helped pull the lace and tulle over my face and I turned to smile at Peyton through the gauzy veil. She looked away like I had caught her eavesdropping. And I guess I had.

AFTER ZIPPING HER purse, Marta stepped back to admire her handiwork. Even Peyton stepped close to Marta and studied me.

They all proclaimed my beauty, but it was Peyton's voice that whispered through the branches.

"You look nice."

My heart melted like ice cream on a hot sidewalk, especially knowing how hard it must have been to dole out a compliment to her soon-to-be-stepmom. Maybe, if I worked hard enough, I could make things new for her, for Stevie, and for Keith. I couldn't replace their mother, but I could be the best stepmother ever. At least I could try!

The other worries I faced were ridiculous, and I chalked

them up to being a nervous bride. A pesky worry that Keith was going to try and make me ride a horse, concern that the kids were going to hate me, even the improbable chance that Keith, who in his single years was rumored to have had a string of cowgirls on his arm, had secretly done something to make his ex-wife run off. What if she wasn't the deplorable person I thought she was? Maybe whatever it was that made her leave would make me want to run away, too. I mean, look at me already. Running away on my wedding day.

Oh no! I hope Keith doesn't give up on me and ditch the wedding. I'd better hurry.

"Peyton Black. You are a doll." I smiled at her. "We need to get back to your dad now, but first, I want you to wear something for me."

I reached up and removed my hat, and then hers.

"Let's trade," I said, placing her hat on my head. I couldn't put myself in her boots, but I could wear her hat today and try to show her how much I loved her dad, loved little Stevie, and loved her.

"Manda." Marta's voice dropped. "Are you sure you don't want to wear that?"

Peyton blinked through the lace as I settled the veiled hat on top of her pretty head. Tugging gently at the ends to make sure it rested prettily over her small shoulders, I said, "If this wedding is a new first for me, then it should be for Peyton, too."

I couldn't make her love me right away, but I could do

that one nice thing for her in that one moment.

"I look silly," Peyton said. "I don't think it would be allowed anyway."

"It's my wedding. I like to be different. If you want to wear it, you can."

"It *is* like you to do everything different than everyone else," she said.

I smiled. "You noticed that?"

"Everyone has," she said seriously, as if breaking a piece of news to me that I didn't already know.

"Then I might as well not have a veil," I said.

"Are you sure?"

"Absolutely. Besides, it looks so much prettier on you," I told her, wondering if it could ever be possible that she would want to be my daughter.

If only we knew why her mother left, Peyton could move on. And that was the final worry I had about marrying Keith—that his ex-wife might show up out of the blue, or that she wouldn't, and then Peyton would always be tortured by her mother's abandonment. And of all people, I knew more about that than Peyton realized.

Someday, I'll tell her all about it.

"Thanks." Peyton focused on the toes of her boots and I marveled at the girl's beauty, her dark hair muted by the lace and tulle, her tan shoulders peeking out beneath, and looking more like her rodeo-queen mother than ever in that moment. But Keith gave her his eyes.

I bent slightly to gaze into those blue eyes, not at all sure she would let herself hear anything I'd say, and whispered. "I'm not trying to replace your momma, sweetie. I just want us to be friends." I held my breath, wondering if I'd pressed too deep into her heart.

She still stared at her boots, but I was close enough to see the slip of moisture trail down her cheek, even through the hat's short veil. Without thinking, I pulled her into an embrace, but I'd gone too far. She gently wriggled away and trudged back toward the wedding party, where her bronco-loving father waited for both of us. At least she'd kept the hat. I wondered again how a mother could leave her children behind.

I wanted to love all the sadness out of my stepchildren, but I had a feeling it would take a while. And then there was that silly worry that Peyton might get her wish and her mother would come back into their lives. What then? She'd vanished without a trace—the divorce papers delivered later the only evidence she was alive and well somewhere.

"Let's go," Marta said. "Your cowboy awaits."

Daddy crooked his arm.

"You sure he's still waiting?" I asked, laughing when I said it. If there's one thing I've learned about cowboys, it's that they aren't good at standing around.

"If he's not, then Daddy and I'll find him and knock him into next week." Marta declared.

For Keith's sake, I headed back up through the orchard

toward the stand of oak trees, because even a cowboy like Keith was no match against Daddy and Marta. When I saw him still there waiting for me, I clutched the hem of my dress, sans slip, and ran to him.

Chapter Two

THE WEDDING WENT off without a hitch, all except for the part where I ran away. But the important thing is, I went back, married my cowboy, and spent the next two weeks rocking my bikini for him in Hawaii. At least he said I did that and more, so I'm going with it. The fact that I got Keith to stay away from his horses for that long had to be a miracle I don't even want to question, because as soon as we got back to Tennessee, he was rocking his cowboy hat on the road again.

I guess I should've just been happy to have him to myself for all that time, but secretly, I wanted more. While I understood the rodeo way of life, it didn't make me miss him less. Truth be told, I looked forward to him retiring from the rodeo the way so many men his age already had. I heard that Pro Rodeo Hall of Famer Billy Etbauer was almost forty-two when he won his last championship, but for the most part, saddle bronc riding is a younger man's sport. Late thirties isn't old, I obviously didn't think so, but in bronco riding years, Keith was getting close.

"I'm so glad you're home," Marta said, pulling a rainbow-colored smock from a closet where a dozen others with equally cheery colors and prints all hung neatly spaced. Back when we first started doing nails at The Southern Pair, we'd sewn the smocks with the prettiest, loudest fabrics we could find because we wanted our customers to feel happy. When I married Keith, I even sewed a few new ones with fringe on them, just to celebrate my new cowgirl side. We wear them all the time now, even when we're helping customers shop.

"Peyton and I played makeup when you were in Hawaii," Marta said, leaning over to pump pomegranate-fragranced soap into her palm.

"I wondered where she got that tube of mascara," I said.

"And the silver eye shadow," she added. "Plus the mani-pedi."

Maybe I underestimated Peyton. She might have a sparkly side somewhere under those brooding teenager eyes after all.

"This place does have a way of bringing out the best in a girl."

"You know it."

The Southern Pair was only ever empty when we flipped the closed sign on the door. From the shiny black and white tiled floors to the hot pink counter tops and turquoise barstools, it was one of the jewels of Castle Orchard, even if I do say so myself. We specialized in upscale vintage clothing, painted furniture, and artsy creations from repurposed objects for locals, as well as tourists looking to take a piece of the South home with them. In the corner, we also had a nail station. In addition to everything else we were, we were nail technicians, because even farm girls like fancy nails from time to time. Or, all the time if you're me and Marta.

Today, Marta studied my nails. "Hmm. I think red and white polka-dots. They'll look fantastic with your white jeans. All sunshine and luscious cool at the same time."

"Okay, but no false ones today. Let's be real."

"You know that's going to take longer," she said. "Your nails are a mess."

"It always does," I replied. "And I don't just mean the nails."

Marta laughed. Large gold hoops bobbled around her face while rhinestone-studded rings tugged at my own ear lobes, casting little jeweled reflections across the pink countertops. I tried to put disappointment about Keith's travels aside and let Marta work her magic. I needed sister time anyway. I'd missed her and the shop as much as Keith missed the rodeo, and my nails *were* a mess.

"I love that new top," Marta said.

We don't dress identical anymore, at least not on purpose. Today Marta wore a canary yellow t-shirt and me a snug, red top with a bedazzled Plumeria blossom across the front. Keith gave it to me on our honeymoon and wearing it made me wish he weren't gone to the rodeo.

"Why didn't you get me one?"

"Because my husband bought it for me," I said.

"I was talking about the husband."

Our laughter exploded into the room, drowning out the country music playing in the background.

"I went on another online date while you were gone." Marta looked like she'd just bit into a sour grape.

"Oh, no." I moaned. "You didn't."

"I did."

"I hope it was better than the last one."

"Nope," she said. "This one was worse."

I could tell by the tone in her voice that she was disappointed. One of the few downsides to small town life is that it's hard to meet a man.

"I'm sorry," I said. "Dating stinks."

"It does. And so did you going off to Hawaii." Marta moved her arms and hips in a mock Hawaiian dance. "Without me!"

"It *was* dreamy," I said. "But I'm glad you were the one watching the kids while we were gone. It made it easier for Keith to relax." The kids usually stayed with Keith's parents, but lately his parents were on a bit of a stubborn streak.

After Keith proposed to me, they'd started taking extended vacations all over the place. I got the feeling Keith had overused them as babysitters since his ex had disappeared. Marta, on the other hand, craved time with anyone's children since she didn't know if she'd ever get married and have her own. She already wore the label of aunt as if it came from her favorite designer.

"My biological clock is ticking like this," she said stamping her foot in a good imitation of Mona Lisa in *My Cousin Vinny*. "And the way this case is going—"

I laughed and joined her for the last line, "I ain't never getting married!"

She gave my nails a sad look. Two had popped off when I'd tried surfing.

"Oh, Sissy," I said. "You are too getting married. Your cowboy just hasn't ridden this way yet."

"Well, he'd better hurry," she said. "I want kids. I wish you could've seen our Peyton's face when she saw the newspaper article about the wedding. I think she would've cleaned this place all afternoon after the ladies made all that hoopla about her."

I wondered if, like me, Peyton hated cleaning up cotton balls and nail clippings, but loved the gossip.

Marta pointed to where she'd taped a newspaper clipping on the wall. She recited by heart. "It was a sweet twist to see the pretty flower girl wear the veil instead of the bride."

"How sweet!"

"You know I had to read that to the customers, don't you? They bragged on her till she was pink as these counter tops."

"Did she get embarrassed?" Even a simple comment from me about anything in front of her friends could splotch her cheeks pink. The time I tried to wipe a smudge on her chin? I didn't even want to think about it.

"She didn't look up the whole time," Marta said. "But I'll tell you what, she couldn't keep that smile from her face either. I think that veil was magical."

"Me, too," I said, remembering how the gauzy fabric hanging from the pearled hat had worked like a curtain hanging between her and the wedding. It was a feel happy hat and veil. Maybe it'd been just what she needed.

Marta smiled. "She told me she felt like a princess."

"A cowgirl princess," I said with a smile. "It's such a shame she doesn't want to be a rodeo queen. That's one way in which I wouldn't mind her being like her mother. Can you imagine the outfits we could dress her in?"

"It's a crying shame," Marta agreed. "So, anyway, let's don't talk about the ex-wife when I'm trying to talk about your wedding. I was saying, while those ladies prattled on about how beautiful Peyton was at the wedding, Esther just had to bring up that slip."

"The slip?"

"The slip!"

"Just great." I could only imagine the conversation. Peyton would have been mortified to have everyone talking about *that*.

"You know what Peyton said?"

"There's no telling." I was dying to know.

But before Marta could answer, Peyton walked into the shop, flushed and out of breath. She pulled little Stevie by the hand and carried that maddening purple phone in her other. I pulled my eyes away from the purple glare, and glanced at the clock. I was still on Hawaii time and didn't realize school was already out for the day.

Peyton narrowed her eyes at me. Had she overheard us talking about her? And the day had started out so well!

I greeted them both with a smile, hoping for the best. Much to my shock and delight, Peyton smiled, whatever had been bothering her suddenly gone.

Stevie exclaimed, "Sissy picked me up from school and we walked all the way here!"

In Castle Orchard, all the way here was a short walk past Bill's Barber Shop with the red and white striped pole in front, past May's Sweets with all those delectable cupcakes in the window, past the candy shop, past the Mayor's office, past the flag pole, past the Magnolia Plate Diner, with its gleaming silver booths and a tree across the street sporting Magnolia blooms really as big as a plate, past the post office, and then to The Southern Pair.

Since I was having my nails done, Aunt Marta sat both of them down on barstools at the counter and popped the tabs on two canned root beers.

"I was just telling Manda about the slip." She said *the slip*, like it was a juicy bit of gossip. I studied Peyton's face to see if Marta had brought on one of Peyton's adolescent pouts, but her eyes sparkled. Today promised to be a good day for her. Thank heaven for small favors.

"Oh that," Peyton said, letting go with a giggle that

bounced around the empty shop. I wished she would laugh that way for just me, just once.

I also would've liked world peace and a sweetener that tasted like real sugar.

"I'll let you tell it," Marta said, plunging my fingertips into a sudsy solution.

"How did they know about the slip?" I asked.

"Oh, boy," said Peyton. "You should have heard ole Esther. Of course, there was no way your missing slip was missed by these gossipy grandmas. I mean, even I saw the sun shining right through your dress."

I almost pulled my fingers away from Marta, but she tut-tutted for me to be still.

"Don't worry," Peyton assured. "I kept moving over to block the sun from shining through your dress, but the preacher kept moving me back."

"How sweet of you." I exclaimed. "The preacher should've left you alone."

Marta shook her head and I envied the way she could so easily relate to Peyton. "Isn't that just like a grownup, Peach? Always telling you where you belong."

"Exactly," Peyton said. "I'm fourteen, almost *fifteen*, but nobody notices, right?"

I wanted to tell her that nobody noticed because she didn't always act like it, but then I remembered she acted exactly like a fourteen-year-old. It was part of the problem I had with her, but nothing I could do about that. Not really her fault, I reminded myself.

"So," Peyton said, stretching out the word until she had my attention. "Esther said the neatest thing about your slip."

"Esther is a gossip."

"She is, but just listen," Marta said. "This is the best part."

Peyton held her fingers in the air and pretended to hold the slip between her finger and thumb, much like I recall doing in the orchard on my wedding day.

"All those ladies said they heard the slip was still hanging in the tree, but Esther said..." And she mimicked old Esther's voice perfectly. "Most definitely not, ladies. I can assure you those big black crows took it to their nests." Peyton's face was all smiles and my heart swelled that sweet old Esther managed to take the embarrassment out of the moment for Peyton. "And then she said, 'I saw those crows flying over the wedding two-by-two with it in their beaks like in Cinderella.'"

And I could imagine it as well—those crows conspiring to get rid of the sad slip for me.

"I think she's right," I said.

Marta had already finished my nails, so I slipped my fingertips underneath the drying light, its blue warmth hardening the polish while we chatted about all the fun Peyton and Marta had.

When I announced that the kids and I had to go home, Marta put up her hands to stop us.

"Hold on! We've got something for you, Mandy." Marta clicked over to the reception counter and pulled out a box wrapped in what could only be called the pinkest of the pinks.

"Peyton helped pick it out."

Lifting the lid of the box, I gingerly pulled a full slip out and spread it over the pink Formica countertop. Immediately a rush of happiness surrounded me. This had to be a happily-ever-after slip. We all three marveled at the swath of white silk.

"Shiny!" Exclaimed little Stephen.

"Don't climb on the counter, Stevie."

"It looks like a silky dress," Peyton said in awe as she ran her finger along the tiny edge of lace. "And not for an old lady." Our eyes met, and I accepted the apology in hers for the old lady slip comment she'd made back in the orchard on my wedding day.

"It's gorgeous," I said. When I saw the price on the tag, I gasped. "Marta. This costs way too much for a little slip."

Marta grabbed a pair of scissors and snipped off the tag. "You did not see that!" She patted my hand. "It's like the ladies told Peyton. A good slip can last for a lifetime, so no price is too high when a bride is starting over, right, Peyton?"

"Yep. Esther said, 'It might be able to last a lifetime, but it's only good for the life of one marriage.'"

I stifled a laugh, thankful again for Esther's candor.

"Well Esther should know," I said. "She's been through

three slips herself."

Marta gave me a knowing glance and even Peyton smiled, obviously forgetting how she had wondered if the old slip was her mother's on my wedding day. We were all giggling like hyenas about that slip when the bell rang and the door flew open. We'd forgotten to flip the sign.

The woman who walked in, fake eyelashes glancing around the room, asked, "Excuse me. Do y'all know where in this town I can find that bronco-riding Keith Black?"

I shot Marta a look that said, "Obsessed fan."

Marta shot me one that said, "Rodeo queen."

Chapter Three

MARTA AND I were still relatively young at thirty-one, but we both gawked at the much younger-than-us, striking, blonde woman standing in the doorway with her sleek physique. She wore a pretty jeweled t-shirt, high-waist denim shorts, and tall cowgirl boots and looked just like she'd stepped out of a country song, just like in the song by that country duo Maddie and Tae.

Then another Taylor Swift wannabe, if Taylor was a young black woman in cowgirl boots, walked in and stood beside her fair-headed counterpart. She wore a cute summer dress so short that I wondered if it was a shirt and she just forgot to wear her pants.

Marta and I shared a glance. Definitely rodeo queens. Not that all queens were like these, but there are always a few if you know what I mean…

Marta shaded her eyes for a moment to tell me their smiles were unnaturally white and too bright.

"So, you girls know him?" the blonde asked.

Peyton started to speak, but I placed my hand on her arm. This wouldn't be the first time random tourists, particularly young women, had walked in looking for Keith. Normally, rodeo fans were a pretty decent bunch, but every now and then men like Keith got fans showing up because he tipped his hat to them as he walked by and they took it as a personal invitation to visit his hometown.

"Most of our customers are women," I said. "He doesn't come here."

"Really?" The blonde looked confused. "Because he told us his fiancé and her sister owned a place where we could get the best manicure in Tennessee." She held out her hands to show us her already-perfectly-manicured hands.

"And," the other woman said, "he said they could help me find an old-fashioned present for my Grandma's birthday—something to make her feel the way she used to feel before she got sick. We were just passing through and thought we'd stop."

Now, that changed things. This was business. Marta and I both started talking at once.

"Not his fiancé anymore," Marta said. "Meet Keith's wife."

"Oh," the fair one said.

She looked hurt, which was strange, right? I looked at Peyton to see if she recognized either one of them, but she obviously didn't, since she wore a narrow-eyed expression aimed at the women.

"Well, congratulations," the blonde said, seeming to gather her bearings. "I've been traveling a lot. I'm surprised my momma didn't at least mention Keith finally got married, again."

I hated how she said the word *again*. Did she have to remind me that I was the second wife? I mean, it should be called first as long as the previous wife is alive. Keith was not a widow, as far as we knew, and it had always seemed to me that the first and second wife labels should be switched in cases of divorce.

Marta and I exchanged the raised-eyebrow look.

"I'm Adrienne," the queen continued. "But call me Adri."

"And I'm Jordynn." The other queen held out her hand.

"Nice to meet you, Adri and Jordynn." I offered my most dazzling smile, the one that makes people offer up their deepest secrets once we've convinced them to choose a color that would improve their mood. Marta wore the exact same smile.

"And you must be Stevie," Adri said, shaking his little hand and moving on to Peyton.

Peyton stared. "You know my dad?"

"You betcha," Adri said. "My big brothers and sister went to school with him."

"So, did you know my mom, too?"

Adri's eyes flicked in my direction, then back to Peyton. "A little. I was practically a little girl back then, but I always thought she was an amazing horsewoman and one of the nicest people I ever knew."

Peyton's face flushed with pride and excitement. "You knew her, too?" she asked Jordynn.

"I knew of her," Jordynn said. "I wanted to be like her when I was little."

"Have y'all heard from her?" Peyton asked.

Adri nearly choked with surprise. "No, honey. We haven't heard from her," she said, while Jordynn focused an undue amount of attention it seemed on the toes of her boots.

Strange.

"Oh." Peyton cast me a look. Blame? Or a cry for help? I couldn't tell.

"So," I said, interjecting before Peyton could ask more inappropriate questions. "Marta has a knack for doing the most adorable nails on rodeo queens."

"So does Manda," Marta said. "Don't let her fool you, but she is much better at creating beautiful things." She motioned toward the furniture and other merchandise in the store.

"Would you have time for nails?" Adri asked.

"Let's see if we can squeeze you two in." I looked up from the appointment book. "You *are* rodeo queens, right?"

"How'd you know?"

"It shows," Marta said.

Jordynn's hand flew to a loose ringlet of hair.

"But in a good way." I assured.

"Well, what other way is there?" Jordynn sashayed over

and sat down in one of the chairs without being asked. Adri followed. Marta and I examined their nails, as if we were doctors examining a rash or a wound, and in many ways we were. Nail doctors, so to speak, and heart doctors, too. We make nails beautiful and then we comfort hearts with the mementos we sell.

"What rodeos are you girls queens of?" I'd met so many.

"Pillar Bluff," Adri said. "I'm the reigning queen, and Jordynn's the lady-in-waiting."

"Oh, so y'all are just a hop, skip, and a jump from here."

"That's right," Adri said with a sigh. "And it's just as hot here as it is in Pillar Bluff. How are we going to make it through the summer?"

"With air conditioning," I said. "Peyton, would you mind turning up the AC, please?"

Peyton, the doll that she was when she wanted to be, turned up the AC and produced cans of Coke from the fridge, kindly handing them to the queens while I discreetly stuffed the almost forgotten silky slip back into its package. I gave Peyton an extra squeeze, not caring that she wriggled away, before I let her and Stevie walk to Daddy's. It wasn't far if they cut through the orchard side of the farm. Marta could have handled both manicures, but since these gorgeous women knew my husband and his ex, yet I had never heard of them, I wanted to stay. Before either of them knew what had happened, they were wearing big smiles and Marta and I were filing their nails and plying them with questions.

"So, I guess y'all are twins?" Adri asked, stating the obvious.

Why do people ask that all the time?

"How could you tell?" I said, chuckling.

"Y'all are beautiful," Jordynn said and Adri chimed in her agreement.

Right then, whether I wanted to or not, I kind of liked them both.

"So, you're coming to Pillar Bluff to watch Keith ride tomorrow, right?" Adri asked.

"Of course, she is," Marta said.

"Of course, I am." I gave Marta a reproachful look. She was always trying to speak for me. Of course, I had to admit it went both ways.

"Oh, good." Adri explained. "Maybe we can all hang out. There's a dinner. All the queens are invited. I'm so excited. So many cowboys. Can you both come?"

"Your fiancé one of them?" Marta asked.

Adri had removed her ring and stowed it safely in her purse before her manicure, but not before I'd gotten a good look at it. At least she was taken, not that I really thought Keith's head could be turned. Jordynn's pretty ring finger was free of jewelry.

"He owns the stables over in Pillar Bluff," Adri said. "Lots of people board their horses there. So, yes, he's a cowboy, but he gave up bronc riding."

I tried not to let my envy show on my face. I knew it

wasn't fair to have been attracted to my husband's fearlessness when I met him, only to wish he would quit riding the rodeo after our wedding.

"I only wish I had a cowboy," Jordynn said. "But I'm footloose and fancy-free, as they say."

"Me, too, honey," Marta said.

After their nails were bright and hard with shellac, I started pulling things from the shelves that Jordyn's grandmother might like. Jordynn had shared that before her grandmother was sick, she'd loved to work in her garden, so I collected an assortment of garden-related items, all vintage and repurposed by me to become comforting decorations on someone's mantle or windowsill. Jordynn gasped when she saw a spade that I'd painted yellow and decorated with a spray of dried lavender, thanking me profusely for finding something she just knew would make her grandmother smile.

"So, we'll look for you at the rodeo in Pillar Bluff," Adri said. She was standing in front of me, her shiny hair swooping angelically around her tanned shoulders. She could obviously ride a horse and her knot wasn't tied yet. And, technically, she wasn't at all a little girl, but I shook away my silly thoughts. I was married to my own cowboy.

No reason to be jealous of this little girl.

"You can bet your boots on it," I said. "I'll be there."

"Oh, and—" she said. "I'm sorry if I upset your daughter."

I smiled at her use of the word *daughter*. It made me feel all warm and sappy, like a real mom might feel.

"It's okay," I said. "Even though she was only nine when it happened, naturally, she still misses Violet."

Adri looked sad. "It surprised everybody in my family when Violet disappeared, and even more when Keith got those divorce papers served to him. Your husband's family and mine have always been good friends. It just didn't seem like something Violet would do, you know?"

She looked at me, waited for a response, and then blushed a rosy red.

"Oh, gosh," she said. "I am so sorry. I shouldn't be saying anything to you." Adri looked like she wanted to say more, but she shook her head.

"Hey," I said. "Let's grab a drink in Pillar Bluff this week." I had a feeling there was more to talk about. While I didn't want to dwell on the past, if Adri knew something that might help me to navigate being part of Keith's family, then getting to know her might be helpful. Plus, I couldn't help but like her just a little.

We exchanged phone numbers and Adri and Jordynn floated out of the shop like angelic beings.

I shot Marta a pleading look. "Can you watch the kids?"

"My pleasure," she said, cleaning up the nail station. "But don't get mad when I feed them dessert for dinner and let them stay up till midnight."

"I wouldn't want it any other way," I said. "Hey. Can I

confess something?"

"Sure," Marta said.

"This is going to sound terrible, but now that Keith's more than just some cowboy I met at the rodeo, sometimes I hate watching him on those wild bucking horses. A part of me doesn't want to watch it anymore. I never know when he might be trampled to death."

I waited for her to chastise me, but I couldn't help it. I loved seeing Keith's skill with a horse, which I had to admit I found sexy, but I never knew when he might get bucked off and trampled like a rag doll. It wasn't like it hadn't happened before.

"I totally get that, sis, but it's not like you didn't know going into it."

"I know," I said. "Just venting."

She pointed a bossy finger at me. "Not that it's any of my business, but put on your big girl panties. Cheer for your husband and trust that all will be well."

"My panties are none of your business," I said, wagging a finger back at her. "And my marriage isn't something you should be commenting on, either. It's against the rules."

"Since when have rules ever stopped either one of us from speaking our minds?"

And that made us both laugh.

"Fine," I said and grabbed a western hat from the window display. I set it gracefully on my head. "Nobody will ever guess I'm just an orchard farmer's daughter pretending to be a cowgirl."

"That's another thing you're worried about, isn't it," she said. "You're embarrassed you're not a real cowgirl, whatever that is."

"So what?"

But she was right. I wasn't used to insecurity anymore. I thought I'd left that all behind when my ex and I divorced, but there was something about rodeo wives and girlfriends that made me question myself. Looking at them, practical and yet beautiful in their western clothing, made my slightly-over-the-top rhinestones feel cheap.

Okay, so maybe they were more than slightly-over-the-top rhinestones. They were all out blingy, but I liked to dress flashy, and Keith liked it, too. At least I thought he did.

"Well, as long as you look hot, no one will judge—definitely not your cowboy hubby."

My heart fluttered, a little bit proud and a little bit nervous, thinking about seeing Keith on the back of a bucking horse again. And trust me, we aren't talking gentle, trained horses, but unbroken, wild horses. And no matter how many times he'd been hurt, he just kept climbing back on. If only the rest of us could do that in life, we'd all be courageous.

"So," Marta said. "What did you make of all that bull crap about Violet? Do you think they really knew her?"

"I don't know why they'd lie," I said.

Marta was just being protective.

She shrugged. "Well, if they did know her, then they

should've known better than to talk about her to Peyton."

I thought about Peyton's question to Adri and wondered, did people hear from Violet?

"I hope she never comes back," I said. "Is that awful?"

"I don't know," Marta said. "I think it would be good for Peyton to know what really happened to her, but, then again, if it's something bad, then she's better off not knowing."

"How could it be something bad?" I asked. "She sent divorce papers. She had to be alive and well to do that."

"That was a long time ago," Marta said. "If anyone's heard from her since then, it hasn't hit the rumor mill." And nothing gets past the rumor mill in Castle Orchard.

"Anyway, we have to stop bringing that woman up," I said. "She's gone. Keith and the kids are my family now."

"Right," she said, but not very convincingly. "That's why you keep obsessing about Violet ever since you fell in love with Keith."

"Ouch," I said.

Marta spontaneously threw her arms around me and squeezed. "Sounds like you weren't ready for the honeymoon to be over. Let's go, I'll help you pack."

"You're right," I said and helped lock up the shop. I closed the door behind us.

"Just find me a rodeo cowboy while you're there," Marta said. "Okay?"

"Be careful what you ask for," I warned. "You might just get your wish."

Chapter Four

"OH FOR PETE'S sake. This suitcase is way too small for all my stuff. I'm going to end up needing something."

"You drive a bug," Marta said. "No big suitcases allowed."

I hefted my pink overnight bag and a pair of my fanciest cowgirl boots, the ones with the fringe up the side, into the back of my yellow VW Beetle.

"Remember these?" I asked.

"You wore those the first time you met Keith. Great choice." Marta and I'd been gussied up in boots and cowgirl glitz just for the occasion, and I admit, I'd only dressed that way for the rodeo. The next day Marta and I were back in our designer jeans and sandals, trying to get rid of our hat-head hair from the night before. That's exactly what I'm talking about when I say I'm not really a cowgirl. When I dress cowgirl for Keith, which I do quite often these days, I'm like those purses people buy on the corner in New York City that look close to the real thing, but aren't.

Daddy walked toward us, coffee in hand. "Now, you be

careful," he said handing me a travel mug for the road.

"What's this?" I peered at the logo on the side of the lidded mug. "Marshall Farms," I read.

He frowned. "It was Marta's idea. Too fancy?"

I looked at the mug, which was light green with red writing and a picture of an apple on the side.

"I love it!"

"I ordered them when you were in Hawaii—before Daddy could put the kibosh on it," Marta said. "I thought we'd sell them real cheap over at The Southern Pair. It might get the word out about his booth at the farmer's markets, you know?"

"I promise to hand some out." I stuffed a few into my bag and let Marta load up the backseat with several more.

In the car, I slipped a pair of jeweled sunglasses over my eyes. I thought they contrasted great with my white, rhinestone-bedazzled t-shirt and chunky, turquoise bead necklace. A look in the rearview mirror confirmed it.

I was no rodeo cowgirl, but this fancy farm girl knew how to pick a pair of sunglasses.

"Tell Adri and Jordynn hi," Marta said.

I gave her a sly look. Was she trying to make me jealous? Because I didn't need any encouragement for that. I was already bracing myself for all his cowgirl fans, most of them as fake as myself, except that, unlike them, I was at least married to a real rodeo cowboy.

I cranked the AC and headed off. The drive over the

wooded hills made me feel a peace I hadn't felt in quite a long while, reminding me that I might not be a real cowgirl, but I was still a country girl at heart. I liked nothing better than a scenic, tree-filled view and a picnic in the grass. I was already trying to figure out how I might lure Keith from the rodeo grounds and into the woods for some rest and relaxation.

Pillar Bluff was only two hours away and was only bigger than Castle Orchard by about a thousand people. Its streets were lined with a few more gift shops, although none that made people feel as happy as The Southern Pair, except maybe the Time for Tea shop, where they served tea in antique cups, and restaurants advertising Southern cuisine to tourists. But Pillar Bluff was most known for having the best rodeo grounds this side of Tennessee, which were big enough to host an annual rodeo that brought people from all over the United States. As I followed the signs to the rodeo entrance, I worried, something I had always done more than Marta.

The thing I was truly anxious about, more than the fans, was running into all those rodeo wives who had known Keith for years. Hopefully, I wouldn't hear any talk about Keith's ex. I hated when they asked me if we'd heard where Violet was or how she was doing, as if I'd be the one she'd call. My more compassionate side knew it was the mystery of her disappearance, the suddenness of it, that made these old friends of hers ask, but my mean side always wanted to ask them why the heck they thought I'd keep in touch with the ex. When Violet decided to vanish, she'd left a trail of trampled people behind her, and some of them still wanted answers. Hopefully, now that Keith had tied the knot, maybe they'd realize that if he was moving on, maybe they should, too.

I SHOULD'VE NEVER come!

I stared up at a tall, beefy cowboy who had a handlebar mustache on his lip and wore a red bandanna around his neck.

"I'm sorry, ma'am," he said. "I can't tell you how many 'wives' come here trying to get back to the RVs. Not gonna happen today."

Behind him sprawled the arena, which resembled a football field, except for all the dirt, the stage on which horses and bulls thrilled the crowds daily, hooves beating into the earth leaving tracks over tracks and kicking up dust to the beat of rock music blaring from the speakers. I'd gotten on the road a little later than I'd hoped and the sun was already climbing higher in the sky. The drop of sweat trickling down my spine from the heat put me in a bad mood, and I was in no mind to deal with this hefty cowboy.

"I really am Keith Black's wife. I even have a key to his RV, see? Because it's *our* RV."

He eyed the key with a suspicious look.

"Everyone wants to marry a cowboy, ma'am, but Keith

doesn't have a wife."

What a funny little man!

Of course, he wasn't so little, but I planted my hands on my hips and stared up at him with a stern look. "Mister, if you don't let me through this gate, you're going to find yourself deep in that smelly stuff in that cow pen over there."

The man gave the cow pen a lazy look, sniffed, glanced at my high-heeled espadrilles and then rested his arms across his barrel chest. They must pick the scariest looking guys to guard the cowboys' RVs. I guessed this one wasn't scared of a little horse manure, or of little ole me for that matter.

"Black'll be signin' autographs later."

A passing cowboy shouted. "Sure, if the old guy's not too sore afterward. I just saw him limpin', but I'll give you mine, sweetheart."

I rolled my eyes and decided to just push past the cowboy guard, but he stepped in my way, gently taking hold of my elbow. I was about to clean his clock when my heart jumped a little at the lanky stud swaggering up.

"I believe I'll take it from here, Bill."

Bill? Should be Brewster or Butch!

"What're you doing here, sweetheart?" He asked, his cowboy drawl making me melt into a puddle, like always.

I didn't know if I'd ever get used to being married to a man who looked like he just stepped out of a western movie. He caught me as I threw my arms around his waist. His shirt smelled like dust. Everything at rodeos was dusty, and, now, so was I, but I didn't mind.

"That cowboy over there said you were limping. And he called me sweetheart."

"That's Slade. He's just mad because he can't beat me. But Bill, here, he's a good guy. Bill, I'd like you to meet my wife of two-and-a-half weeks."

Bill erupted into smiles and congratulations. "Pardon me, ma'am. I hope I didn't offend."

He doffed his hat.

Now, how could I stay mad at a man with such good manners, never mind how late they were in coming?

"You just keep on keeping those girls away from him," I said.

"Oh, he's in good hands here, Mrs. Black. I keep all those girls away."

All?

I didn't miss the look Keith shot him.

Bill added, "Of course, you don't have anything to worry about. Keith's about as boring as an old mule. Can't get him to leave his trailer half the time."

That sounded better.

Keith said a farewell to Bill and grabbed my hand. Together we walked past pens filled with cattle and horses toward rows and rows of RVs filled with rodeo people until we got to one I recognized as ours.

"You come to watch me ride?"

"Does a rodeo queen wear a crown?"

He laughed. "But you hate watching me ride."

"I love seeing you ride. It just terrifies me to watch."

"I'm glad you came," he said.

Keith kissed my forehead in mid-stride, the scent of dust and sweat tickling my nose.

"It's awhile before I'm up, but I need to get on over there. Cheer for me, cowgirl."

"I will. And you be careful out there," I whispered, ignoring the endearment.

Keith called all the girls in his family 'cowgirls'—he even called Marta a cowgirl, which was even funnier than calling me one.

"Don't get hurt."

"How about you stop worrying and just tell me good luck." He wrapped his arms around my waist and pressed his mouth against mine.

I tried to keep it reserved in case someone was watching, but Keith's lips were soft and persuasive. I'd never been one to care if a man had a muscular physique, but that was before I married a rodeo cowboy with rock hard abs and shoulders to go with his biceps. If I was that lucky, I was going to enjoy it, and right then, the heat of his body pressing up against mine almost made me forget where we were. Just when I felt like we were back on the beach, a breeze swept through and the barn-related odors reminded me that we weren't still in Hawaii. I pulled away, wrinkling my nose.

"What? Do I stink?"

I laughed, knowing he would stink a lot more when he got back from his ride.

"I'll send Quentin by to check on ya," he said.

"Good luck, babe." I gave him a peck on the cheek.

"I'm gonna need it," he said and straightened his hat.

He didn't seem to be limping anymore, if that cowboy had even been telling the truth. If anything, his long stride reflected a good mood. He was glad I came. I could see the pride in his face, and it made me happy. If only being a bronco rider's wife was as easy as showing up to see her cowboy ride.

QUENTIN, A COWBOY on Keith's support team or whatever he called it, knocked on the camper door. He held an arm load of goodies.

I remembered Marta's comment about finding her a cowboy and wondered if she'd ever met this one. He lived in Pillar Bluff, but he was in Castle Orchard working for Keith all the time. Although, maybe Queen Jordynn was more Quentin's type. I'd have to ask Keith if Quentin would be open to meeting a blonde, white woman who looked just like me.

"They sure do treat the cowboys and their families good," I said. "Look at all this food, Quentin."

"You hungry?" He set it all on the tiny table and turned to offer me a hug. I gasped at his strength.

"I don't think I feel like eating right now," I said, catching my breath and popping the tab on a Coke.

"Alrighty," he said. "You might want to head over in a few minutes. You don't want to miss it."

Of course I didn't. Keith rode all the time. He'd be fine like always.

Quentin handed me a badge on a red lanyard. "You'll need this to get in."

"Quentin?"

"Yes, ma'am?" He stood with one hand resting on the side of the door, the other about to place his hat on his head.

Oh, boy, Marta definitely has to meet Cowboy Quentin. "Manda?"

"Oh! Sorry," I said, shaking my head. "Just distracted by this heat! I was only asking you, is Keith okay? I heard someone say he was limping earlier."

Quentin looked out the door, toward the arena. "Keith's fine, Manda. Don't you worry yourself, okay? He's as happy as a kid with an ice cream cone that you're here, so cheer loud and let everyone know you're his wife." He winked.

My jealous side wondered if the comment about letting everyone know was more than a joke, but that would be silly, right?

He let the door close and I sat down at the miniature table, all those shrink wrapped cakes and cookies spread out on the cheap table top Formica wasted. There was no way I could eat when my husband was about to ride a wild horse. Restless, I changed into my Miss Me jeans and the fringe-adorned boots, grabbed my bag – a fringe and turquoise thing from a fellow rodeo wife at my wedding shower—and stepped out of the RV. Dust tickled my nose and a roaring rose up from the arena a short walk away. My chest tightened as I picked my way past the RVs and toward the place where my very own cowboy was about to be whipped and jerked and possibly thrown from a wild animal. What Keith did for a living never failed to make me weak in the knees, in ways that were both good and bad.

The roaring got louder the closer I got to the stands. The sun was high in the sky and I pressed my hat down and popped on my sunglasses. I could hear the announcer, all full of wit and grit, explaining what was happening over the loud speaker.

"Hi."

I stopped, turned. A woman stood beside the barrel trash can with a big smile on her makeup-less face. Now, I'm not judging. I'm just saying she had no makeup on and her highlights were way overdue, and I am the kind of person who notices something like that. Call me shallow, but I also noticed that her clothes didn't match and her dull brown hair was twisted up in what I think was supposed to be a bun. The spacey look in her eyes sort of scared me, so I looked around to see if she was with anyone. When I looked back, I saw my mother's image for a split second and I froze. It wasn't her, of course, but that was the look Momma'd had in her eyes during that last year she was with us. Something wasn't right with this poor woman, either.

The woman grinned, her smile white and brighter than I'd expected.

"Hi." She repeated.

Homeless?

I know it's not my best self that finds meeting homeless people, or really any person in need, uncomfortable. My heart goes out to them, I truly want to help and, frankly, have given clothes, food, and even money to charities, but I've never gone down to serve soup and bread at the shelter over in Nashville like Marta does. The one time I tried it, I broke out in a sweat when a homeless man held out his grimy hand, a soup bowl clutched between his filthy fingers. All I had to do was ladle soup, but when I saw that look, Momma's look, in his eyes, I'd frozen. Marta had to wrench the ladle from my hand and give the poor man some soup. I am not proud of this fact, but it's the truth, and if I'm not as good and brave as Marta, then at least I'm honest.

I flinched now when this woman reached out to touch my arm.

"Hi." I felt the beginnings of a panic attack.

There was something about the combination of how sorry I felt for that woman and how much I loathed being in this predicament that confused my senses. Dr. Phil might be able to dissect my feelings, tracing them back to some random scare I had when I was a child, or a deep sadness about being abandoned by my Momma, but all I know is that when I'm around someone like this poor woman, I get emotional and I want to run.

The poor woman reached into the trash can and grabbed a semi clean napkin, held it out to me.

"Here, honey." She didn't sound homeless.

I waved it away. "I'm fine. Just so much dust around here. It's in my eyes."

She nodded like she would understand. "In all the years I've been in rodeo," she said. "I've never gotten used to the dust." She held her hand out. "I'm Judy."

I gingerly shook it. She was skinny and definitely not as old as I first thought, but even though her words were sound, her eyes told me she wasn't all present in the moment, either.

A lot like Momma.

"Nice to meet you, Judy." I noticed she wore a silver western-style bracelet similar to the one I wore on my own wrist, a gift from Keith, and her nails were manicured and painted with a clear coat of polish. Kind of fancy for a homeless woman and I wondered if it was a special bracelet. Someone who loved her must have given it to her, same as with mine. She saw me staring and with a vague smile she touched the bracelet, rubbing her fingers across its stone. It made me smile, despite my awkwardness. Every girl deserves a good manicure and a beautiful bracelet, trust me. Not only did I have both, but both were popular at The Southern Pair. They always brought happiness.

"I'm Manda," I said. "Keith Black's wife." I didn't know

why I said that when she probably had no clue what I was talking about.

Her eyes widened. She looked at the sky, started swaying from side to side. I noted her western boots, also newish, if not outdated. The look in her eyes reminded me of my mother when she would be right there, but leave us in her mind, sometimes for hours at a time. A wave of sorrow rushed past me, and I willed it to keep going.

"Nice to meet you, Judy." I turned to go.

"That Black. He's a champion," Judy called out.

I spun around. The lady stood there, smiling serenely as she fingered her bracelet.

"You've heard of him?" I asked, surprised that someone like her would know one rodeo cowboy from another, but then I heard the announcer from the arena. Maybe she picked up easily on things she heard.

"Cowboy Man. He's a champion." She started picking at her cuticles. "On the news."

I offered her a weak smile. This poor, poor woman.

"Yes, he's in the news a lot around here," I said, backing away. I felt bad about leaving her alone, and yet I was about to be late. "Now, you have a good day."

"Everyone knows Cowboy Man's name," she muttered, and then she launched into a string of utterances I couldn't understand. "Excuse me, what is that cowboy's name again?"

"Keith," I said, realizing I probably shouldn't even answer this woman's questions, lest I confuse her, but she stood there with a lonely look on her face. I didn't know how to help, but I felt sorry for her. At a total loss, I reached into my bag and grabbed a twenty, stuffed it into one of the travel coffee mugs, and handed it to her. She took it, her eyes filling with surprise.

"For me?" Her eyes sparkled like a child's.

"That's right. A present." I nodded. "Nice to meet you, Judy." She looked at the mug like it was a Christmas gift.

I hoped she would be okay, but I didn't know what else to do. I walked away, which was something Marta would have jumped all over me for. In some ways, Marta and I were very different. She loved helping anyone and everyone. I did, too, but I preferred distance. Maybe it made me a bad person, but I didn't like being reminded of Momma.

I rushed off.

"You better hurry!" The woman called out. She had no idea I only wanted to get away from her.

I flashed my badge to the guard and headed to the seats right behind the chutes. Amazingly, one was still empty.

THE STANDS WERE filled to the brim with spectators, waving cheap fans bearing advertisements for new trucks, eating chili cheese dogs, and wearing cheery straw hats that looked like they'd been stomped by a horse. Everywhere I turned, people wore smiles and their eyes were filled with excitement, seemingly unaware of the sweat beading above their eyebrows. I sat behind the chutes right in front of a group of obsessed rodeo fans even though I could've sat by the other wives and families in the tent down on the ground. This was right where I'd sat the first time I ever saw Keith. Just like then, the fans were cheering and hooting, excited from the adrenaline, and, no doubt, from the beer that was being sold by vendors walking through the stands.

"Go, Black!" The roar of the crowd going wild was almost deafening.

A rattling of iron gates down in the chutes sent a vibration up into the bleachers. My heart leapt in my chest like the horse Keith was about to mount. The horses waiting to be ridden were always frisky. Well, more than frisky. They were mad. They wanted out, and as they snorted and pressed their sides up against the chutes, seeing Keith lower himself onto the back of one made my heart leap, and I do mean in a bad way this time.

In an attempt to calm my nerves, I rubbed the surface of my own western bracelet that Keith had given to me when we were dating. Peyton had one a lot like it, also a gift from Keith, and it made me feel like we were somehow connected when I wore the intricate silver band, even though I knew she didn't think so.

I smiled down at the bracelet, thinking it would've been fun to bring Peyton with me, but the forceful rattle of the gate below drew my attention. All I wanted at the moment was for the next eight seconds to be over. I didn't want Keith on that horse.

Like I said before, I was a terrible cowgirl.

When I first met Peyton, she looked me up and down and snorted, a little bit like the horse she'd just been trotting around the circle of the corral. My bejeweled jeans and blue t-shirt with the western swirly designs and rhinestones across the front didn't fool her. When her gaze rested on my bracelet, her eyes had widened.

"Where'd you get that bracelet?"

"Your dad." I smiled.

She'd reached down to touch her own bracelet, and it was the first time I knew that like mine, hers was a smooth circle with an engraving of a rose, but I'd mistakenly thought she'd think it special. I wanted to apologize to Peyton for encroaching on the special gift her daddy had gotten her, but she was jabbing a finger at my boots.

"Where'd you get those?" Peyton demanded.

"Also your dad." I popped out the pointy-toed boot and turned to show her the four-inch-heel.

"Well, I don't think he meant them for riding, but whatever."

Feeling chastened, I'd followed her into the barn like she was the parent and I was the child.

"Okay," she said, after walking me through the barn and into a large circle pen. "Say hello to Lizzie."

I slowly approached a beautiful—and enormous—black beast that I couldn't ever imagine sitting on. As I stood there, watching her flanks shiver from the bugs, chills went through me. My most recent experience on a horse was fresh in my mind. My backside hurt just thinking about how I'd landed in the dirt on the other side of the pen.

"That's good," Peyton said. "She likes you. Now, you need to get to know her a little better. Let her know you're in charge."

I trudged behind her walking through the soft dirt beside the huge horse, sad that my boots were getting dirty. I accepted the long stick with the slender leather strap hanging from it.

"A whip? I am not hitting her."

"Don't be stupid," Peyton said. "That's not what it's for."

Deciding to ignore her huffiness, I turned my attention back to Lizzie. She was gentle while Peyton showed me how to exercise her. Riding her couldn't be too bad, could it? I decided to go for it, but the first time I planted my cute boot into the stirrup and tried to swing my other leg over Lizzie's back, I promptly fell off the other side. Lizzie, bless her heart, stood still. I love that horse. I really do, but that day, it just wasn't working between us.

To make matters worse, Peyton started laughing, and when I stood and dusted the dirt off my jeans, the first thing I saw was Keith home from work and sitting up on the fence, a big smile on his face. Needless to say, that was the last time I planned to ride Lizzie. After that, my job at the ranch was grooming the horses.

Eventually, I fell in love with all of Keith's horses, but those horses weren't anything like the ones in the saddle bronc bucking contests at rodeos. Nothing. The horses they use in rodeo bronc riding are beautiful, sleek, and powerful, not afraid to use that power to let you know who is in charge. And when they first jump out of the chute, they're pretty sure it's them. It takes a tough cowboy to turn that attitude around, one like my husband.

THE CHUTES RATTLED as the cowboy, my husband, leaned over the horse preparing for his ride. I have to admit that before Keith, watching cowboys buck on the backs of horses was exciting. The cowboys themselves seemed powerful and strong, and yes, I admit it, sexy! I'd be lying if I said the out-and-out masculinity of it wasn't something that attracted me to Keith. Of course, I never thought I'd actually get the chance to talk to him, let alone become his wife. And like so many things in my life, I owe it all to my sister.

Marta and I used to sit with all the other fans hooting and hollering for the cowboys to stay on for their eight seconds. We were single and a bit wild, but always ladies. I didn't chase cowboys, but if I was in the right place at the right time, they were welcome to chase me. That first time I saw Keith ride, I knew he was doing it right, even though I hardly knew anything about how the cowboys were judged or the precision and strength it took to stay on. I've learned since that there's lots more to saddle bronc riding than just getting on and staying on for eight seconds. The cowboy's form matters. Even how the horse bucks counts, which I think is kind of unfair, but Keith says that's how it's supposed to be.

Another rattle from the chutes jarred me. Horses snorting, cowboys waiting for their cue to swing the gate open—a dangerous job if you asked me. Beyond them, cowboys with ropes sat on the backs of horses poised and ready. I love those guys, now that I know they're not mere cowboys who look like they just stepped off a rodeo poster. They're the 'pick up men' who snatch the cowboys off the horse after their eight seconds are up, assuming they stay on that long.

The bucking horse in this case was brown dappled with white. Beautiful, but mean looking, nostrils flaring. Keith's nostrils were flaring, too! Every time I saw him ride, I was amazed that my gentle man could be so transformed.

The horse shivered, a lot like Lizzie back at the ranch when I groomed her, but it wasn't to get the flies off its back. This horse only wanted to get the cowboy off its back and it did its best to send Keith flying, even before the gate was flung open.

Come on, already. Open the gate.

The announcer was busy filling the crowd in about Keith, getting them riled up for the ride. Then he roared over the loud speaker into the arena.

"Friends, let's give a big welcome to three-time world

champion, Keith Black. Come on now, let's show 'em some love!"

And as they say, the crowd went wild as the rock music blared over the loud speaker.

I know. The rock music always surprises me, too. The first time I ever saw bronco riding, I was expecting to hear a little Toby Keith, instead of Guns and Roses. And speaking of guns, a gunshot sounded and the men who'd been holding the gate were now pulling on the ropes and swinging it wide open. The horse reared its front legs high, its mane flaring like a flame, its body flexed and full of power and the energy of a freight train. My husband, hanging on for his life, literally it seemed, wasn't just a man anymore, but a cowboy, and I hated it.

Hated it. Loved it. I was so proud! So scared. Amazed. Worried. In real time, it's only eight seconds, right? But in a wife's time, it's all in slow motion. Every time the horse's hooves hit the dirt, my heart burst open just a little more.

Keith's legs, encased in flapping black-fringed chaps, held tight in the saddle and his hand was gripped tightly to the hack rein. He was straight up in the saddle, boots locked in the stirrups, rocking with the rhythm of the bucking horse. Hooves hit the dirt with a mighty force as the horse's body jerked into a rocking back-and-forth-up-and-down, motion. The horse was really ticked off and it made my heart slam around in my chest with each rock and roll of that beautiful beast.

And oh, let's face it, that man! My man.

What a picture! I wished Peyton was there with a camera. All I had was my phone camera and I didn't have time for any of that. The horse was bucking just like you want it to. Even a rookie rodeo observer could see that *this* – my husband! – was how a cowboy should look on a bucking bronco, everything in crazy, fast motion from the waist down, and yet every muscle in Keith's upper body taut and in control, his jaw tight, face determined.

Oh, heavens to Betsy. Be strong, baby.

You don't even have to be a rodeo fan to know that a wild, bucking horse is unpredictable and that Keith could go swinging off into the dirt at any moment. At that point, he could be trampled and broken, even killed.

Eight seconds was all he needed. The horn sounded. The radio announcer's voice came over the speaker.

"Now that's how a saddle bronc rider does it. Let's give that cowboy a hand!"

"Whooooooo!" I yelled with the roaring crowd, but I stayed seated for now. "Way to go, baby!!!"

When the pick-up man helped Keith slide off the horse and he landed in the dirt, perfectly unscathed, I stood. Keith walked across the arena, plucked his cowboy hat off the ground, adjusted it on that beautiful head of hair, and punched his fist in the air. Even as scared as I'd been eight seconds before, I was now yelling with joy and relief. I waved at him, waiting to see if he would remember what he'd always done, back when we were dating.

He remembered, not even breaking his stride as he blew a kiss to me. Several hats swiveled in my direction, but I didn't acknowledge them. I was too busy watching my hunk of a husband walk out of the arena.

"Well, I'll be darned," said the announcer. "What a cowboy. What. A. Cow. Boy."

Oh, be still my heart. If a rodeo wife has to put up with her husband putting his life on the line, she might as well enjoy the rest of the cowboy, right? And all those rodeo fan girls are right. There's just something about a cowboy that makes a woman weak in the knees.

"Ladies and gentleman, if Black keeps riding like that, he just might win the whole purse." I cheered.

The crowd was still going crazy when I yelled, "Go baby!" I turned to the bewildered fan beside me and said, "That's my husband!"

She smiled. "Lucky girl."

But then I heard the announcer say something I knew Keith wouldn't like. Not. At. All.

"Folks, at thirty-seven-years-old, Keith Black has still got it! He's gonna be sore tomorrow, and all you folks over thirty know what I'm talkin' about, but Black's still got it."

I hurried out of the stands to meet him coming out of the chutes. Behind me I heard a familiar voice.

"He's a champion, isn't he? Everyone knows that cowboy's name."

Surprised she was still there, I turned to see Judy standing beneath the bleachers, the mug still in her hand. She was waving at me. I smiled and kept my eye on her until a man walked up and offered her the crook of his arm. He wore a lime green t-shirt with a white logo I couldn't read from where I stood. Maybe someone from the homeless shelter she came from was there to help her out. I wasn't sure how that all worked, but it was obvious she was in safe hands. When Keith called my name, I turned away.

He held his arms open and I fell into them. Now isn't that just like in the movies? Only the movies never accurately depict what a cowboy who just got swung around by a wild horse would really smell like. Of course, I didn't care.

"You watched?" His grey eyes stared at me from a dirty, sweaty, but beautiful face.

I nodded and his smile was priceless. I kissed his cheek, then wiped my mouth. This made Keith roar with laughter. I laughed, too, but thought of Judy and how I'd flinched when she touched me. I could have sworn I heard her voice again saying, "That cowboy's a champion." I turned to look for her, and sure enough, there she still was with her friend, eating a hot dog and waving at us.

Keith raised his hand and she giggled, whispering something in her friend's ear. He didn't smile as he turned her away from us in a protective gesture.

"Who was that?"

"Judy," I said. "Sadly, I think she's homeless or maybe

from some kind of institution."

"*You* talked to her?" He put a heavy emphasis on the word 'you,' reminding me that he knew I didn't feel comfortable around people with, um, problems so to speak. I just shrugged, not telling him that she thought she knew him, maybe even had a little crush on that cowboy from the news. He got tired of the obsessed fans quickly, even though he was always gracious and kind, and this one wasn't even in her right mind, it seemed. I thought of the dirty napkin she'd pulled out of the trash can for me and shuddered.

"I'm glad you came," he said, giving me his full attention, gently wrapping his arm around my shoulders. "I was missing my cowgirl. In fact, I was thinking—"

"Keith!" We both spun to see a young woman holding a microphone, followed by a camera man and queen Adri.

"Hi!" Adri squealed and hugged me like we were old friends, but when she turned to do the same thing to Keith, I have to admit that my barbs went up. How ridiculous is that? I stepped out of the way, feeling immature, but instead of hugging her, my husband held his hands in the air like an outlaw.

"Oh no, you don't want to hug me young lady. I'm filthy."

She backed up, as if remembering her exquisite western clothes, and prattled on. "The news wants a few quotes from the two of us, since we're both from the area."

"You're from Castle Orchard, right?" The reporter held

the microphone close to Keith's face. He took it right out of her hands.

"Yep. Just down the road from here." He handed the microphone back to the young reporter who took the opportunity to ask queen Adri about her reign as Miss Pillar Bluff Frontier Days.

She gushed and gushed. I watched, taking mental notes in case I ever had to deal with reporters myself, which I doubted would ever happen. Adri knew how to work that camera and everything she said was adorable, witty, and even smart. Keith broke out in a smile, and I wondered if he noticed how she kept laying her hand on his shoulder, patting his arm, talking about how Black Ranch had sponsored her when she was running for queen.

We had? He'd never even mentioned Adri to me. Why wouldn't he have told me about her? I chastised myself. What was there to tell? She was just some queen.

Just then the camera lady held the microphone out to my face and I realized I'd missed the whole conversation and she seemed to be waiting on me to answer a question. That's when Keith took the microphone again.

"This here's my bride," he said, pulling me close to his side, resting his hand on the curve of my hip just a little bit lower than was appropriate, and I didn't even care that he was filthy. I flashed a dazzling smile that even Adri would've been envious of.

"Lucky girl!" The camera lady exclaimed.

"That's what everyone keeps telling me," I said with a smile.

Keith smiled encouragingly.

"So, Keith," the girl with the microphone said, "are you gonna be sore tomorrow? The announcer seemed to think so."

"Well now," he said, his drawl a little stronger even than it was back on the ranch at home. "I don't reckon I know what you're talking about."

She giggled, her nerves giving her away. I felt a little bit sorry for her. Keith was a very good-looking man and standing there fresh from riding a wild horse, he commanded a presence that made you feel at awe. He might have been older than her, but he wasn't too old to look at. Heck, he was older than me and he was my husband.

"Well, you're thirty-seven, Keith, not twenty-seven." More giggles.

"Don't make a bit a difference," he said. "I'll be alright."

"Some folks say you're thinking of retiring. Is that true?"

He didn't even glance at me. "We all have to retire some time, but don't worry. It won't be any time soon for me."

Excuse me? I didn't say it out loud, but I just can't express how worried that made me. Keith was young and strong, but those boys he was riding against? Some of them were eighteen, twenty-two, and so forth. An injury for them might be easier to heal from than for Keith. I wanted to give Keith an earful, but the look on his face told me tonight wouldn't be the best time. Riding against younger men might be hard on a man's pride. On a cowboy's pride. I leaned closer to him, trying to look supportive.

After the interview, Keith guzzled down a bottle of water someone handed him and shot it into the nearest trash can. Wiping his mouth on the back of his hand, he gestured toward the concessions.

"Looks like Adri knows your homeless friend, what did you say her name is? Judy? You sure she's homeless?"

"Yes. Judy. And no, I'm not sure if she's homeless, just not quite all there." I watched with interest as Judy and Adri chatted. The gentleman in the green shirt stood patiently beside Judy, sometimes contributing to the conversation as he stood with his arm bent so that Judy could rest her hand in its crook.

"Adri's a nice girl," Keith said. "She has a knack with people who aren't quite all, well, you know what I mean. Adri likes everyone."

Even me.

I searched his face to see if by chance he was attracted to Adri but his face only looked like he was stating the obvious. And of course he was.

"She really is." I begrudgingly meant it, too.

"I've got some things to do before I can get cleaned up if you want to hang out with her for a little while."

I figured why not. "Plus, there's shopping over in the tents," I said.

"Go gab with the girls and shop till you drop," he said.

"You know I will," I said, not at all minding that he was throwing stereotypes all over the place. I did love to shop. I accepted his sweaty kiss, and the way he pulled me to him as if we were the only two in the arena made me forget my petty insecurity about Queen Adri.

IT TURNED OUT Judy wasn't homeless after all, but she did have some kind of mental condition and lived in a special home where her green-shirted chaperone worked. I learned all of this from Adri and Jordynn, who magically appeared at my side after Keith left for the camper. The queens suggested I join them for a bite to eat over at the Old Time Village where people in old-timey clothing strolled and we could get an ice cream cone for a dollar and an entire barbecued turkey leg for five bucks. Yes, it's true, a whole leg, as well as stunningly beautiful Native American jewelry you'd never find at Macy's. I wouldn't doubt if it was where Keith bought the silver bracelets for Peyton and me, although shops with similar wares could be found at any rodeo in the country. We even had some in The Southern Pair.

"Of course," Adri said, "I didn't ask what she was in the home for, but whatever her condition is, it obviously makes her forget who she is."

"I got the feeling she still knows her way around the rodeo scene," I said.

Adri shook her head sadly. "Her chaperone said she used

to work with horses before she got sick. I can't imagine ever losing the ability to ride my own horses! I wish I could think of something nice to do for that poor ole cowgirl."

"Maybe some of the other queens could go with you for a visit," I suggested, having no idea where this fantastic idea had come from. "You could wear your crowns. Maybe she'd get a kick out of it."

"I love it!" Adri exclaimed.

"And it would give the rodeo some good press," Jordynn added. Spoken very diplomatically.

"You were so at ease with her, Adri." I said. I didn't dare admit that I never felt at ease around people like Judy.

She shrugged. "Didn't Keith tell you? I had an older brother who's in heaven now, but he had some pretty difficult special needs. So, I like spending time with people like Judy. It's a way I can honor my brother's memory and use all this for good." She motioned like Vanna White in her pretty green and white rodeo queen outfit and sash, complete with a white cowgirl hat that had a shiny crown pinned to it. It reminded me of my wedding-veiled hat and Peyton.

"He didn't mention your brother," I said. "But I'm sure he was going to."

"You are brilliant," she said. "I'm going to schedule that visit, and I wouldn't doubt Keith would want to go, too. He loved my brother."

He did? Why, oh why, do cowboys keep things so close to their vests?

Adri hugged me, and I couldn't help but hug her back. She was a total do-gooder. So much for my opinion that rodeo queens were brainless and shallow. I begrudgingly wondered if Keith's rodeo queen ex-wife had a better side, too. In my mind, she was a monster, therefore all rodeo queens must have been cut from the same cloth, but Adri wasn't.

"So," I said, when the conversation lagged. "How long have you known Keith?"

Adri's face lit like the sun itself and I braced myself for the announcement that they used to date.

"I've known him since I was little." she exclaimed. "He's friends with my big brothers. He dated my big sister in high school. He's never mentioned me?"

"Nope," I said, trying not to sound happy about it.

"Hmm. We're old family friends. Keith is even the one who introduced me to my fiancé."

"How well did you know Violet?" I asked.

Adri and Jordynn exchanged glances.

"We didn't hang out or anything," Adri said. "But sometimes she came to family dinners, that sort of thing."

"And you?" I directed the question at Jordynn.

"Oh," she said with a dismissive wave, "I didn't really know her. I'm a barrel racer when I'm not doing this queen thing. Violet Black used to be a great barrel racer, too, so, of course, I looked up to her. When she left, it was a big disappointment for a lot of us younger riders."

"Hey, does it make you uncomfortable to talk about this?" Adri asked, looking apologetic.

"Of course not." I lied, wanting the information more. If I could give Peyton some kind of reason to put her dream of finding her mother to rest, maybe it would help.

"We're pretty far apart in age," I said. "So, I never got to know her well when she moved into town. I was still in school."

"Nice," Jordynn said. "Married an older man, did you?"

I didn't like the way that sounded. "Only by six years," I said.

"Good for you," Jordynn said. "I want a man who's a little bit older than me. I want a mature man who knows what he wants."

I smiled. "I agree. Anyway, I wasn't close to Violet, obviously, so I don't know exactly how it all happened, even though I've heard Keith's side, and some gossip, too."

"Well," Adri said, "there were rumors and stuff around the rodeo circuit when she left. But most of the rumors couldn't have been true if she had Keith served with divorce papers."

I tried to imagine how Keith would've felt having the papers served to him, not even knowing where Violet was or why she'd left. I remembered all too well how I felt when it happened to me, but at least my ex hadn't disappeared. He'd left me for another woman, all out in the open for everyone to see and talk about.

"What'd people say?"

"That she was kidnapped," Jordynn said.

I wasn't shocked at this statement. I'd heard it before, but didn't believe it for a minute, knowing that Violet's lawyer had been given strict instructions to let Keith know she was fine, but didn't want to be found.

"But, of course, that was shown not to be true," Adri said.

"Some of the gossips say that she died," Jordynn said. "Or that she's living off in the Caribbean with some man."

"It's so sad, especially for the kids," Adri said. "I never got to know them, but my mom heard that Peyton has never accepted that her mom would just leave her and her little brother like that."

"It's hard to accept that a mom would choose to leave you when you're just a kid," I said, speaking from more experience than Adri or Jordynn knew.

"I'm so glad Keith and his kids have you," Adri said, offering me another one of her spontaneous hugs.

By the time I was ready to get back to Keith, I found myself liking both Queen Adri and Queen Jordynn.

"If you girls ever need another manicure, or a memorable gift, come on back to The Southern Pair."

"You know we will," Adri said. "But we'll see you at dinner tonight."

I WAS DETERMINED to ask Keith why he hadn't told me

about his friendship with Adri before, especially the queen sponsorship, but when I stepped into the RV and found him stepping out of the shower with nothing but a towel wrapped around his slim waist, his muscles rippling up into a 'v'—I forgot what my question was.

"Hey, cowgirl." He wore that half-smirk, half-smile I loved so much, and of course, the towel.

How can a man be this good-looking and be mine?

Out loud, I said, "You're forgiven."

"For what?" He sauntered toward me, reaching me in three steps.

"I already forget."

"Good," he said, nuzzling my ear as he pulled my t-shirt out of the waist of my jeans and began loosening the fancy belt buckle I'd found among some objects in an estate sale as I was shopping for The Southern Pair. I knew someday I would need it. "Because I don't like my wife being mad at me."

I liked how he said 'wife'.

"Hey," I said, laughing. "I brought something to wear that I picked out specifically for an occasion just like this one. You'll love it." I turned toward my suitcase, but he caught my waist, pulling me backward against him. I was done for after that.

"I'm sure it's pretty, but, trust me, you don't need it." He pulled my t-shirt over my head and planted a kiss on my shoulder, sliding his hands around my waist.

Emboldened, I slipped my fingers beneath satin straps and slid them off my shoulders. Spinning me around, he bent to place his lips on the soft skin at the tops of my breasts. I reached for him, and all the worries I'd carried with me from Castle Orchard went away with the yank of a towel.

"You think you can kiss all my worries away just like that, cowboy?"

"You betcha, sweetheart." His mouth pressed gently against mine, then grew more persistent as he found the clasp of my bra. He unsnapped it with one hand and there in the safety of the RV, I forgot about everything, except our bodies entwined like newlyweds should be. I wish things could have stayed that way a lot longer, but maybe it's like some people say. The honeymoon can't last forever.

Chapter Five

SOME WOMEN HATE the idea of being a trophy wife on their husband's arm while he shows her off at fancy dinners, but I say, give me my crown.

That night, I had on the cutest western outfit in black with just enough rhinestones to light up the smiles of anyone in the room, and enough sparkles underneath to light up Keith later again that night.

I loved being on my husband's arm as we walked up the sidewalk toward the Morris House Bistro, a restaurant that used to be a house in the historic district close to Pillar Bluff's downtown. I happened to know the owners, who lived most of the time in Cheyenne, Wyoming, of all places, where they had a sister restaurant that served the same menu. I'd been to both restaurants, having gone with Keith to Cheyenne Frontier Days the year before, and Morris House Bistro had become my favorite restaurant in both the North and the South.

The bistro's windows glowed with happiness as we walked up the sidewalk, and as soon as my boots clicked over the gleaming hardwood floors and I saw the candlelit tables in the middle of a large room that had been restored with love and attention to old but fine things, I decided that even if the party was boring, my heart for restored loveliness would at least enjoy the good vibes.

"Amanda! Is that you?" My old friend, Dante, pulled me into a warm embrace before holding me out to study my face. "I'm so glad you made it." He grinned broadly, his round face making me grin too.

"I didn't know you were in town," I exclaimed. "How will Wyoming survive while you're here in Tennessee?" When Trace came out of the kitchen and spotted me, he hurried across the room.

"You're in town, too?" I asked. "I'm so glad to see you both!"

Trace and I went through the same routine and, after they shook hands with Keith, they ushered us toward the head table.

"These seats are for the rodeo chairman and his wife," Dante whispered. "And they are really excited to meet your husband."

"And here come the queens," Trace whispered conspiratorially.

I saw numerous glances in my direction and wondered for the tenth time if any of the queens thought I was as old as rocks compared to them. I couldn't help but wonder, as well, if any of them had set their sights on Keith before he met me, and worse, I wondered if he'd dated any of them. And just like that, there went my dignity, again. How could I not trust my wonderful husband? I watched the queens walking gracefully around the room and remembered that sometimes it wasn't about trust. It was about simple biology. The queens were all young, but many of them not too young. Adri, after all, was old enough to get married. I texted Marta my thoughts, using the moment to check on the kids, too.

"As if he only dated rodeo queens before you," Marta texted.

"He was married to one," I texted back.

"You are his only queen now," she replied. *"And kids are fine. Peyton has been riding Lizzie. Stevie has been helping Dad."*

"Sounds like fun," I texted back.

"So is taking on all your nail appointments. When are you coming home? And where r u eating?"

"Morris House Bistro. Trace and Dante in town."

"No fair! Hugs to them."

"Gotta go. Cowboys and queens await."

"Bring me one."

I shoved my phone into my pocket and settled in for dinner. For the next hour, I was in dining heaven. Some of the guests might have been expecting a chili supper or juicy steak since it was a rodeo event, but it was a treat having baked macaroni and cheese, fried green tomatoes from the bistro's garden, shrimp and grits, and fried catfish with everybody's favorite, warm bread pudding. All was going well, until Keith stiffened at my side. I turned to see him staring at his phone, reading a text.

"What is it?" I leaned in to look, but he evaded me,

standing quickly and stepping out onto the porch. I followed.

"Manda! Are you leaving?"

I sighed, holding in my frustration, and turned to embrace Adri.

"Are you having fun?" I asked, steering her away from Keith who was talking heatedly into the phone.

"A blast," she said. "I love this stuff." She was decked out in a beautiful pink and white fringe leather outfit with a crown-studded western hat and lipstick to match.

"So many cute cowboys, right?"

She blinked innocently, fiddling with her big fat engagement ring.

"But not for you. You're getting married!" I took the opportunity to ply her with questions about the date, the decorations, and the location. Apparently, she wasn't into the rodeo queen decorations for a wedding and wanted an indoor church wedding with everything in black and white. Serious sounding, and kind of boring, but I didn't tell her so at all. Besides, a girl like Adri didn't need all that bling. As drop-dead gorgeous as she was, she would be the decoration, as they say. When Adri turned to answer a question from one of the other queens, I took the opportunity to look for my husband.

I caught sight of Keith through the window. He was still talking on his cell, his boots pacing the yard just outside the patio. He was careful to look under control, but I knew he was wound as tight as the wild horses he rides for fun.

"Your wedding decorations sound elegant." Adri was back at my side and I did my best to focus on the conversation with her and all the queens. I tried not to watch Keith, wondering who he might be talking to. Were the kids alright? When I'd just texted with Marta, she'd said they were. Was something wrong with Daddy? My heart clutched at that thought. Maybe it was just business.

"September first." Adri repeated. "I want you and Keith to come to my wedding, Manda. I'll send you an invitation." Her eyes sparkled and lit up her pretty face and I was genuinely touched that she would invite us, especially after Keith had obviously forgotten to invite her to ours.

"I'll put it on my calendar."

She squealed her happiness and laced her arm through mine. "Now, the others have a bunch of questions for you." And by the others she meant the queens. "They all want you to do their nails, but you'll have to promise me you won't do theirs better than mine, okay?"

"It's a deal."

I had to put whatever was agitating Keith at the moment out of my mind. The queens dazzled me with their smiles, their lipstick, crisp sashes, and, yes, I hate to admit it, their sincerely adorable personalities.

Why do they have to be so nice?

You know the type. Not only are they beautiful and adorable, but they're genuinely nice, too. Makes it hard not to like them. I wondered for the tenth time that day, had Keith's ex-wife been like these girls once, before whatever happened between her and Keith happened?

"We have to go," Keith said, taking me gently by the elbow as he nodded to the smiling queens.

I barely had time to say goodbye to Dante and Trace, praising them for their amazing food – and it *was* divine – before Keith calmly ushered me down the steps and into his old blue refurbished Chevy truck. I had loved that truck the first time Keith took me for a ride in it, and we'd ended up down by the creek, lying on a quilt spread in the bed of it, staring up at the stars.

"What's going on?"

The engine roared to life and he turned to look at me. I'd never seen him so wounded looking – but angry, too – since I'd known him.

"Your dad called."

"He did?" I dug my cell phone out of my purse, and there were a string of new text messages from Marta. I huffed. "Those queens distracted me."

"They have a tendency to do that." If I wasn't so worried about that phone call, I might have asked what he meant by that. Instead, I was imagining Peyton running away, or something worse. It had to be awful from the look on Keith's face.

"What's wrong, hon?"

He swallowed, his Adam's apple bobbing, and stared

ahead without driving away. His toughness was gone, obliterated. He looked like his horse had just trampled him and he'd come in last place.

"Is it the kids?"

"No, no." He patted my knee. "Well, sort of."

"You're worrying me."

"Peyton got a phone call."

"And?"

I was really getting worried now. If this was about a boy, I needed to let Keith know, this was bound to happen sooner or later. Or was somebody hurt? Maybe Peyton's best friend, Pia?

"Is Pia hurt?"

"No, no," he said. "Nothing like that."

"Keith, if you don't tell me what's wrong, I'm going to—"

"It was Violet. The phone call was from her."

An icy chill spread between my shoulder blades.

Violet.

"Violet?" The name caused a flutter in my chest that spread to my fingertips.

I pressed my palms to my forehead. That woman. She was eight or nine years older than me and not originally from Castle Orchard, so I hadn't really known her, but what I did know of her now, I didn't like. Plus, I did recall that when I first opened The Southern Pair with my sister, it had been too quaint for Violet, and her best friend, Kim, to shop in. I couldn't imagine that one item in my store would have leapt out to be owned by either one of them, anyway, unless it was something for bad luck. Like Peyton's phone. That was an item that brought bad luck. I wished I'd taken it from her weeks ago.

"Peyton's—mom, Violet? She called?"

"Do we know another Violet?"

As a matter of fact, we knew two others – one from church and one was Peyton's math teacher – but I knew reminding him wouldn't have gone over well at that moment. I chose to let his sarcasm slide past me instead of jumping on him for sounding like a downright jerk.

"Violet called Peyton's cell? Why?" I knew I should've taken that phone from that girl ages ago, but it had obviously held good memories for Peyton, and she'd clung to it the way Stevie clung to the blankie his mother had made for him, even though he couldn't remember her anymore. When kids cling to stuff like that, it's best to wait until the connection is lessened before taking them away. Sometimes, you can never take things away, not even to give them a new purpose, like the things in The Southern Pair.

When Keith's hand searched out mine, I squeezed back, struggling with why Violet might have called. I guessed her being dead was out of the question, but maybe she was in the hospital on her dying bed, wanting to talk to her daughter for the last time. Maybe cancer.

Now, don't get me wrong. I wasn't wishing Violet dead – even though she might as well have been with having abandoned her kids – but I couldn't imagine why she would violate the agreement that she herself had drawn up and signed along with hers and Keith's divorce papers. He got the kids, the house, and all of the important things, while she took her part of the money, gave up her parental rights, and wouldn't return – ever. Keith only had to promise not to look for her.

"Is something wrong with her, or what?"

"I think she's okay," he said softy.

My cheeks flooded with heat and my chest swirled like an angry tornado. How could that woman burst back into Peyton's and Stephen's – and Keith's – lives after the lengths she had gone through to get rid of them in the first place? How dare her.

"Then why?" I demanded.

"I don't know." He barked, slamming his palms onto the steering wheel, causing me to jump back. Immediately he laid one hand on my knee. "I'm sorry. But don't you worry. I'm going to find out."

It occurred to me that while Keith wouldn't have wanted her anywhere near Peyton or Stephen, he might want to know where Violet went off to when she left everyone hanging. If I were him, I might've wanted closure.

"I'm going to call that two-bit lawyer who sent the divorce papers," he said. "I'm going to call the police if I have to. I won't let her just swoop back into Stevie's and Peyton's lives after what she did to them."

And to him.

I couldn't believe it. Keith's ex-wife had called, just like Peyton had always said she would. I wished again I'd taken that phone away from her. There was nothing good that had ever come from holding onto that phone, except keeping Peyton from accepting the truth that her mom was never coming back.

Sighing, I realized that Peyton might have been right all along.

"DO YOU WANT me to drive?" I offered.

He straightened abruptly, snapped his seatbelt in place, and threw the truck into drive.

"No, thanks. I'm fine."

"Okay." Fastening my own belt, I watched the road that led toward Castle Orchard.

"The rodeo isn't over," I said. "You still have to ride again tomorrow."

"No crap."

Tears stung my eyes. Keith did a lot of things that bothered me, like being on the road a lot, refusing to retire from rodeo, and attracting beautiful women – which I knew wasn't his fault – but one thing he never did was be overly angry with me.

"My kids need me," he said, softer. "I'll come back to Pillar Bluff early in the morning if this turns out to be a hoax or misunderstanding."

"A hoax? Do you think someone is pretending to be Violet?"

"I don't know what to think." He stared fixedly on the road, his jaw still working like it did when he was stressed. "I'm just fishing for reasons. Hoping."

I nodded, not saying much else on the two-hour ride home, not voicing the dozens of questions I had. I knew I shouldn't borrow trouble, as Daddy always said, but all the possibilities rolled through my mind like a bad movie.

Did Violet want the kids back? No judge would let her have them, surely.

If she wanted her stuff back, it was too late. Except for the stuff I let Peyton put in her bedroom for memory's sake and all the photos in the hallway. I'd sold the rest online and put the money in Peyton's savings account. And thank heavens, because I can't even tell you how sick I was of purple dishes and furniture! A little purple in my clothes? Sure. Lavender accents here and there? Okay. But no more full blown purple in my life. It was all hot pink and turquoise from here on out.

I looked at my husband, all the cowboy in him whipped out for the moment. His brawny chest even looked a little smaller beneath his leather vest, and I was reminded that I didn't know what really happened between him and Violet. Nobody did.

I'd asked for details once and he'd clammed up, telling me it didn't matter anymore, but from the looks of him slumped behind the wheel, I knew for sure he hadn't been honest about the impact of his divorce. The truth was written, as they say, all over his face.

It did matter.

Chapter Six

I'M NOT AS up on the Internet as Peyton, but even I know how to Google, so on the drive back to Castle Orchard, instead of talking to Keith who was beyond stressed, I Googled 'Violet Black'.

Typing in her name reminded me of some gossip I'd heard at The Southern Pair.

"GIRL," TRUDY HAD said as she followed me, jabbering through the aisles looking for a special something for her husband. "You're lucky you won't have to deal with the ex."

"I agree," I said, having no idea the ex would still manage to wiggle her way into my marriage eventually. "What does your husband like to do?"

"He used to build things with his dad, but since he passed away, he just sits in front of that TV watching home improvement shows."

"Sounds like he's lost his tools," I said.

"He definitely has," she said. "And his mojo, too. Now, about Keith's ex. You're going to be a better momma than her for sure. That Violet sure couldn't have been a very good mom to leave her kids. Who'd do such a thing?"

"Well," called Esther, the slightly wrinkled woman who had been through three slips herself and presently sat with her nails soaking in sudsy solution. "There are times when I wanted to leave my kids – and my husband, too."

"Esther!" I exclaimed, peeping at her over the aisle of what else, repurposed wedding items.

Things the ladies let loose when they're getting their nails done sometimes just floor me. It's as if they walk through the shop doors, and when that bell rings, throw all their inhibitions aside. And sometimes, they need to.

"I'm just telling you the truth," Esther had said. "When I was young, my kids drove me crazy. Sometimes, I wanted to lock myself away."

Trudy and I'd exchanged a glance and I pointed at a repurposed jewelry box with a broken heart painted on top. Trudy smiled sadly at the box and shook her head, then she pointed at a dragonfly. I nodded and picked up the tiny figurine, a symbol of strength and poise that only comes with age, and handed a nice hammer to Trudy for her husband.

"But you loved your kids, Esther," Trudy said as she paid for the hammer and for the dragonfly, too.

"Well, of course, I did," Esther said. "But that didn't keep me from hiding in the closet sometimes. I just needed a moment of peace and quiet."

Marta began to rub cream into Esther's wrinkled, and probably tender, hands.

"You coulda never left your kids, Esther. I know you're a softy." Marta picked up a bottle of almost garish red polish, Esther's favorite.

Esther huffed. "I could have. Trust me. I just didn't."

But Violet had.

As I'd wrapped the dragonfly for Trudy to give to Esther, I'd remembered how once, right after Marta and I had pulled one of our twin sister switch tricks on our momma, she'd locked herself in her bedroom. Daddy had slept on the couch until she was ready to come out.

Two days later she emerged, her hair floating around her head like a halo and said with a smile, "Where are my girls? Come here darlings."

KEITH WAS DRIVING too fast, but I didn't dare say anything. Instead I stared at my phone screen, watching as 'Violet Black' filled the search results on my smartphone's screen. I thought about Esther's story and Violet's. Esther might understand what could make a woman want to escape, but there was a big divide between hiding in a closet for a few minutes of peace, or even locking yourself in your room for a few days, compared to disappearing on purpose forever.

As I scrolled down the screen on my phone, most of the search results were from Violet's rodeo queen days. The most recent showed the divorce of beloved couple Keith and Violet Black, along with a string of stories about her disappearance. Pictures and pictures of them with shiny belt buckles, hats, and pretty horses populated the screen, a few with the children, but most without them. I knew for a fact that Keith's parents had spent lots of time watching Peyton and baby Stevie during the rodeos, but surely she would have missed them. Then again, she and Keith were rodeo royalty and were treated like it, according to stories I'd heard. Maybe she enjoyed it a little bit too much. I clicked onto a picture of Keith and Violet riding side by side on their horses in the Pillar Bluff Frontier Days Parade. They really did look like western royalty.

And, wow, I'd forgotten how beautiful she was. Violet Black was a gorgeous woman with rich, flowing brown hair that reminded me of the queens I'd just met that night, flawless olive skin, like Peyton's, bright brown eyes and, of course, a tiny little body to die for. Sucking in my stomach just a little, I looked out the truck window to get refocused.

Why am I torturing myself?

My eyes fell back on my smartphone screen and the other results. A site called *When Life Gives You Apples* stood out. Wondering what that had to do with Violet, I clicked on the link.

"Oh. My. Gosh."

"What?" Keith.

"Did you know Peyton has a blog?"

"Sure," he said. "*When Life Gives You Apples*. She called it that because of all the orchards in Castle Orchard, and it's something we've always said, even before we met you. When life gives you apples—"

"Make applesauce," I said along with him. "I wonder why she's never told me about it."

He shrugged. "You know Peyton. She likes to keep some things close to the vest."

Spoken like a cowboy dad. Scrolling down, I was met by vibrant pictures – good photos even on a smartphone – of Peyton, her best friend Pia, Stevie, Keith, and none of me. My eyes lingered on a recently posted photo that was obviously several years old. Violet's smiling face beamed out at me. My stomach twisted a little more.

I ran my finger over the touch screen of my phone and scrolled down the web page in front of me, loving the colors, all red and green, but hating the topic of the recent blog post.

'An Open Letter to My Mom: In Case She's Reading This.'

If you didn't know Violet had abandoned her daughter, looking at the picture of her smiling while holding a toddler Peyton on her hip might lead you to believe the opposite of the truth.

Dear Mom,

I cried when you called. You called from a blocked number, so I couldn't call you back. I waited a long time, but something must have come up. I hope you are looking for me online, like I do you all the time, and that you see this.

Next was a very cool photo of Daddy's old red rotary phone, the one our own mother had loved to sit and talk to her friends on, curling the chord around her fingers, laughing and smiling. Her lipstick had always seemed to match the phone. I had to strain my eyes to read the words beneath the photos.

Did you know I have a stepmother now? There's a lot I can tell you about her later, but really, she isn't that bad.

I leaned back in my seat. Not that bad? To say I was stunned would be a serious understatement, but that's what I was. Not that bad. It made my chest tighten.

Not bad.

I know you're probably worried about Stevie and me, but we're okay. Dad takes good care of us.

Maybe not this week, I thought as I studied an adorable picture of Stevie giggling, forever giggling, on the front steps of the farmhouse. Both Keith and I had been gone too much. After this rodeo, I vowed not to do anything like this again. The kids needed a parent at home, and it obviously would have to be me since Keith had rodeos for the rest of the year. If I did another rodeo, the whole family would have to go.

And we have a new Grandpa.

Smiles! Of course she included a picture of my dad in his orchard, dressed in overalls atop his tractor, smiling. I loved her even more for taking it. But when in the world had she taken all these photos? To me, her camera had just been one more gadget, and she loved gadgets almost as much as she loved her horses.

Maybe I'd been wrong about how Peyton spent her time.

He doesn't have the best horses, but they're sweet, and he has an orchard. He's the coolest thing about Dad marrying my stepmom. I have an Aunt now, too. You would like Aunt Marta. She's my stepmom's twin, she's funny, and she paints my nails in The Southern Pair shop for free.

I smiled thinking of Peyton's new love of manicures.

Next, a photo of Peyton's nails painted blue with tiny sunflowers, the way Marta had painted them just a few days ago.

So, what about you, Mom? Are you okay? Where are you? Where have you been?

Yes, Violet, where have you been?

Are you really coming home?

I gulped.

Here, Peyton inserted a stunning close up of a brilliant purple garden violet. I recognized it from the violets bursting from their terra cotta pot on Dad's front porch. I didn't have one reason to like Violet, but if she actually saw this blog post and didn't call her daughter again, she was worse than I thought. But did I want her calling Peyton again? Of course, I didn't, and yet—

I glanced at Keith, his jaw locked once again in concentration, and wondered what would be best. I chewed my lip, worrying about it before exhaling in frustration. It didn't matter what I thought. She would either call, or she wouldn't. I had no control.

No matter what, you're still my mom. I still want to see you.

Please come home.

Love always,
Peyton

Lordy, what is it with Mothers not being there for their children?

I wished I'd been there when Violet – or someone pretending to be her – had called. I would've taken that phone no matter how angry it made Peyton, and I would've demanded to know what in the world she was thinking, calling after all these years?

Chapter Seven

THE LOOK ON Peyton's face when we walked through the door made me want to cry. I'd never seen a smile like that, all full of hope and happiness, in all the time I'd known her. Still dressed in her jammies, she threw herself into Keith's arms.

"Mom called!!"

Keith gave her a squeeze, but couldn't seem to think of what to say. I shot my dad a helpless look.

"Let's all sit," he said.

His face was tired, tiny wrinkles etched into the corners of his eyes, as he motioned for us all to join him at the oversized kitchen table. Even Marta, who'd been conked out on the couch, wandered through the doorway in her bathrobe and sat down. Only Stevie was asleep up in the room he called his at Grandpa Marshall's house.

I studied Keith's face, but couldn't isolate just one emotion there.

"Isn't that great, Daddy? Mom! She called."

Dad poured coffee for the adults, pausing in front of Peyton and then, despite a chiding look from both Marta and I, poured her some, too. He then poured a heaping plop of creamer into her mug. She sipped at it like she'd been drinking it all night. I looked at Dad. She had.

"What?" he asked, the picture of innocence.

"What'd your mom say, cowgirl?" Keith reached for Peyton's hand, but she was too excited to hold his.

"Lots of stuff." Peyton drummed her fingers on the table, rattling the spoon she'd laid beside her cup. "But she didn't say where she was calling from. It said private caller or something like that."

I glanced at Marta to see what she knew, but she just shrugged.

"Are you sure it was your mom?" Keith asked.

"Of course, Dad. Don't you think I'd know my own mom? And you want to know the best part?" She smiled and didn't wait for him to guess. "She's coming here!" She giggled loudly, a sure sign she'd had too much coffee and had been awake way too long.

Keith caught my eye, and I didn't miss how his pupils flashed.

"When?" I asked.

"She didn't say, but—"

"Then how can you be sure?"

"Because, A-man-da." She sounded my name out, each syllable dripping with sarcasm. "She said she was. Why would she lie?"

Right. Why would she do that?

"And, why," Peyton continued, "would she go to the trouble of calling if she wasn't really coming?"

Now that one, none of us had an answer for. My mind went to Peyton's blog and I wondered if this phone call might be related to that. How many posts had she written about Violet? It could be some cyber-stalker calling her. I'd heard of that sort of thing. In fact, I never had liked the freedom of the Internet. Who was to say that all of Peyton's blog followers were legitimate?

"You made it sound like she was coming tonight," Keith chided.

Peyton stood, ready to argue with her dad, who had just driven all the way from Pillar Bluff. We all knew how this was going down. Someone needed to stop her. I stood, but then Marta touched my arm and I sat.

"Maybe she is," Peyton said. "What does it matter? My mom called!"

"I misunderstood," he said. "I thought she was coming tonight."

"I never said that." Peyton countered.

"Okay, so we have time," he said.

"Exactly!" Peyton exclaimed. "I need to get my room organized. Maybe Mom will want to sleep in it on her purple couch."

I was proud of myself for not moving a muscle or saying a word when Peyton mentioned this.

"Peyton," Keith said, once she'd calmed down some.

"I'm supposed to ride tomorrow." He looked too tired to make the long drive back tonight, but I was pretty sure he wouldn't listen to me. "I've got to get back to Pillar Bluff. We'll figure all this out later."

He stood, grabbed his keys.

"You're leaving right now?" Marta.

"Keith. Right now?" Me.

"You're leaving?" Peyton ran around the table and threw her hands around his waist, no longer angry at him.

She tried her happy smile, but I saw how it wobbled in the corners now that her dad was leaving her to process this huge event on her own. But even though I didn't like it, I did understand. He had to make a living.

"My mom called, Dad. If you leave now, you might miss her."

What a tragedy that would be!

Keith paused and wrapped his arm around Peyton.

"I love you forever and ever amen, girl."

My heart melted. I loved that cowboy so much. He stood with Peyton like that a long time while Marta and I plucked napkins from the red hen napkin holder in the center of the table. Like so many things in that kitchen, it was our momma's. Using it made me feel like she was near, but of course, she wasn't.

My dad, always calm in difficult situations, sipped his coffee, only his glistening eyes betraying his feelings.

"Listen, cowgirl." She looked up at her dad, arms still

wrapped around his waist. "We can't even be sure it was her. It might have been someone playing a trick or something."

Tears spilled down her rosy cheeks. "Who would do that, Dad?"

He smoothed her tussled hair away from her forehead, making her look more like a ten-year-old than a teenage girl.

"I don't know, honey."

"Nobody," she said with conviction. "She's coming. Soon. I know it." She pressed her cheek into her dad's chest.

Keith cast me a look full of confusion and worry. We all knew Violet wouldn't come, better not come. Someone would have to explain the truth to Peyton, since she didn't seem to be listening to her dad.

Grandpa Marshall stood at the ready as Keith jingled his keys. Keith held Peyton at arm's length, bent at the waist, looked at her with those eyes that I remembered in my dad's own face when he told us our mother had left us.

"Peyton. I don't know who called, but I promise I'm going to get to the bottom of it when I get back."

"It was my mom." She tried to shrug away, but didn't struggle when he gently pulled her back in front of him.

Marta and I were about to finish off the napkins.

"Now listen to me. Don't cry." Keith caught one of Peyton's tears with the tip of his finger. "Remember? I told you before. Your mom had to go, cowgirl. She said she wouldn't be coming back."

"But she just called me, Dad."

"I don't know what this is, but even if she comes, we can't just let her show up after all these years, cowgirl. She has to go through the authorities to make that happen."

"No." Peyton was shaking her head. "Aren't you the authority in our family? You can let her come if you want to!"

I heard it in her voice, that conviction that enters a person when they refuse to accept the truth. It's what keeps people going in the hard times, during wars, during tragedies. This, for Peyton, was her great tragedy. My eyes burned and I fought an almost overwhelming desire to let out a sob, both for Peyton and for me, for Marta, because our mothers had left us all behind.

"She knew what she was doing when she left, Peyton. She left instructions with a lawyer releasing parental rights. I haven't wanted to force the issue with you because I knew it would make you sad, but I see now that it was the wrong thing for me to let you go on believing this—this fantasy. I shouldn't have let you keep the phone. Now—"

"No." Peyton jerked away. "You aren't taking my phone. And no. No. It's not a fantasy. You're lying about the stupid papers." She stormed upstairs, her bare feet pounding the hardwood so hard I worried the balls of her feet would be bruised in the morning. Marta followed. Right on cue, Stevie came out of his room, rubbing his eyes with one hand and dragging his stuffed horse in the other.

"Dad? Mommy?"

My heart melted and I couldn't stop that sob anymore.

Stevie had been calling me versions of Mom, Mommy Mandy, and just plain Mommy for a while now and I loved it, but right now, it was also a reminder that Peyton probably could never think of me that way. Who could blame her? For Peyton, mom was the woman who had abandoned her. It's not right. And it's not fair. I know better than to think any mom is perfect, but one thing I do know is that moms aren't supposed to leave you, at least not by choice.

"I LOVE YOU forever and ever amen, Dad." Stevie lay his head on his pillow. It'd taken a while to get him back in bed, and all the while we could all hear Peyton crying down the hall, even after Keith and I stepped outside and stood together, leaning against his truck.

"I want to stay here with the kids," I said. "I know I'm not going to be Peyton's favorite person right now, but she needs a parent here."

Keith pulled me into his arms. "Thank you."

"Don't leave." But I didn't mean it.

"You know I have to."

And I did know. Rodeo was our livelihood for the time being. We stood like that for a while, me not knowing how I should feel. A part of me wanted to tell him that Peyton needed her Daddy more than she needed me, but wild horses waited, and he couldn't not show up. It was a paycheck. It was his reputation.

"Be careful," I said, careful not to let any of the comments flying through my head escape my lips.

"I always am."

"Hon?"

"Hmmm?" He was rubbing my back, his breath warm against my neck, his heart pounding from the excitement of the evening against my shoulder.

"Do you think it *was* her?"

"I don't know. I can't imagine who'd pull a joke like that on a kid."

"Me, neither."

"I don't think Violet's going to show up here tomorrow, but I'm going to call the sheriff, just in case some weirdo – or Violet – tries to cause any problems."

"What would she want after all this time?" I asked.

"The kids."

My breath caught at hearing Keith saying it out loud. "How dare she?" Even I was surprised at the conviction in my voice.

I squeezed Keith tighter, my wife and mama instincts flooding my heart. I wanted to say something to relieve the tension I felt in my husband's spine, but all I could do was squeeze Keith tighter, as if in doing so, I might squeeze her out of our lives, out of the kids' lives, where she belonged. Where she had chosen to be.

Chapter Eight

KEITH HAD TO stay in Pillar Bluff for another week. I should have questioned it at the time, but since almost a week had gone by with no more calls from Violet, the fear that she would show up had subsided to worry. Maybe it was like Keith thought – just some kind of prank. I was anxious to get back to the home I now shared with my husband, so after a couple of days at my dad's, I decided to take the kids back to the ranch. Stevie adjusted wherever he was just like the Transformer toys he liked to play with, but Keith and I had agreed over the phone that getting them back to their routines would be the best thing for Peyton.

"Why can't we stay with Grandpa?" She was sitting at the table while I busied myself making breakfast. It felt good to be back in my home, our home, even if Peyton didn't want to be there without her dad.

"He's a mere five miles away," I reminded her. "You can see him every day if you want, but we need to be home."

"Why?" she demanded.

"Because this is our home," I said.

"Doesn't feel like home," she said, staring at the table's

surface as if it held some answer as to why. I didn't believe her, but I decided not to comment further. The supposed call from Violet had disrupted her world, opening a Pandora's Box of troubles that were better off locked away.

"Have some oatmeal," I said, placing an antique purple bowl filled with oatmeal and raisins in front of her. I'd found the bowl in the shop and hoped it would calm her, because after all, just because your mother isn't there for you doesn't mean you can – or even want to – stop remembering. Even I didn't want her to forget her mother, only the idea that she was coming back.

"It's your favorite—cinnamon raisin oatmeal," I said, tapping the table with my index finger, next to the bowl.

Peyton shifted her attention to her glass of orange juice.

"That's Stephen's favorite, not mine. My mom would've known that. See?" She took a long drink, and smacked her lips. "You don't even know me."

I sighed, truly wanting to know her. Why wouldn't I? Even if it seemed like she might never warm up to me, I wasn't ever giving up.

"Sorry," I said as kindly as I could. "Please eat it anyway."

One thing was for sure—at least Peyton's teenager attitude was back to normal.

"When's my dad coming home?" She sounded frustrated, and I was right there with her. I couldn't have been happier when Peyton's best friend, Pia, knocked on the door and right behind her stood Marta.

"Marta gave me a ride," Pia said as she entered all giggly and happy. She offered me a kiss on the cheek before she grabbed Peyton and they ran up the stairs to Peyton's room.

"I love that girl," I said. "She's so good for Peyton."

"Me, too," Marta said. "It's too bad she has a momma who's as stiff as the flagpole downtown."

"I know," I said. "Being loyal to Violet to the point of ignoring me is ridiculous. We should be classier than that for the girls."

"Some people aren't classy," Marta said, pouring herself a glass of sweet iced tea, even though it wasn't even nine-o-clock in the morning yet. I offered her Peyton's bowl of untouched oatmeal. Marta wrinkled her nose, but grabbed the spoon.

"Guess what," I said, happy for an excuse to lighten the conversation. "I found you a cowboy." I told her about Cowboy Quentin.

Marta squealed. "When do we meet?"

"Soon," I said. "Don't you want to know what he's like?"

"Is he a cowboy? Friend of Keith's?"

"He lives in Pillar Bluff, but he and Keith work together on ranch things a lot. He even works here sometimes."

"Then why haven't I seen him?"

"I don't know. He'd be hard to miss in this little town. He's exceptionally handsome."

"What does he look like?"

I laughed. "What are we, writing a romance novel?"

"That's a great idea," she said. "If he were my cowboy romance hero, how would you describe him?"

I thought for a moment. "Okay, I'm no writer, so this will sound corny, but I would describe him as a very tall, broad-shouldered, exceptionally fit man in his thirties with shaved ebony hair and skin the color of umber. His eyes are kind."

"Now aren't you the novelist!" she exclaimed. "Umber, huh? Like toffee brown?" Marta and I often thought in shades of nail polish.

"I'm not sure a novelist would say that, but yes. And he wears Levi's, crisp, button-down shirts, favors black boots and black cowboy hats, but I've also seen him in t-shirts and it looks like they just don't make them big enough to fit across his broad chest."

"Yummy."

We burst into laughter. "And since I know you're not looking for a fling, you should know that he's probably one of the nicest men I've met on the rodeo circuit. Keith says Quentin avoids the party life and that he hasn't dated in a long while."

"Poor thing," she said. "I wonder why?"

"Because he's waiting for a girl like you," I said. Keith hadn't shared why Quentin hadn't dated and I hadn't pried anymore. Guys have the bro code, you know.

"Well, if he's interested in a loud, white girl and doesn't

mind that she looks just like his friend's wife, then I want to meet him."

"If you'd come to visit me more often, you might just bump into him – with a little bit of help from me."

She grinned. "It sounds like I might enjoy that."

We burst into giggles, and for a few moments we were back in our rodeo fan days, before rodeo became a part of our family.

"Hey. Speaking of cowboys, when's Keith coming home?"

"In a few days, but even if the rodeo is over, he has a lot to do before then with ranching business. He's never going to be retired if the ranch isn't running the way he wants it to, and I want him to retire. I have to be patient."

"The ranch isn't going well?"

"It is," I said. "But he's a stickler when it comes to running things. We have to think long term. Plus, he's been feeling a lot of pressure lately."

"Pressure? Keith is always stone-faced calm, to me."

"Well, he's my husband. I get to see another side of him. I think he's also working harder on everything just to prove he's still got it, sis." I told her about what the rodeo announcer had said about his age.

Marta opened her mouth like she wanted to say something, but bit her lip.

"What?"

"Nothing." She held her hands up, palms out. "I'm not

getting in the middle of it."

"Since when do you not get in the middle of anything?"

She laughed. "Well, I was just thinking, if he's under a lot of pressure, he might need his wifey. You don't think you ought to go back to Pillar Bluff again, do you? You could drive over and have lunch with your hubby and be back by dark. I'll be here for the kids."

"I don't need to go to Pillar Bluff. The rodeo is over. He won his prize, otherwise known as a paycheck. Now he has work to do." I wasn't going to admit to Marta how lonely I was without Keith there, or how Peyton and I were constantly at each other's throats.

"You miss him."

"He's working." I was worried about how hard he'd been working, too, but I knew whatever he was working on was for us.

"But what kind of ranch business takes this long?"

"I'm still figuring out the horse business," I admitted. "But it doesn't matter. He'll be on his way home any time."

"I don't see why he has to stay overnight. It's barely a two-hour drive."

"It would be a waste of gas to drive every day," I said. "Honestly, what's with you, Marta? It's all fine. I trust Keith."

"Do you?"

I glared at her. I tolerated a lot from my twin, knowing it was a two-way street, but I didn't like her talking bull crap about my husband.

"Cut it out, sis."

She huffed and drank her tea. I huffed back.

"So, what's up with you?" I felt defensive.

She patted my hand. "You've been worried all week, that's all. I've noticed."

"I've been worried about Peyton," I said.

"About more," she said, ignoring my frown. "And frankly it shows in your face."

Despite my frustration with my sister, I touched the corners of my eyes. Nothing a cold compress and an infusion of herbs wouldn't help.

"You two are newlyweds," she said, snapping me back to attention.

"And your point is?"

"You have to keep the spark going."

I laughed. And everybody says I'm the crazy one. "Not that it's any of your business, sis, but the spark's not out."

"Mm-hmmm," she said, placing a hand on her hip.

"Mm-hmmm," I said, placing both hands on my matching hips.

"Well," she said, grabbing her spoon again and dragging it through the oatmeal. "I'm just saying that with everything Peyton is going through, she and Stevie need a dad around, and you should make him hurry home."

"They have a dad," I said sharply enough to make her pucker her red lips. I did the same. We were mirror images when angry. I stared that girl down until she let her shoulders drop.

"Fine," she finally said. "I know it's none of my business."

"You're right," I said. "What my husband is doing in Pillar Bluff, and anything about our marriage, isn't any of your business."

"And your point?"

"Oh, whatever. You'll say what you want anyway, so go for it."

"Okay," she said, not backing down. "It's not just the kids I'm thinking about. Don't think I'm crazy, but I know you have a little jealousy thing about rodeo queens and cowgirls, so I just thought you might be worried about him, you know—"

My heart skipped a beat, but I didn't let it show.

"No. I don't know. I haven't been worried. And how dare you insinuate what I think you are."

The chastened look on her face made me feel better, but only for a moment. I plopped down on the barstool opposite her.

"Do you really think I should be worried?"

She shrugged, and I didn't know whether to slap her or joke it off. Of course, I couldn't joke it off. I'd been cheated on before, and if anyone knew how a relationship could change overnight because of a cheating spouse, it was me, and Marta had witnessed my whole sad journey.

"I'm sorry for upsetting you," she said.

"I'm not upset." I lied, but as what she suggested sank in, I wondered.

What if some cowgirl turned his head? He was going through a lot, and I could see how the attention might catch him at a vulnerable time. But would he do that to me, the way my first husband had? I felt my cheeks go hot with the thought of it.

"Now, don't worry," Marta said. "I'm just trying to help."

I shook my head, ridding myself of such thoughts. Marta was lonely, so she was stirring the pot in my marriage.

"Bless your heart," I said. "I love you for caring, but you're not helping." I slapped the tea towel onto the counter. "I think what you need is a man, sissy. That way you can stay out of mine."

She huffed. "That's not nice."

"Sorry," I said.

"No, you're not."

I shrugged. "I'm sorry a little bit."

She sighed. "Fine. Don't listen to me if you don't want to, but don't blame me when he does what all men eventually do to their wives."

"They do not," I defended, praying fervently that I was right.

"And you're right a little bit," she said. "I do need a man, preferably a cowboy of my own. When can I meet this

Quentin?"

I stared. It was hard to believe she was a grown woman for a moment, but then I couldn't help but smile at the sincerity in her face. I thought about how long she'd been waiting to meet a good man. Maybe causing drama for me and mine was how she was dealing with it.

"This is so high school," I said.

She smiled. "It always is."

I laughed with her. It was way too easy to slip into old habits. Sometimes I missed those days when we were single together. I knew she did, too.

"I'll definitely make sure you two meet."

"Thank you," she said. "And I'm sorry. I'm meddling, it's true. I'm sure I'm wrong. Keith isn't doing anything bad, but that doesn't change the fact that newlyweds shouldn't be apart this much."

"True. I'm getting tired of my teddy bear. I want the real one."

"Stop right there," she said. "No details about your sex life."

"So much for writing that romance novel," I said.

We giggled like two teenagers.

"Did you know," she said, "that in the olden days a warrior had to take a year off from battle to be with his new wife?"

"What days were those?"

She shrugged, adjusting the red frames of her blingy

reading glasses and studying an old issue of *Bride* magazine I'd left on the counter. "I don't know. I read it in some magazine at the shop."

"I do miss him," I confessed. "But what if I go to Pillar Bluff and Violet shows up here while Keith and I are both gone?"

"Trust me. Daddy and I won't let her near them." I knew it was the truth.

"What would my excuse be for showing up in Pillar Bluff, again? Keith's going to think I'm way too spontaneous."

"Um, he already knows."

"That's true." I grabbed my phone to text him. "There, now he's expecting me."

"Hooray! You get over there and scare those barflies away."

I felt my smile fade. "Do you still think I should be worried? Be honest, sis."

"That's not what I said. Nix the barfly comment. I was being silly."

"Right. I mean, you're the one who is always saying nothing to be jealous of."

"Exactly, so please forget what I said earlier. Don't be jealous. Besides, look at you. You have nothing to be jealous about." She ran her hands in a curvy pattern through the air.

I shook my head, trying not to be amused. "Do you realize how self-serving that sounds?"

"Well, the truth is the truth. And I think you're beautiful." She giggled.

My phone buzzed with a text from Keith. "I'll leave in the morning. And I'm staying the night."

"Now you're talking. And you can take this. Suzie came by yesterday with it." Suzie was our Mary Kay rep. Marta reached into her bag and offered me the brand new tube of pink lipstick.

"It came early!"

I walked over to the mirror next to the front door. The lipstick made me feel a little happier. I smiled brightly when Peyton and Pia paused on their way out the back door and Pia said, "Where did you get that lipstick?"

Pia was a girl after my own heart.

"It is pretty," said Peyton, albeit begrudgingly. Well, what do you know?

I dug through Marta's bag and pulled out the tube of lipstick.

"You girls come here." I popped the lid off.

Each girl leaned forward and pursed their lips while I dabbed a little color on their pouty little mouths, enjoying this moment and knowing it would be gone in a few minutes. They popped their lips and smiled in unison, and I don't care what anyone says, when everything else in the world is going wrong, it's good to have one thing a girl can count on.

But Peyton needed more than lipstick to make the smile

on her face glow. She needed a mom. I hoped that in her heart of hearts Peyton knew she could depend on me someday, but just as Peyton offered me her pink lipstick smile, her cell phone rang. Her face transformed to joy. I knew instantly it wasn't because of me.

"Hello? Mom? Mom!" She whispered to all of us. "It's my mom!"

My heart dropped to my toes. For a second, I thought of reaching out and taking the phone from Peyton, giving Violet a piece of my mind, asking her why she thought she could abandon her kids and just breeze back into their lives any time she felt like it, but Marta slapped my hand down. Instead, I had to sit there and listen to Peyton talk to her mother, shyly, not like talking to a mom should be, and then see the tears well up in her eyes as she pressed the off button.

"She had to go." She scrunched her face. "Something about movie time."

"Did she say where she was calling from?"

"No." Her lip quivered. "And—she's not coming."

We all sat, Pia, Marta, and I, watching Peyton, nobody sure what to do. When the lonely tear trailed down her cheek, it was her best friend who pulled her into her arms, while Marta squeezed my hand in an effort, I knew, to calm my heart.

But it didn't work. I was not calm. In fact, there might as well have been a herd of horses running inside my chest. I wasn't going to let this woman gallop in and out of Peyton's life without a fight. I was going to Pillar Bluff and have a talk with Keith. We needed to find her and we needed to decide together what to do about Violet's ghost, somehow resurrected in this house. And we needed to throw away that darned phone and all the negativity attached to it. Peyton must have sensed my thoughts because when I looked at the phone, she gripped it until her delicate knuckles were white.

Chapter Nine

"HI THERE," I said to the receptionist of the Two Sycamores in Pillar Bluff. "I need a key to my husband's room, please."

When I told Keith I was coming, he'd arranged to have the RV taken home and moved over to the adorable bed and breakfast he knew I loved. In the room, I threw myself on the bed, exhausted. Keith was meeting with a rancher about twenty miles out of town about some horses and wouldn't be back for a few hours. That didn't sound anything like a clandestine affair, or like he was keeping it a secret from me, now did it?

I dialed Keith's number on my cell. "Hi, honey. I'm here."

"Hi, sweetheart." His voice made me melt into a puddle. "I'm afraid I'm going to be another couple hours."

I sighed. "It's okay."

"Why don't you go shopping or something? Or to the new library. Did you know they remodeled it and it has a coffee shop? We need to bring the kids."

"Did you say a library and coffee?" A book sounded nice,

preferably one that would get me in the mood for love. I chuckled at the memory of making up cowboy hero descriptions with Marta. I had one for Keith, too, but I wasn't sharing it with anybody.

He laughed. "Yes, and then I'll call you when I'm on my way back to the bed and breakfast, but don't wait on me if you want to eat."

"That sounds like more than two hours."

"I'll try to be faster."

"Okay." Hanging up, I called my friends, Trace and Dante, at Morris House Bistro to see if they were still in town.

"Hey, guys. I'm in the mood for macaroni and cheese, and I'm in town." They returned the message right away and told me to come right back to the kitchen. "Okay, I'm stopping at the library first, and then I'll be over."

At the library, I bought a coffee. I was dying to check out some books, but wasn't sure when I'd be back to turn them in, so I settled with perusing some house design books in a quiet corner and enjoying my coffee. I could have stayed all day, but I wanted to see my friends and then, hopefully, Keith would be back. On my way out, I was surprised to bump into Judy from the rodeo. I smiled at her as I passed, but her face had a look that said she had no idea who I was. Instead, I smiled at the person who was helping her. She wore the same t-shirt Judy's friend at the rodeo had worn.

The library was close to the bistro, so I left my car there

and walked. I was still thinking about Judy as I walked toward the entrance, so, at first, I didn't even notice who Trace had paused to talk to out on the restaurant's patio. And then I saw him. Who could miss that rust-colored shirt I'd bought for Christmas, or those trademark boots? And guess who was sitting across from my husband?

"Adri," I whispered.

I wanted to speed dial Marta right away, but something told me I needed to handle this on my own. I loved my sister, but I had to be my own person with my husband.

My heart was in my throat. I thought I heard sirens. I don't know, but there might have even been smoke shooting from my nostrils and out my ears. Adri had her hand in the crook of Keith's elbow and was dressed in one of those little country girl numbers that belonged on a very young, leggy country singer. The only problem with her outfit was that she completely pulled it off, like it was designed specifically for her lean itty-bitty body, and definitely not for my curvy one.

But this was Adri, I reminded myself. My new friend. And my husband, whom I trusted – didn't I? And yet, there they were, together, Adri's hand now slipping across the table to touch my husband's.

Mercy. Am I crazy?

"Mandy?" I didn't realize it, but I'd walked right up to his table.

I offered a weak smile. What was going on?

Keith reached out and took my hand. "Sweetheart. What are you doing here?" His voice was suddenly that of a stranger.

Of a cheater. A swindler.

"How fun to see you again so soon," Adri said, her eyes sparkling. Probably from her fascinating meal with my husband.

I glanced down. It looked like they hadn't eaten, but both had half-finished glasses of iced tea. But still, why wasn't Keith at that ranch meeting that was supposedly taking him so long? Or with me?

Adri smiled, all innocence, and I wanted to throw up. Instead, I drew myself to my full height, which in my heels was almost six feet, and smiled. Whatever was going on, the whole world didn't need to know about it.

Instead of asking Keith what he was doing there, I said, "I just left the library and am stopping by to say hi to Trace and Dante. Didn't I tell you what my plans were?"

Keith's face went white as my meaning sank in, but what could he do without creating a scene?

"Mandy!" Trace appeared beside me and swept me into his arms.

"Trace!" He settled me down and I pasted on a smile, pretending I wasn't seeing my husband sitting at lunch with a lovely young woman after lying to me about where he was.

"Are you sitting here? I can pull up a chair."

Keith jumped up to grab a chair and Adri made a big

deal about what a great idea it was. My blood was at a full boil now and by the look on Keith's face, he'd noticed.

"Yes, have a seat, sweetheart." He motioned toward the chair, and I thought he looked trapped.

How dumb was my husband to meet a woman here, at the restaurant of my friends? It didn't make sense. I wanted to freak out, to scream, and to hit him over the head with my purse. That's exactly what I would have done when I was single, but I was a married woman now. I had rights to this man, whether I decided to keep him or not. I shot him a withering look. If Adri noticed, she didn't blink.

"No, thank you. Y'all enjoy your visit," I said sweetly, as if I'd known all along the two were meeting. "I'm going inside to talk to Trace and Dante. It's why I came. I'll catch you later, cowboy."

Trace not missing a beat, offered me his elbow and we walked through the doors of his restaurant. He led me across the gorgeous, hardwood floors and through the swinging doors into the kitchen.

"Bless your heart, you look like you could use some sweet iced tea."

I downed half of it before muttering an embarrassed thank you.

"Now tell me. What is going on?" Trace crossed his arms over his bulky chest. "You look ready to punch someone."

I gulped the rest of my tea and handed him the glass. "I think my husband is a no good, two-bit, drunk cheater."

He looked doubtful. "Are you sure? He didn't look drunk when I saw him."

At that moment my phone buzzed. It was Keith, but I didn't answer.

"Is that your husband?"

"Yes."

"Are you going to answer it?"

"I don't know what to say."

He sat on a stool beside me. "Well, you are welcome to stay in here for as long as it takes you to calm down."

"I'm calm."

He raised his bushy eyebrows. "Honey, your face is so red I'm about to douse you with water. Why don't you just let him explain?"

Dante walked up and kissed me on the cheek. "Hi, sweetheart." He offered me a mimosa.

"Thank you," I said. "Why can't you two be here all the time? Why must you live in Wyoming?"

"We love it there," Trace said.

"Yeah, yeah." I sipped my drink. I tried to smile. "This is perfect."

"She thinks her husband is cheating on her," Trace said.

"Oh no. Do we want to kick him out?"

"No, he's with Adri, so I highly doubt he's cheating."

"Oh, no way he's cheating."

"You know her?" I asked. "And, anyway, he lied to me. He's supposedly out of town at a ranch, but obviously not."

Tears sprang to my eyes. I fanned them dry until one of them offered me a box of tissues. I pulled out a handful.

"I should've put on waterproof today." I moaned.

They nodded.

"But I just hate how difficult it is to get that stuff off, you know. I don't know how those rodeo queen types do it. I wear as much makeup as the next girl – okay, I wear more—but I like to wash it off at night."

They both nodded again and I felt sorry for them. They probably felt like we were back in college, me having a boyfriend meltdown. Only now I was a mature woman having a cowboy meltdown.

"So, you two know Adri?"

"We do," Trace said. I didn't wait for them to say how.

"What I wouldn't give to throttle that girl. She tricked me. Pretended we were friends. And I thought she was so nice. She's obviously a total B."

"Adri? A bitch?" Dante stared.

"No, she's a B," I said. "I'm a mom now. I don't curse."

"Okay, a B," Trace said. "Listen, Mandy. She's not a B."

"Yes," I said. "She's a husband stealer!"

Trace chuckled.

"What?"

He just kept chuckling until Dante joined in.

I stood. "My husband is obviously having an affair and you just don't understand."

Trace's lips formed a flat line. I pointed my hand in the

air and said Scarlett O'Hara style, "I am not going to stand by and just watch it happen, either. As soon as I calm down, I'm going back there and give him – and her – a piece of my mind."

Trace patted my shoulder. "Your husband isn't having an affair, Mandy."

"Did you not just see what I saw? The two of them all googly-eyed? How do you explain that?"

"I heard them talking, and there were no googly eyes, except Keith's when he saw you."

I perked up. "Really?"

"Really. If it makes you feel better, in passing, I heard them talking about a special home for people here in Pillar Bluff. She probably wants him – and you – to donate something. We know Adri's family. They dine here a lot and we've gotten to know them when we are in town."

"Oh," I said, considering changing my tune.

"Adri is real big on places that help people with mental disabilities. You probably know all about her volunteer work and her queen platform."

"But why would my husband lie about where he was, if that's all it is?"

"I don't know," Dante said. "There might be a simple explanation for that, too, but that's between you and your husband."

I remembered how at ease Adri had felt with Judy, our talk during the Pillar Bluff Rodeo, and how she shared her passion for volunteering at places like the one Judy lives.

"I'm an idiot," I said.

"Not an idiot, but I seem to recall, you *were* always a hothead."

"But why doesn't she go to Castle Orchard to meet with Keith? Why here, at a fancy restaurant?"

"We're not that fancy, and you'll have to ask them, but I am ninety-nine percent positive there is no funny business going on between your husband and Adri."

I took a brave breath and stood to go. "I'm sorry about this, you guys. You must think I'm crazy. I swear, I've grown up, but this… this just threw me for a loop." I smiled. "And she's so young and beautiful, you know? I feel old around her."

They took in my outfit, which I just want to say was a pair of adorable designer jeans, a gold t-shirt, and the cutest leopard scarf you've ever seen.

"I don't think you will ever get old," Trace said. "Does Marta still look this good?"

"Exactly like me," I said.

"Then you both look just like you did in college."

I loved him for that little fib. "Hey, do you two still have that mac and cheese?"

Dante disappeared for a few moments and returned with a heaping bowl of homemade pasta saturated with golden cheese.

"This is my nanna's mac and cheese recipe."

I took a heaping bite, savoring the cheddar on my tongue. "I hope we have this in heaven."

"I don't know about that, but her recipe is the best. And when you're finished with that, it's nanna's bread pudding."

I wanted to bury my face in it. Whoever said carbs were out has gone off the deep end.

Chapter Ten

BACK AT THE bed and breakfast, I put on a pair of my best yoga pants and one of Keith's favorite hot pink tops with my new lipstick. When I'd left the restaurant, Keith and Adri were both gone. I'd checked my message when I got to the car.

"I'm sorry," the recording said. "It's not what you think. Please let me explain. I'll see you later, back at the room."

But he wasn't there. I prayed I hadn't scared him off. Deep down, I knew I couldn't, but old insecurity stirred up unreasonable ideas that made me jealous. After all, he had lied.

As I waited, I rehearsed an apology for my part, me jumping to conclusions, but couldn't think of the right thing to say. First, I'd demand an explanation for why he lied, but before I could come up with anything, I heard the door unlock. It swung open and there stood my cowboy, his face full of regret and uncertainty. He held his hat in his hand and looked so adorable; I gave up my last shred of anger.

"I'm sorry," he said.

"I'm sorry I didn't trust you," I said. "But please, honey,

explain. Why did you lie to me?"

He gave me a sad look. "It's okay. I can see how your mind might run away with crazy ideas, sort of like you did at the wedding." He smiled then, and I could tell he was used to me melting at such antics. I struggled to look neutral. I wanted him to explain first.

I huffed, hiding a smile. "What's that supposed to mean?"

He smiled softly, glancing down at my outfit. "It was supposed to be a joke." His eyes traveled over my hips and lingered on the pink fabric stretched across my breasts. I'd chosen that shirt, knowing full well it'd get my husband's attention.

"Oh, well, sometimes you aren't funny."

"Sometimes I'm not," he said. "Usually I'm not."

We both laughed a little. Again, he was right.

"So, that's what you're wearing when I take you out dancing tonight?"

"Do you have a problem with my yoga pants?"

He closed the door behind him.

"Only that I want to take them off of you." He reached for me, and his mouth was warm on mine, silencing anymore undo apology. His hands traveled around to cup my bottom, and the tender action was so familiar, yet unexpected after so much fury the hour before, that tears sprang to my eyes.

"I guess we can discuss the details about what just happened later."

"Good idea," he said.

He pulled my hips close, kissed me even closer, and all the heat that'd gone into my being mad at him escaped through hot skin and warm, wet kisses.

KEITH LEFT THE bed and breakfast early in the morning. More horse business, of course, but he promised that when he got back, we'd talk about Violet. In the meantime, I was happy with his excuse. He'd actually come back from the ranch early and was on the way to the bed and breakfast when he ran into Adri at the gas station, of all places. When she pitched her idea about him helping her with some public service announcements related to her favorite charity, they'd walked over to the bistro for a quick drink of iced tea. That was when I appeared and misunderstood the whole thing. I was almost too embarrassed to meet Adri for breakfast this morning, but, in Adri fashion, she showed up at the bed and breakfast to join me. How could I say no when she was already down in the lobby?

"I'm sorry," I said as soon as I walked into the dining room.

"Oh, me, too." We embraced and we were like little and big sister.

"You poor thing," she said. "That must have looked awful, finding us together like that. I'm so embarrassed."

"Don't be," I said. "It was all me. I'm ridiculous."

"You are the farthest thing from ridiculous."

I laughed at her over-the-top attempt to calm me down after I'd treated her like a slut after my husband.

"Oh, sweetie," I said. "You are too nice for your own good. Let's not talk about that nasty little incident again."

"Agreed," she said and we opened our menus.

The waiter poured me another cup of coffee from the silver carafe sitting on our table and I let him. I'd been meaning to give up caffeine, but couldn't bring myself to do it even though Keith always teased that Daddy must have given us a lot of coffee when were little to make us so energetic as adults. The truth was, he had, but it wasn't what gave us all our energy. If you asked me, it was our energy that required us to drink more coffee than most people, just to get anything out of it. I just wished I could muster the energy that I usually brimmed with.

"It's so sweet that you came to see your husband. You missed him, didn't you?"

"Yes," I said. "But you know how the rodeo life is, being a queen and all."

"It's an exciting life," Adri said.

"Exciting it is, but I have to admit, I'll be ready when he retires from the rodeo. I know he's sore about the 'old man' rumors."

Adri's laughter rang through the restaurant. I smiled at how she could be so carefree. I didn't even know why I'd told her something so personal.

"I'm sorry," she said. "It's just crazy that Keith would be considered old."

"It bothers him, what people say about him needing to retire."

"Does he want to?"

"I don't know. Does a cowboy ever want to stop being a cowboy?"

She laughed. "Never, ever."

"Right. And he doesn't appreciate people saying he should, and neither do I. It is one thing for me to want him to retire from it, and it's quite another for others to say it. He's a good man. He wants to do the right thing for me and the kids, but that doesn't make it easy. He loves bronc riding."

I think that just saying those words out loud opened a little door I'd previously closed off to Keith. I might not have been a very good cowgirl, but I loved my cowboy.

"He really is a good man. I'm lucky." I wanted to share about Violet calling, but I wasn't sure Keith would be okay with that, or what reaction it would bring from Adri, so I kept quiet for now.

"I know the feeling. I'm lucky to have mine, too." Adri held up a cranberry-iced scone. "Here's to good men."

I held my own scone in the air in a mutual toast before popping a large bite into my mouth.

"And here's to maintaining my curvy figure," I said.

Adri and I chatted and laughed through the rest of

breakfast. Her energy revitalized me and her idealistic approach to life and love made me want to surround myself with happy things. Heaven knew, I had a whole shop of them back in Castle Orchard. Maybe what I needed was to go to work and help people find mementos of happiness. I wondered if we had an item in the store that would make me feel confident again. I hated feeling out of control.

If only I were still as idealistic as Adri, and if only love was really as easy as it seems when you haven't yet come up against obstacles like cheating ex-husbands, mysterious ex-wives, and grief for lost mothers, and lost children that have a way of seeping into the cracks of your life, covering everything with a hazy film that would even make a rodeo queen's rhinestones turn dull.

Chapter Eleven

IT WAS SCHIZOPHRENIA that my mom was diagnosed with. One time, when we visited her at the home Daddy had to put her in, he was mortified to find her wandering the halls, crying out senseless things. He was told it was time to check into a more secure facility that handled people like her, so he said no and took her back home to live with us. Bringing her home seemed to do the trick, at first.

In the weeks before she left us, everything was crystal clear for her. We knew it couldn't last, according to her doctors, but we hoped, the way children and lovers do, that she was cured. She wasn't, of course, and so, when she took her own life during that brief reprieve from her illness, the shock and betrayal I felt stayed, while all the loving memories were lost for a while as the bottom fell out of my world. It didn't matter if I stood in her kitchen surrounded by all her things, the happy memories attached to them didn't permeate my grief.

Over the years, the lost memories came back, but the grief never left, having wrapped its tendrils around my heart as secure as the Cinderella buns Marta and I weave into the hair of prom queens as an extra service to the nail salon once a year. In the past, I wouldn't have dreamt of going into homes to visit people with mental problems, the way that Adri did. The idea would have terrified me, but on that day, I decided to make a change. It had helped Marta to deal with mom's death. We were twins, after all. Maybe it would help me, too.

"I'll be back in a couple of hours," Keith said after a long lunch together, if you know what I mean.

I leaned in for a kiss, no longer in the mood to talk about Violet. It'd have to wait. Besides, Keith was in a hurry to get back to his business meetings with ranchers and whatever business people he needed to meet with. He didn't ask my plans, and I didn't tell him what they were.

JUDY'S PLACE WASN'T really called a 'home,' like I kept referring to it. The sign in front of the sprawling building read Cottonwood Manor. I walked through the sliding doors, not even sure they would let me in to see her. After all, I wasn't a real friend or family member. Maybe it was ridiculous of me, but seeing Adri's passion for places like Cottonwood Manor, and Keith's desire to support it, had filled me with a conviction, or maybe Judy's smile had simply given me a guilt complex. Judy, for some reason, kept popping up in this crazy time I was having, so maybe God was trying to tell me something, trying to use Judy to open my heart.

Open heart or not, just looking at the entrance of the manor brought back sorrowful images of my mom when she lived in a place very similar to Cottonwood Manor. For a moment, I thought I might leave. I didn't want to remember Momma that way, but, taking a deep breath, I pushed my panic aside. Walking past the flowering plants, placed at the entrance to invoke a peaceful feeling, but failing, I pushed past my fears.

There was another feeling I had that I couldn't put my finger on, but I wanted to see Judy. Something about her condition did trigger sad memories of my momma, but something else, maybe her smile and the innocent way she talked about my husband, had also endeared her to me.

The floors were so shiny; they looked as if nobody ever walked on them. The fluorescent lights cast a yellow pallor on everyone, even healthy visitors, and the fake silk flowers were as ugly as I remembered from momma's place. I never understood why they had real flowers outside and fake ones indoors. When our mother was in a place like this, Marta and I had hated the silk flowers then, too. We'd taken in potted flowers for our momma and her 'friends' in neighboring rooms.

"Your name?"

"Manda. Amanda Black to see Judy."

She referred to a log, running her ringed, manicured hands down a handwritten list, and I waited for her to notice I wasn't on it. I wasn't sure what I'd say to convince her to let me in.

A moan carried across the room and settled in a chill around the nape of my neck.

"Nooooooo."

I turned to see an elderly man sitting in a wheel chair near the exit doors. He was crying.

"Please," he whimpered. "Turn the music down."

Of course there was no music, but it made me think of my mom. She heard things, too.

When my mom took her own life, Daddy told me my anger was wasted, that she probably didn't know what she was doing when she did it. It could've even been an accident, but we would never really know. Deep down, I felt like I knew. Momma seemed coherent in those last weeks, and she'd chosen to leave us, instead of fighting anymore; instead of fighting for us. Now, looking around at people lost somewhere in their minds wandering the halls, waiting in their wheelchairs by the doors hoping for a visitor, I was sorry for always blaming Momma. As a kid, I couldn't have placed myself in her shoes, but now I wanted to forgive her. At least I could try.

It wasn't as if she'd literally abandoned me for no reason, like Peyton's mom had her and Stevie. I wondered if Judy had children and if they ever saw her. I ran my fingertips along the bottoms of my eyes in an attempt to staunch tears stealing down my cheeks. I was glad I'd forgotten to take off my sunglasses, even though they now felt garish with their blingy frames in a place like this. I left them on anyway.

"Amanda Black, you say?" The receptionist smiled up at me, making no mention of my sunglasses, or wet cheeks, of course. She would be used to seeing sad visitors.

"Yes."

"Do you want me to call your husband and tell him you are here, hon? Or do you just want to go on back?"

I sniffed back my tears. "Excuse me?"

"Your husband, Mr. Black."

"My husband?"

She nodded, still smiling. "He's with Judy now."

Keith. My husband was here. In Judy's room?

"No need to call," I managed to say. "I'll just – join them."

"It's room 213."

I turned to go.

"Other way," she said, still smiling. Such a patient woman she was. I turned down the opposite hallway, finally pulling off my sunglasses, so I could have a better view.

I KNEW KEITH agreed to help Adri in her compassionate pursuits, but visiting Judy by himself was a little over the top. Had he been bitten by the same do-gooder bug as Adri? Maybe he wanted to support Adri's cause more directly than a check and being a spokesperson, but surely he would have told me.

I counted the doors. Were there really more than two

hundred rooms in this place? How terribly sad. I pictured the families absent of grandpas and grandmas, and in some cases, moms like my own, and dads.

The smell was something I'd never forgotten. It was a mix of cleaners, air fresheners, and body odors that didn't matter there where nobody was trying to impress anybody else. Passing a woman in curlers, sliding her walker down the hall, I recalled Marta and me trying to fix our mother's hair when we visited. She was a beautiful woman and we knew she wouldn't want to be seen looking terrible as the nurses tended her. We had done her hair every weekend, doing it up in styles that made her smile when she looked in the mirror, even though she didn't recognize us much of the time.

This place could sure use some of those new air fresheners Marta and I sold at The Southern Pair. The stuff they used at Cottonwood Manor reminded me of a department store bathroom.

210...211...212...

I stopped at Judy's door.

213.

Chapter Twelve

I WISH I could say I had a better reaction when I saw what I saw inside that room, something compassionate and considerate, a rushing forward and offering a comforting embrace, but my mute button had been pushed. I just wasn't at all prepared to see my husband sitting on the bed beside Judy, holding her hand while she slept.

Cowboys weren't supposed to cry. Why was he crying?

The image before me depicted my husband like a character in a movie, shiny trails mapping a streaming pattern down his shadowed cheeks. That was when I started to fit the broken pieces together.

A glance around the room lifted the veil—a framed picture beside the bed was of a rodeo queen next to a cowboy whom I recognized instantly; a purple hat encircled by a gleaming rhinestone tiara, resting on an antique dresser; and a framed eight by ten photo of Judy and two smiling children, only I now knew it wasn't Judy because the kids in the photo were my kids. Peyton had the exact same picture on her bedside table back at the ranch.

"Violet," I whispered.

Keith's eyes found me, his eyes wide. He ducked, brushing the back of his sleeve across his face. He sniffed, tried to get himself under control. I felt, as much as read, the embarrassment in his eyes, the worry about what I might think, and then the compassion as he let go of her hand and walked toward me, to reassure me.

I backed away, thinking about running. This was worse than our wedding day. Much worse.

I turned, ready to flee.

"Mandy. Stop."

I did, not turning around to face him, but believe you me I didn't want to. I knew something wasn't right, although my brain hadn't had time to process what my heart already knew. I couldn't run.

I let Keith take my hand. I glanced back at Judy—no, Violet—still sleeping, and followed Keith out to the parking lot. How I'd walked right past his truck parked by the main doors of the manor without noticing, I have no idea. Inside the truck, Keith started it and cranked on the AC.

"Holy cow, Keith. What is happening?"

He said nothing for a long while. I also couldn't find any words, which was not like me at all, but what was left to say? In my mind, during my most jealous thoughts, I'd rehearsed what I'd say to Violet if she ever came back, what I'd tell Keith if he ever decided he would take her back – which I know was a ridiculous worry – and none of it fit this situation.

With all my humorous quips and usual quick-wittedness gone, I reached for Keith's hand. He didn't just take mine in his own, but gripped it until my fingers hurt.

"Ouch," I whispered, making a feeble attempt at teasing.

"I'm sorry," he said, loosening his grip, but only slightly.

"Honey," I said. "I don't know what to say. Have you known all this time?"

"No," he said, his voice thick with emotion. "I just found out a few days ago when Adri brought me here for a tour because of all that spokesperson stuff she wants me to do." He stared straight ahead, his jaw rigid. "I was walking past her room and Adri said, 'Let's go see Manda's friend Judy.'"

"We weren't really friends," I mumbled. "She's just that lady from the rodeo…you know. Then I saw her again at the library, and—well, she's sweet."

"Yes." He said. "But I took one look at the pictures on her dresser, of Peyton and Stephen, and I knew she wasn't just some lady."

"I had no idea," I said, afraid he'd think I set this up or something, although that would have been pretty complicated to do, even if I'd known.

"Ever since then, it's been… some kind of nightmare."

"I can't imagine. What a shock." Everything I said sounded staged, inadequate.

He could only nod his agreement.

"All this time, we all thought—you thought—"

"I know. I was so wrong." He sank his chin low. "I

should've known something wasn't right. She wasn't the kind of woman who would've abandoned us." He looked at me, the depth of his broken heart fathomless in his eyes. "I can't believe she went through this alone."

"It's so sad," I whispered, grasping at words, but they evaporated like clouds, too insubstantial to hold the weight of reality.

Keith's face transformed into a grimace, like the people who picked up something in The Southern Pair that reminded them of something sad, something painful. I reached over and squeezed his shoulder, thinking of Judy's treasures inside her room, neatly organized on her dresser. Things with happy memories attached that must have made her smile.

"Oh, honey," I said. "I'm so sorry."

And then he did something I've never seen a cowboy do, certainly not my husband. He leaned his forehead against the steering wheel and sobbed. I had barely gotten over seeing my husband crying silently at Violet's bedside, and now he was weeping.

Keith was my western romance novel hero. He didn't cry.

But he did. His whole body, those muscular shoulders of his that had absorbed my own tears in the past as I'd confided to him about my lost babies and about my mother, shook like a silent earthquake.

"Oh gosh, Keith." I whispered into my hand, my own

cheeks growing wet.

I dried them quickly in the hem of my t-shirt. This wasn't my pain. This wasn't at all what I'd wanted for Keith, for Peyton, or Stephen, back when I'd insisted on getting rid of their mother's things.

I still couldn't believe it.

Judy is Violet?

Even though it was pretty awkward in the cab of the truck, I scooched real close to my husband, reached around his shoulders and waist, and held on. He obliged by turning and pulling me close to him. He cupped the back of my head in his hands and cried into my hair. I didn't say a thing, certainly not that he was about to squeeze me to death, but just held on to him, letting him pour it all out.

Keith needed me, and it reminded me that I'd been all about myself lately. All I'd talked about was what I needed from him lately – for him to retire, to be at home with the kids, to get rid of Violet's things, to help Daddy more at the orchard, to affirm me, to answer his phone – and I'd given very little thought at all to what Keith might need, or even that he had needs. He was so strong, such a man – such a cowboy – that I thought he was too tough to ever be vulnerable.

When his tears turned to choking sobs as he fought to regain control, I fished around in the cab of the truck until I found a purple bandanna that I recognized as Peyton's. I pressed it into his hands, and turned away while he dried his eyes, blew his nose, and cleaned himself up. I was glad for tinted windows and a large pickup cab. My poor husband. My poor kids.

No, Violet's kids.

Chapter Thirteen

"Young early-onset Alzheimer's."

"What?"

"It's why she'd fade away sometimes, forget to change Stephen's diaper, forget where Peyton was. She went to a doctor for help when Stevie was still a baby, and was diagnosed when she was only thirty-four. She didn't tell me any of this, just apparently started getting everything ready, and, less than a year later, she left us while she still could."

"But she's way too young." I did the math and realized she'd have only been three years older than I was right now.

"It's not common, maybe five percent of all Alzheimer's cases, or something like that," he said. "Apparently, it happens. The doctor told me about rare cases like hers, where the people were in their thirties. Hell, I looked it up on the internet and only managed to find two." He looked at me, his eyes wet. "Two cases buried in a search list of tons of articles about older people. Maybe there were more, but—" He choked up.

"I'm so sorry," I whispered, dumbfounded.

So this was what Keith had been up to all this time. Not

just ranch business. I wished I'd been there with him, although something told me he'd needed to do it himself.

"Can you believe, in one of the cases I found, a man was only twenty-nine?" He shook his head in disgust. "Violet won the damned Alzheimer's lottery."

I choked up, too. I tried to imagine what it would have been like for Violet, a young mom, to forget to feed her baby, pick up Peyton from school, and not know what was wrong.

"I should've known something was off," he said.

"You couldn't have." I used a dry corner of the bandanna to clean up my own face. I knew I looked hideous with my makeup smeared, but it didn't really matter at that moment.

"So, she planned everything?"

"She made a living will while she was still in her right mind. She set things up with that lawyer to divorce me without having to see me, to make it look like she was just leaving."

"But why? She could've just told you, and then you could have taken care of things. You and the kids could have visited her…and…" I thought of the sad visits to my own mother, the pain in my daddy's face every time he looked at her.

"I wish she would have done that," he said.

Maybe, I thought, he wouldn't if he had seen what my dad had gone through. Violet had known what was coming. She wanted to save him, and their children, from seeing it happen. For a moment, I was struck by the deep love she must have had for him. My heart fluttered.

I didn't let that little twinge of jealousy even make its way into the open. I didn't know if Keith had thought of it, but we probably would never have married if Violet hadn't done what she had. The impact of her decision on all of us was too difficult to fathom. Had Violet done the right thing? She must have seen it as an impossible situation. No answer was right. And it was too late to go back anyway. There was no solution at all. None. I didn't even need Daddy to remind me that this moment called only for compassion, even if it was hard to understand. And so unfair.

I thought of Peyton, who must have been right about her mom the whole time. Even though she was young when Violet left, she remembered, and she knew in her heart that her mom would have never left her and begged her dad not to get her a new phone number or phone. And she must not have been lying when she said Violet had called her, although I wasn't sure yet how Violet had managed it in her condition; a good day maybe. A flash of memory.

Why does God let stuff like this happen to the people I care about? I thought of the snapping plate, with the purple ring, of Peyton's crumpling face as it broke in two.

"She didn't want you and the kids to see her waste away," I said.

My own mom had tried to stop us from the pain of seeing her like that, however misguided her actions. She couldn't have arranged to disappear, the way that Violet had. By the time they knew what was wrong with her, it was too far in. Taking her life was all she knew to do. It was the only thing she could control.

Maybe Violet was smart to have taken action while she still had her mind. It was still terrible, but I got it. At least she hadn't done what my momma did.

"How did she hide it?" I asked.

He leaned back in his seat, his shirt damp at the collar. His tanned face, always so boyishly cute, was filled with lines and edges under his three day shadow. I reached out, attempting to smooth his mop of hair that stood out at all ends. He nudged my hand away.

"I'm fine," he said but he didn't look it. "I should've known," he said. "She was seeing some kind of specialist in Nashville, but I didn't know the real reason. She'd just had Stephen, so it seemed normal that she might be getting some lady stuff done. She didn't act worried about it, so I didn't worry either."

Ah, the age old trick to keep men out of our business. I thought about the times I'd done the same thing myself, back when I was still trying to have children of my own, before the doctor told me I'd probably never be able to get pregnant again. One time, I didn't even bother to tell my exhusband that I was pregnant, and that later, I wasn't.

"So, she set all this up? With the lawyer and everything?"

"She did it all before she could get worse. And this…"

He gestured toward Cottonwood Manor. "She paid all of this in advance with her part of the money. I'm glad I gave her extra."

"You did?"

He nodded, slumping a little deeper into the seat. "I arranged with the lawyer to let her have even more than her share, just to keep her away. I was so angry."

"And it enabled her to be taken care of," I said.

He turned toward me. "But don't you see, honey. I signed those divorce papers, and it was for nothing. I was so angry. I couldn't believe she was asking for money. I just gave her what she wanted and a hell of a lot more to get rid of her."

I didn't say anything. How can a current wife argue against her husband for divorcing his ex-wife? When he looked at me, I'd never seen eyes so filled with grief, even in my father, except in the mirror after I lost my baby girl.

"And you know what's worse?" He didn't wait for me to answer. "That I didn't even dig deeper."

"But you didn't know," I said. And what if he had?

"I was hurt; I didn't try hard enough to find out where she was. Mandy, don't take this wrong, but..."

He placed a rounded fist over his mouth and then placed his hand on my knee, I guessed to reassure me about what he was about to say.

"I'm not that kind of man. I wouldn't have divorced my wife if I'd known she was sick."

He'd said, *my wife*.

And he wouldn't have married me. That was sobering, but it didn't feel like a bomb, much to my surprise. In that moment, as my husband tried to swim to the top out of an incomprehensible situation, I decided to step out of the role of wife and mother, and into the role of his best friend. Being a wife was too hard right then, but let's face it, if we weren't best friends, then what kind of marriage did we have?

"I know you would've done the noble thing," I said. "And she knew it, too. Maybe that's why she did this. To set you free."

And then he struggled with tears, not letting himself cry, but the effect was worse than if he had just wept. I didn't really know what to do, except be there for him, not have anything to compare this to. The only thing I could equate it to was death. Death and loss were always a shock, and accepting it took a long time. This would take a long time.

And why Violet and Keith, Lord? It wasn't fair.

He banged the steering wheel then.

"I didn't want to be free. The kids needed her." He looked at me, apologetically, and I loved him for that small reassurance. "I would've taken care of her. I...would've wanted to say goodbye."

The urge to swing open the truck door and run away surfaced again. In order to keep from grasping the door handle, I turned and grasped Keith's hands. He was going through something that nobody could understand. Surely nobody I knew had ever faced such an impossible, unfair, and devastating situation. Keith let go and cupped my face in his, kissed me, hugged me, and kissed me again.

"I am so sorry," he said. "Everything I'm saying must hurt your feelings, cowgirl."

I shrugged, refusing to let this become about me, for once, I had to admit. My former selfishness was emblazoned across a big banner in my mind. I wanted to rip it down.

"Are you okay?" he asked.

"Cowgirls don't cry, Keith. You should know that." He was the one who always said it.

"I guess cowboys do," he said, a sheepish smile crossing his face.

"About that," I teased. "I didn't know."

"I love you." He brushed my hair back with one hand, held my hand in the other. "What would I do without you?"

And there, that was all I needed to hear.

He wasn't going to run out and divorce me because of this, so I knew that no matter what happened in the next part of our lives, I could handle it.

"How did you end up here, this morning, anyway?"

"Besides serendipity? I think I was trying to atone for my sins," I said. I gave a half-hearted laugh, only halfway joking. "I felt bad that every time I ran into Judy, or anyone like her, I freaked out, you know? Because of Momma. So before we left Pillar Bluff, I wanted to see her –my friend Judy – to see if I could be a better person… like Marta and Adri. Like you." I didn't explain how I felt drawn to Judy. I didn't understand it myself.

He shook his head. "What are you talking about? I know those situations make you think of your mom, but you never treat anyone poorly."

"But it's what's in my head." I sighed. "I know, it sounds silly to someone like you."

He shook his head, reached out, and fluffed one of my stray curls. "Not silly at all. I'm not good. But I'm impressed you came. I assume a place like this brings back sad memories for you."

"It does," I said. "I almost left, but I wanted to see Judy. I couldn't get her out of my head."

"Me neither," he said. "Ever since you pointed Judy out at the rodeo that day."

"You didn't recognize her then?"

He shook his head. "Not at first. Not until I saw her in her room, all those pictures, some of our things, on her dresser. She looks so changed compared to when I last saw her. Older, I guess." I knew Judy was only about three years older than Keith, which meant she was barely forty. I could see how he would be surprised.

"I think she recognized you," I said, remembering how she seemed to be such a fan of his at the rodeo.

"On some level, she did," he said. "A doctor explained it to me yesterday morning. On some plane, deep inside, she has memories and recollections, feelings, but she has trouble remembering what's what. Although she still has flashes of clarity, like when she called Peyton's number."

Like my momma at the end, I thought, when Marta and I were fooled into hoping she had been cured from her schizophrenia.

"They say that in a few years, those will be gone, too. She's advanced more quickly than they expected."

"Poor Peyton," I said. "In a way, she's been right all this time. How amazing that Violet recalled Peyton's number. What if we'd made her change it?"

"We'd never have found her, if we'd taken that old phone away and changed her number."

Keith squeezed my hand. He sat up straighter in his seat and was Keith the tough cowboy again, transfigured right before my eyes. We sat there for a long time, just holding hands, and listening to the country radio station, until we were interrupted by Keith's cell phone chime.

"Peyton wants to know when we're coming home."

My phone chimed, too. "Same message."

"Tell her we'll be there tomorrow. And let's not tell her about her mother, yet."

I texted her and she replied, K.

"So, when you called the lawyer, that's when you found out where Violet was?"

"Yes," he said. "But only that she was in this town."

"That's why you were helping Adri with her cause?"

"Not at first," he said. "Strange coincidence, isn't it? I

just felt drawn to contribute. Adri's a good fundraiser."

I thought about what Daddy would say, about God working in mysterious ways. And in The Southern Pair, there are never any coincidences when a customer sees an item that reminds them of the past, or what they are hoping for in the future.

"Why didn't you tell me?" I asked.

"I was going to, cowgirl. I just needed to figure it out for myself. I'm sorry."

"Okay."

"Forgive me?"

"There is nothing at all to forgive," I said, meaning it. It wasn't as if he had a handbook to tell him what to do in this situation. Of course, no matter how strong I was trying to be, it didn't stop a sudden wave of nausea from sweeping over me.

"Hey," he said, rubbing my shoulder. "Are you feeling okay?"

"It's just all the excitement, I'm sure," I said. I took a deep breath, wanting so much to be stronger.

"You look a little pale."

I offered a weak smile. "I'm fine. So, we need to decide. What are we going to do now?"

"I don't know," he said. "But Mandy? I hope you'll be there – to help, I guess. I understand if it's too awkward. If you don't want any of this anymore, I understand."

Could he be serious?

"I'm not going anywhere," I said. "And that's a promise.

He sighed, his relief obvious, but not as much as mine. I didn't bother to share with him the earlier itch I'd had to jump out of the truck and run away from it all. Thank the good Lord it was only a thought. Whatever came, I could take it. Of course, I'm not a seer into the future, or I might have sprinted while I still could.

Chapter Fourteen

VIOLET JUDITH BLACK.
Her full name was spelled out in the divorce papers, drawn up while Violet – who called herself Judy – was still of sound mind. What Keith had never seen before his visit to the lawyer was her living will. In it, she made all the provisions needed so that her kids would need not even know she had passed when the time came for her to die. It also contained a paragraph that I read to myself several times, just so I could get comfortable with it before moving on to the task at hand.

"And if my ex-husband and children ever find me, I will probably not remember them. I want them to be told that I loved them. Keith Black will always be the one love of my life and my children, whom I love dearly, my reason for doing this. And if Keith is remarried, I know it will be to a woman worthy of loving him and my children. This woman, in her shock, might think of leaving when she finds out about me, but I pray she will stay, and I thank her for it."

I read it until the lines started to blur, trying to picture Keith's reaction, how he'd felt when he read that paragraph.

I could only imagine. Violet had thought of everything. I called Marta, and read the words to her.

"Oh, that poor woman."

"I know," I said. "I'm not saying she made the right choice, because I don't think she did," I said, again thinking of Momma. "But it was obviously made out of love."

"Obviously," Marta agreed.

"But I don't know if Peyton will understand."

"Y'all are going to tell her?"

"Someday."

"Good. Because she deserves to know."

"Hey, sis?"

"Yes?"

"When I first walked into Cottonwood Manor, I almost panicked. It made me think of Momma, when she was at that home outside of Castle Orchard, but I stayed."

"I'm proud of you," she said. I let those words sink in.

"I decided to forgive her," I said.

Silence, then a sniff.

"When are you two coming home, honey?"

"This afternoon. We just have one more thing to do, and then we're leaving."

Since the shock of finding Violet, a longing to see my family and the kids had swelled inside of me. I couldn't wait to get home.

"Hi, Judy."

She wore a lavender outfit that must have been from her rodeo queen days and her eyes filled with a smile when she saw us. I didn't know why, but I suddenly felt shy, as if meeting Judy for the first time. She didn't seem to mind. She was apparently a huggy person because she quickly walked in our direction and bestowed hugs on both of us.

Keith leaned over and kissed her on the cheek, an act that was full of all the innocence of a brotherly kiss to her, but I could see that it was a familiar gesture, as well. I ignored the blush of his cheek when he glanced my way and the way that she simply glowed when she looked at him.

"Hello, Cowboy Man."

"Hello, Violet," he said.

"Who's Violet?" she asked, her voice filled with childish innocence. She looked at me. "Oh, are you Violet?"

"No," I said. "Violet is, well, she is a friend."

She nodded. "Oh, I understand. I hope she can come by for a visit soon."

"So do I, Judy."

"Please," she said with all the elegance and poise of the rodeo queen she used to be when she was young. "Have a seat."

We all three squeezed around a tiny garden-style table. She served us vanilla sandwich cookies and water in dainty purple cups that she said was tea. Keith ran his fingertip over the rim of the tea cup and I wondered if he was recalling the broken china plate with the purple ring from his argument with Peyton.

Judy was a talker, and so after a while, her chatter, however random it was, made me feel less awkward. Keith on the other hand, had loosened up right away. Violet's letter had freed him just a little. His face was not joyful, but happy as he gazed at her. Perhaps he was trying to find a piece of Violet in Judy's face. I tried not to figure out what he was thinking, what all of this meant to him, what it was going to mean to us in the future. For now, I was just going to be here beside him.

I could see a little spark, despite her dull brown hair and plain skin, of what Keith might have seen in her at one time. And she was witty! Maybe wittier than me, so I could see why Keith always laughed at my jokes. Judy's jokes were silly and their meaning was lost in her funny babble, but her sincerity was contagious. Keith and I were both laughing with her when a nurse came in to take her vitals and give her some medicine.

She cried like a child because she didn't want the medicine, which made me cry, and Keith's protective instincts come out.

He interjected. "Does she have to take it right now?"

The nurse reassured him. "This is the way it always is, Mr. Black. She will be okay. I promise."

The nurse was gentle with her, and after Judy took the pills, she told her she was a good girl, which made Judy smile. After she left, just as the nurse had said would happen,

Judy went back to normal, or at least what was her normal.

She moved to a cushioned rocking chair, all grace, and studied Keith. "You look like a cowboy I know," she said.

"Who's that?" He was smiling at her, a teasing look that I recognized.

"Oh, he's a wild dog rider."

Keith chuckled. "Oh. Do you mean a wild horse rider?"

She giggled. "Yes. Yes. That is what I said. A wild dog rider."

I didn't know if I should laugh or stay silent. I wasn't yet accustomed to these conversations with Judy, but Keith, always the gentleman knew what to do. He just nodded, agreeing with her.

"What's his name?" Keith asked. By now, we both knew who she meant, but we played along.

"Man," she said. "His, c…c…cowboy man, is his name."

I smiled at this. I couldn't help it, but I did place my hand over my mouth so that I wouldn't hurt Judy's feelings.

"And who are these children?" Judy asked, pointing to the picture of herself with Peyton and Stevie. "Do you know?"

I watched Keith's Adam's apple bob up and down. "Those kids," he said. "Are named Peyton and Stephen."

"Lovely names," she said. "I bet their mother is proud of them. Don't you think?"

"Yes. I think she probably is."

"Is that woman their mother?" She pointed at the photo

again.

"She is."

"Nice woman," Judy said.

"Yes. She is."

After a while, Judy nodded off in the rocking chair. Keith and I stood to leave. I had brought my bag inside, in hopes of offering to give her a new hairdo the way I had for Momma, if she wanted me to, but she was obviously too tired. We would have to do it on a future visit.

The realization that there would be another visit, without even having discussed it with Keith, surprised me, but it felt right. Strange, and it gave me a little bit of a stomach ache to think about it, but definitely right.

"We'll come back," I whispered to Keith, knowing he would have come back whether I had said it or not. Better to be a part of this than a bystander.

I clutched Keith's arm and reached for the door.

"Keith Brown." Judy, or maybe in that moment, Violet said.

Keith released my arm from his and spun around. Her eyes were open and she was smiling.

"Yes?"

"Keith Brow…brow…No… Black. He's a star."

I watched Keith's face transform from a surprised smile, to sadness, and then fighting back tears.

"I knew he would come see me, someday," she said.

Keith still didn't answer, being too choked up and all.

"My friends, they laughed at me, but I knew someday Keith Black would come and autograph this for me." She stood, walked primly over to her dresser. She paused to straighten her knickknacks, and the thought occurred to me that Violet and her things were proof that The Southern Pair was filled with providential, if not magical items that connected people to their happier selves, but even our inventory of mementos had limits. Judy's mementos connected her to the past somehow, but sadly, they couldn't heal her from Alzheimer's. She opened an antique drawer and pulled out an old issue of a western magazine and held it out for us to see. She smiled at us from the cover, as did a younger version of Keith.

"That," she said, "Is he. That's he. Keith Black. And his girl. Doesn't she look like such a nice person?" She pointed at the image of herself.

I answered for my mute husband. "Yes. She looks like a nice person. I think she is a very nice person."

She nodded, gazing at the magazine cover. "And she... You can tell she is just crazy about c...c...cowboy man. Don't you think?" She smiled in a way that, beyond the lined eyes and bare face, reminded me of some of the old queen pictures Peyton had hanging in her room.

"Yes," I said. "You can tell. She loved..." I swallowed, hating to say it despite the situation. "They're a great couple. I am sure of it."

She looked at me, her head tilted in the way a child might when trying to figure something out. "Do you think he loves that girl in the picture, too?

My heart split right in two. Keith was still silent. "Yes," I said for him. "He loves that girl." Because it was the girl, the forever young Violet that was part of his past.

She smiled, looking happy. "I thought so."

Keith turned away and I tried to engage Judy by talking about horses while he collected himself. When he turned back, she held the magazine out to him.

"Could you please have Keith Black autograph this next time you see him, Cowboy Man?"

"How about now?"

"No, no." She said. "When you see him is fine."

Keith smiled sadly. "I sure will."

We said goodbye then, and I noticed Keith was extra gentle as he let his ex-wife hug him and kiss his cheek. She giggled like a seven-year-old, which made Keith smile sadly.

I hugged her then, mostly because she wouldn't have it any other way.

"Come back to see me, cowgirl."

I almost told her I wasn't at all a cowgirl, but I knew she wouldn't believe it.

"We will."

"I like that cowgirl, Cowboy Man." She fiddled with the fringe on her vest. "I like her." It took me a moment to figure out that she probably meant me.

"That cowgirl...she likes you, too, Judy." And I was telling the truth.

Chapter Fifteen

OVER THE NEXT few months, I did what I could to help Keith find out who else knew about Judy. We decided not to tell Peyton or Stevie for a while. We didn't know how long, but we just knew that now wasn't the right time. Judy's parents, sadly, were passed on. There was one aunt and a couple of cousins who Keith said Judy never even knew before her illness, so we didn't contact them. The only other person who knew about Judy was her brother, whom Keith had already reconnected with. Apparently he had stopped visiting at least a year ago because his presence, unlike Keith's, sent her into confused rages. Keith said they had always been close, so it would have been difficult for him to endure. Still, her brother checked on her by phone and made sure everything was okay on a regular basis.

"Will he develop Alzheimer's, too?" I asked once.

A shadow passed over Keith's face. "He says he doesn't know. He's older than her, and so far, he has no signs. He said he doesn't want to be tested for the gene."

I blinked back tears when I realized the implication of Keith's words. This could affect Stevie and Peyton someday.

Dear God, please not the kids.

Keith didn't look like he wanted to talk about it right then, so I didn't say it out loud.

"So," I said. "Do you think Pia's mom knew?"

"If Kim knew, she would've told me," Keith said.

"Are you sure?"

"I'm positive," he said. "But the question is, do I tell her? Judy didn't want anyone to know. Not me. Not even her best friend."

Great, now I'm going to have to forgive Pia's mom for being so rude to me. All I can say, is, it's hard to be humble sometimes.

"Do you want me to explain it to Kim?"

He smiled. "I don't think that would be a good idea."

I shook my head, relieved. "Just make sure she knows that we are telling Peyton when the time is right. Not her. And not Pia. Pia can't know. She'll tell Peyton."

"Good point."

And that was the kind of stuff we talked about in between his rodeos. It kind of killed the romance, most of the time, even as we grew closer and closer. Not that we didn't still want romance, but it was kind of awkward to talk about Judy and then go kindle the fires, if you know what I mean. When I confided to Marta one evening after we closed The Southern Pair for the day, she told me to stop worrying.

"Sis, you have your whole life for romance. Don't worry, it'll rekindle itself. Right now, what's important is your family, and, as weird as it is, you have a new member in that family."

"A new member?"

Marta shrugged. "Now you're going to worry about Judy's well-being, too. You already do. And you like her, admit it."

"I do," I said. "And do you know what's even stranger? Keith still loves her, and I don't care. If he loves her, then so do I." Even as I said it, I felt the truth shock through me.

I didn't think I could ever fully accept Violet. It was just too hard. But Judy was different. I found that I could view her as a different person, apart from Keith's wife. With Judy, everything had changed and because I'd never known anyone else who'd gone through this, I was making my own rules.

Marta had hugged me then. "Sis, this is the weirdest thing I've ever heard of, but I am so proud of you for handling it so well."

"It's not too awkward? I'm not crazy?"

"No, and yes. You have to be a little bit crazy to deal with a shock like this."

"True," I said. "So, tell me about your love life?" Marta had managed to bump into Quentin all by herself when he brought Keith's RV back from Pillar Bluff.

Marta gave me a secret smile, but didn't say anything.

"Sis, is there something I need to know?"

"Maybe."

"Do tell."

"For now, all I can say is that Quentin keeps coming around in those boots and Wranglers."

We squealed together and for a minute I felt the way we had in the past, lost in fun adventures involving boys and laughter.

"I miss life not being complicated," I said.

"Oh, sis. It has always been complicated. That's life."

"But for me, it's going to be more complicated forever." I gave her a sad smile. "I'm sorry. I keep going back to the same stuff. You are probably sick of hearing about Judy."

"Not at all," she said. "It's serious business. How's Keith doing with all of it?"

"At first, all he wanted to talk about were practical things like how we were going to get up there to visit Judy, making sure she is being taken care of, coordinating with her brother, etcetera, etcetera, even though her brother has been doing okay without us, before we knew."

"That's a man for you," Marta said. "Problem solvers."

"But I've also sensed a change in him, sis. I thought he would be freaking out, you know? Beating himself up forever and all that, but lately he's been calmer, like he accepts it."

"It must be hard for him, to find out after all this time that she left him and the kids out of love, and not because of the opposite. I would feel so guilty for moving on, at first."

"That's what I thought at first, too," I said. "But you know what? I think it's the other way around."

"I'm not following you."

"Think about it. All this time Keith hasn't had a word from his ex-wife. She divorced him, humiliated him even, by leaving no trace or reason, only those divorce papers and an agreement to give him the kids."

"Sounds hard to me."

"Yes. But now he knows that she really didn't abandon them, at least in her heart." I sighed. "Of course, she might have considered that the kids might need to know their family health history someday, but maybe she thought it was best not to know. Whether it is right or wrong now, she thought she was doing a good thing, the right thing."

"I'm not sure if she did the right thing," Marta said.

Marta wasn't the only one who had offered her opinion on Judy's decision.

Daddy told me, "It seems wrong to us, but at least she is alive. Who's to say why she thought it was best. Who knows why your mom decided to do what she did? It doesn't matter anymore. We've lost her. Keith and the kids lost Violet, but now they have Judy." I'd hugged Daddy on the spot.

Keith didn't talk much about their marriage, but he'd confessed in the past that although they'd had a good relationship, sometimes they had their differences. Now I wondered if their differences were related to Violet's symptoms. I'd been reading as much as I could find, and sadly, people with the disease changed, often becoming completely different in personality.

"But it turns out that she really did love him," I told

Marta. "He needed to know that."

"Sis, you amaze me with that big ole heart of yours. Come here now." I didn't think my heart was big enough, to tell the truth. I found myself whispering a prayer for help more often than anyone would believe of me.

Marta sat me down in one of the chairs at the nail station.

"You need a makeover."

"What's that supposed to mean?" I fluffed my hair and glanced in the mirror. "We don't do makeup."

"Let me rephrase that," she said. "You *deserve* a makeover, and you know I keep a bag ready just in case some poor soul needs more than nail polish. You never know when there might be an emergency. Now, you just settle back and let me do my thing. I'm going to get you a Diet Coke and some peanuts, and when I'm done with you, you're going to feel like the Top Model."

Diet Coke and peanuts were our mother's favorite treat, even after she was sick. She'd said her mom had taught her to love them, too.

I THINK MY queasiness started with the peanuts, but it got worse that night when we were all sitting at the big farmhouse dinner at the ranch. I was basking in the glow of having Keith home from the rodeo, all of my family together, and, to top it all off, we were seated around a new, but antique, table Keith had bought me along with new place settings in yellow and cobalt blue. Everyone was having a great time enjoying dinner, until everything spilled out. And I do mean everything. The mashed potatoes, the steak, and even the homemade bread that Dad and Marta brought over with them. All that food gone to waste.

Keith looked panicked. Even Peyton ran to my side, gently taking my arm.

"Are you okay, Mandy?"

I noticed Marta looking at dad and the two of them were oddly smiling as they quickly lay several towels over the mess and ushered everyone away from the table and out onto the back deck. I sat in a cushioned deck chair.

"And how is this funny? Why are you two smiling?" I heaved again, but thank goodness there was nothing left inside my stomach.

"Don't talk." Dad brought me some 7-Up from the fridge and a package of saltine crackers.

"What are these for?" Keith asked. "She's tossing her cookies."

"Just give her a couple." In the meantime, Peyton dabbed my forehead with a damp rag, worry playing on her face.

Dad and Keith went back inside to clean up, the sweet men that they were, while Stephen, Marta, and Peyton sat beside me.

"That was gross," Peyton said. "I've never seen anyone throw up like that. There was so much!"

I gave her a weak smile, but felt too tired all of a sudden to laugh.

"It was wild," Stephen said.

"Kids." Marta chided.

"Well, it's true," Peyton said.

"It's true," I said. "I've never been that sick, except for when I was…"

I calculated time in my head and thought it might have happened in the RV in Pillar Bluff when I surprised Keith at the rodeo, or in Hawaii, or maybe even before that. Keith had been away at so many other rodeos we'd barely managed romance lately, although I don't think we've ever been closer.

Marta leaned in and stared, her eyes shining.

The memories, the booties, the soft fabrics and yarn all rained down in dream bubbles, settling around my waist. The moodiness, the fact that my period had stopped coming and I hadn't even noticed because I was always so irregular anyway. And I didn't even take the pill anymore because of the doctor's sad prognosis that the chances of my ever getting pregnant again were slim to none.

But doctors are sometimes wrong.

"Pregnant," I whispered.

Peyton's face lit up, and the most magical thing happened. She smiled, laughed. "A baby!" She even hugged me.

"Oh, baby," I said. I kissed her face and she didn't even care. She kissed mine, too, and then she ran in to tell her dad the good news.

So much for my sharing it with him first. Of course, if that girl was happy, then it was fine with me.

Marta squeezed my shoulders, careful not to jostle me as Peyton had in her joy, which was good because I was still nauseous. In fact, now that I thought about it, I'd been nauseous several times lately, but I'd paid little mind to it even though I should've known. Sadly, I had a lot of experience at being pregnant and already knew that I was one of those women who threw up well past the first trimester, sometimes throughout the whole pregnancy. It wasn't related to my complications, according to the doctor, but it had felt like a cruel trick on top of everything else.

I placed my hand against my tummy, aware that the night's nausea was proof of a miracle. And was I imagining it or was my tummy already starting to puff out?

"If I could just have one more miracle," I whispered to Marta.

"It'll be okay," she said, knowing the full implications of a pregnancy for me, the worries and the precautions we would have to take. "I'll be there for you."

"I know."

"So, right now, it's all joy."

"It is," I said, and then Keith was gently pulling me out of the chair and hugging me ever so softly like I might break, and truth be told, I thought I might. The look in his eyes was filled with wonder, and with fear. He knew all about my earlier pregnancies, and about Sarah, my sweet baby I got to hold for a short time before she slipped away.

"I love you," he said. And the way he said it, strong voice hoarse, his face vulnerable and filled with the same wonder Stevie had on his face, made me think, why did I ever feel I couldn't trust this cowboy of mine?

Chapter Sixteen

EVEN THOUGH MY nausea hadn't subsided much, just as I expected, I didn't let it stop me from helping during harvest time at Daddy's orchard. This was my favorite part of the year and I always pitched in to help outside, but my dad and Keith still put the kibosh on that one. I was relegated to the kitchen with Marta.

"When are you telling Peyton about Judy?"

"Soon," I promised, even though every time Keith and I talked about it, we thought of a new reason she might not be ready. "We've just been so busy getting ready for this little surprise." I patted my belly.

"Well, don't wait too long," Marta said. "It worries me to think that she won't know Peyton even a little bit if you don't tell soon. Who knows how long Judy will have any memories left at all?"

I knew Marta was right. It worried me, too. Judy's flashes of memory were so unpredictable, and always scattered. One could never be sure what it meant to her when she seemed to recognize someone. Maybe she did, maybe she didn't, but Keith thought she could still remember him somewhere deep inside and that she might recall the kids. Many of the things she said were too specific to be anything but a memory, but how much she connected her memory of Keith to the visitor whom she called Cowboy Man, was anyone's guess.

"I'll tell her soon," I told Marta. "I promise I'll talk to Keith about it tonight. Let her enjoy another day without having to worry about it."

"She worries about it every day," Marta said. "She's still waiting for her mom to show up. Have you forgotten about the phone calls?"

I hadn't forgotten. It had turned out that occasionally, during a clear moment, Violet would manage to find a free phone at Cottonwood Manor and call people she used to know. Naturally, one of those people was Peyton. She hadn't called since summer, but Peyton didn't know it was because we had requested that the Manor be extra careful about phones around Violet.

"I will tell her, soon." I promised.

I felt terrible that Peyton still didn't know, but Keith and I had good reasons for waiting. There had been a lot to work through with Judy's appearance in our life, not to mention the new baby.

"Good." Marta rolled pie crust into a perfect sphere. "Because if you don't, I will."

My heart leapt. She sounded serious. I would talk to Keith about it tonight, for sure.

To prepare for the special harvest celebration we had created for the community and tourists a decade ago, we made pie after pie, jam after jelly, and anything else we could make with apples from tarts to bread. We lined the shelves of The Southern Pair and invited everyone who came in to join us. The family day at our farmhouse was designed to sell apples and promote orchard farming and organic practices, but it had evolved into much more over the years, offering an excuse for the community to come together. Dad, the pushover that he was, even let local fruit farmers and bakers sell their own produce and other foods at tables spread with red and blue tablecloths in the sprawling front yard.

Keith, wanting to add his own touch, since I was part orchard farmer and part ranch woman now, brought over his gentlest horses and he, Peyton, and Stephen gave the children rides for free. I loved seeing my family take part in the festivities in that way. It was like a marriage of my two halves. But the best part of the day was Peyton, who when she wasn't giving rides, took photos of everything to add to the website she had created for her grandpa. She was excited to have an excuse to post pictures and blog on the Internet since Keith had made her take down her own website for the time being – and I don't even want to tell you about how mad Peyton was about that.

At first he'd had her take it down because of the whole random call from her mother business, but once Keith and I knew the truth, we'd agreed it might do her good to stay off it for a while, especially if she was attempting to contact her mother via that blog. Violet had been an intelligent woman, and it wouldn't have surprised us at all if on a good day she managed to figure out how to use the Internet and search for Peyton. It sounds crazy, but after accepting that Violet had an elderly person's disease, nothing about it could surprise us anymore.

Keith didn't think there was any rush to tell Peyton, but I knew better. Marta and I both knew not to underestimate how deep a daughter's longing for her mother could be, so I did what I could to let Peyton know we all loved her. Letting her help us with selling apples and peaches on her website was small, but it took her mind off her mom a little bit, at least she seemed to like it.

With my much more sophisticated camera, Peyton took pictures all over the orchard during the harvest. The best pictures were of Marta and me baking, men harvesting the fruit, and of the apples themselves. A few days earlier, Marta and I had prebaked most of the items. Peyton had taken extra care photographing the baked goods and produce as we packaged them for the big day. In twenty-four hours, she designed the site, managed to get it listed in various search engines and whatever else they list Internet stores on, and there it was, getting hundreds of hits a day and almost as many orders. Many of the customers were local, living in Castle Orchard or Pillar Bluff, so they either picked them up or we delivered them. We had a fruit stand, too, like all the farmers in the area, so it served as a pick up site. We also had commercial fruits that were loaded into trucks and delivered professionally, but as long as we were local, Peyton and Estefan, the son of one our long-time employees, helped out.

Estefan, dreamy Estefan, had a license and a truck, so we let him, Peyton, and Pia deliver many of the orders. At first I noticed Peyton was shy and quiet around Estefan, but eventually she opened up. I could see he was as smitten as she was. Peyton had a beautiful personality, when she wasn't being a haughty, ill-tempered teenager, and for the first time, Keith was made aware that a boy might think she had a beautiful little figure. This was made apparent when she walked into the kitchen of the ranch house one morning, ready to meet Estefan, who waited in the driveway with a truck full of products to deliver, and Keith went ballistic. I'll tell you right now that I fell deeper in love with that man for the kind of parent he was. I recalled the conversation very well.

"What?" Peyton had demanded.

"Those shorts are too short. Go change."

"They are not. I wear them all the time."

"Around the house, but you aren't wearing them on a date with a boy."

"It's not a date!" She looked shaken at the thought, but not all together uncomfortable with the idea.

"Peyton," I said. "Go change them."

"You're siding with him? He's a man. Dads don't know anything about style."

"I'm siding with him on this one. Not on style, but on the degree of skin you are showing in those shorts."

"But you let me wear them all the time." She gave me an imploring look and Keith gave me an accusatory one.

"Those are at-home clothes," I said. "They aren't appropriate to wear around a boy when you are a teenager." I watched her stomp, huff, and spin around, eventually reappearing with another slightly longer pair of shorts that were deemed appropriate by her dad.

Keith and I smiled at each other. Since we'd learned the truth about Peyton's mother, this parenting thing between Keith and I was starting to be a team effort. No more did we mistrust each other's motives when it came to the kids. I also appreciated Keith's efforts to be more involved when he was at home. He had even started doing those video chat things with the kids when he was gone, and they loved it. We all felt more connected than ever, and I have to hand it to him. A cowboy can be a good dad. That didn't change Peyton's longing for her mom, but she finally started to blossom in the sunshine of her dad's attention, smiling more, and being less of that haughty, ill-tempered girl.

"Good job," I told Keith, whom I could tell didn't like having to lay down the law.

"I hate telling her to go change her clothes. It makes me feel old."

"Well, my daddy had to do it when Marta and I were kids. Girls want to stretch their wings and push their limits.

They want to impress the boys. Marta and I were the same way."

"And look how old it made your dad." His hand encircled my rounded waist, pulling me close to his hard chest. My heart fluttered.

"If you tried wearing short shorts," he said. "It must have been hard for him, fending off the boys."

"Worse," I said. "Try miniskirts!"

"Scandalous." He had pressed a kiss against my neck in that little place between my shoulder and ear that always shivered when he whispered to me. "Of course, they do make miniskirts for grownups, you know."

"Hmmmm." We kissed. "I'm afraid that with my expanding waist line, my mini skirt days are over."

He'd hugged me gently, my rounded belly pressing between us, and offered to make me a cup of chamomile tea.

"No," I said. "I'd prefer decaf coffee. I've heard it still has a teeny-weeny bit of caffeine."

"Like you need caffeine," he teased.

"How do you think Marta and I keep up with each other? It takes lots of coffee."

He turned and popped a decaf coffee pod into the coffee dispenser. "I'm pretty sure it's not with coffee. I think you two were just born that way." He set the blue cup carefully in front of me and lay his hands on my stomach. "And I won't be surprised if this one doesn't turn out the same way."

He had kissed my tummy then, donned his hat, and left me to have a moment of peace in the kitchen. Of course, as soon as I saw the taillights exit the driveway, I downed my decaf and started cleaning the house. I probably shouldn't have done that.

THE HARVEST CELEBRATION was in full swing and even though moving around the kitchen was like maneuvering with a bowling ball tied around my waist, I was keeping up pretty well with Marta. At some point, I finally had enough and had to sit in the rocking chair in the corner. Marta brought sweet iced tea and I didn't even ask if it was decaf. I was beat, but everything seemed okay. It was normal, everyone said, to be tired this far into the pregnancy.

The contractions started just before lunch, right about the time Daddy walked in for a break. He looked exhausted from all the interactions during the family day, but he knew something was off as soon as he saw me. If he was scared, too, he didn't show it. Daddy was always calm, always knowing what to do.

Even though Keith wasn't there, having left to take the horses back to the ranch, Daddy was as capable as anyone who could have gone through that moment with me. He ordered Marta to stay with the kids because they would be scared. I knew it was torture for her not to be with me, her twin, but our dad wasn't going to let even a doctor near his daughter without his being there with me. Later, someone would comment about how noble he was to take care of me for Keith until he could get to back to me, but Marta and I both knew that he hadn't done it for Keith. He'd done it for himself. He was our father.

Daddy had been there the last time it had been too early, and I'd held my living, breathing, short-lived baby in my arms, while my then husband was off doing who knew what with his mistress. Daddy would be there for me now, and it gave me courage to get through whatever might come next.

"Daddy," I said. "It's just like always."

"No," he said. "Not this time." A storm raged in his eyes even as he calmly walked over to the old-fashioned, red rotary phone on the kitchen wall, dialed 9-1-1. For a moment, I felt I saw Momma's image holding the phone, overlapping Daddy's, like two pieces of film on top of each other, but then Daddy hung up, blurring the image, and sat down beside me on the couch. I didn't tell him about Momma, but I felt comforted, and I absorbed the strength of Daddy's grip when he took my hand. Without asking my permission, he prayed, his words choked, halting, and powerful. Very powerful.

Please don't take this one away.

It was all I could add to his prayer, and that not even out loud right in the middle of my cramping physical pain and my searing emotional ache, but my dad filled in, his voice not shy at all, not doubting, but full of trust and conviction.

When the paramedics burst through the door, they

stopped for a split second, possibly moved by the sight of Daddy's hand resting softly on my stomach as he prayed—who wouldn't be moved by that—and then they'd rushed forward. One of the EMTs, a woman who reminded me of the receptionist at Cottonwood Manor, worked busily around me and said, "Amen, and amen." It made me think of Judy, and if she would ever get to meet Keith's and my baby, the sibling of her own children; the children she hadn't even seen since we discovered her living in Pillar Bluff. And did I want Judy to meet Keith's and my baby? I was startled to realize that I did.

Chapter Seventeen

EVERYONE WAITED ON me hand and foot after that, scared and worried, but happy the contractions had stopped and the baby was okay. For the next few weeks I was supposed to rest, so I took up knitting. Keith thought it was a hoot watching the blankets and booties pile up, but I think the fact that I was knitting baby things excited him more than my actual knitting talent.

"Knitting," Marta teased. "I thought you hated knitting."

"That's because I didn't really know how to do it right," I said. "This time, Peyton hooked me up to one of those video sites on the Internet. It's the neatest thing. I learned how to knit baby booties just by watching videos. You should try it."

"I don't have time for that," Marta said. "I have my work and yours to do, too."

"Sorry," I said. "I miss the shop so much!"

"Well don't. I'd rather have you knitting and the baby safe."

I smiled at her. "The baby is going to be fine. The doctor

only said get extra rest as a precaution. I have a good feeling, sis."

She smiled back, but no joy reached her eyes. I wanted to take her worry away, but there was no way I could. I'm not saying I wasn't worried myself. Of course I was, but I'd reached a point, during that terrifying moment when Daddy was bowed before me with his hand on my stomach, that brought me peace. I figured that being relaxed might be good for the baby, so I chose to surround myself with happiness instead of worrying about what I couldn't control. Besides, everybody else was doing the worrying for me, everyone except for little Stevie who didn't know any better than to feel joy about a coming baby.

"I even taught Stephen how to knit on one of those little looms." I showed her a baby hat I'd helped him make.

"Nice," Marta said. "What's Keith going to think of you teaching his little cowboy how to knit?"

"Nothing," I said. "Stevie taught Keith how to do it, too. The little blue hat is his."

Marta laughed. "Y'all are about as crazy as, well, I don't know what, but I like it."

"How's the Peyton and Estefan friendship going? She gets all shy and defensive when I ask her about it."

"They're as cute as two split peas who found each other."

"Well, keep an eye on them."

"Don't you know it," she said. "I remember all the tricks."

"Well, you should."

She playfully pretended to slap me with a piece of yarn. "I had a partner in crime, you know. And do you remember the time we got into trouble with the Jackson twins?"

"Girl, do I. That was awful, but fun."

"It was your fault."

"How did I know they wanted to break into the city pool?"

We laughed at the memory. The Jackson twins had been grounded for twice as long as us.

"Now scooch over here and let me do your hair," Marta said.

"What are you trying to say about my hair?" I asked. "I like my ponytail just fine, thank you."

"You do?"

I leaned until I could see into the living room mirror. "Okay, I do look a little dowdy, don't I? So, fix me up." I set my knitting aside.

I loved when she came over and fretted with my hair. She even did my nails, using the peel off gel kind of polish so that it wouldn't hurt the baby. I didn't know if there was anything to beauty product chemicals being dangerous, but why push it when I'd already had such bad luck with pregnancies?

"Speaking of boys, what's up with Quentin?" I asked. "I've been so obsessed with this baby, I haven't asked. I'm sorry."

"I'm obsessed about your baby, too, so no apology necessary. And who knows? Maybe someday I'll be having one of those."

"Oh, really?"

"Well, I don't want to get my hopes up, but if Quentin asks me to marry him, I'll say yes."

I squealed; the baby did a somersault.

"Oh!" Marta pressed her hand into my tummy and we cried.

Those jabbing little legs unleashed emotions I'd been hiding beneath all those knitted baby things.

"Oh, honey." Marta grabbed a tissue out of the box. She patted my shoulder. "There, there, sissy. You just cry. You have every reason. Your baby is kicking!"

Every kick was so precious. I couldn't even speak without sniffling more.

Marta laughed. "Now, get to work on those baby booties, you hear? Make pink and blue, and some green and yellow. Since you refuse to find out the gender, we need to be prepared."

The phone rang and a country song blared into the room. "Excuse me," she said. "Hot cowboy calling."

"You mean Quentin?" I asked.

"Same thing," she said, and sashayed out of my room with the phone pressed to her ear.

Once she was outside, I called my own hot cowboy.

"Hey, cowgirl. Everything okay?"

"The baby kicked, hard."

I heard a little gasp.

"Not just flutters, like before, but really hard kicks. You'll be able to feel it, too, now."

Silence. Then, "That's great, cowgirl. I'm coming home right now."

"He or she might not kick again right away," I said. "So you don't need to rush."

That night, that little rascal kicked so much neither Keith nor I got any sleep.

"Dear Lord," I said, out loud so Keith could hear. "Please don't let it be a bronc rider."

This made Keith laugh out loud.

"Sh-sh," I said. "The baby will never calm down if you are so noisy."

"You mean it can hear me?" he asked.

"You've had a baby before." I reminded him. "You know they can hear noise."

"It's been a long time," he said. "I'd forgotten about all this." He bent over my stomach, kissed it, and began to whisper.

"Well, you probably need to talk louder than that." I teased. "If you're going to keep the poor baby awake anyway."

"Okay," he said, and to my surprise broke out in a country sounding rendition of rock-a-by-baby. Somehow, as he sang, I managed to fall asleep, and I guess so did the baby, because it didn't kick again until morning.

I TOOK MARTA'S advice about the colors, but a baby can only wear so many booties, sweaters, and caps. Eventually I started knitting other things out of boredom. That's how I started knitting scarves, hats, and even small lap blankets for Adri to hand out during her volunteer adventures in Nashville.

"I could use some extra scarves and hats for the home in Pillar Bluff," she told me during a visit as she sat on the opposite end of the couch. We were going through stacks of things I'd already made. "Before we know it, there'll be snow."

"How about this one," Stevie said, handing Adri a bright purple scarf. "It would look good on a snow man."

Adri wrapped it loosely around Stevie's neck. "Yes, I agree. Let's have some more purple, and some pink, and then some blue for the boys. I'll take them to Cottonwood Manor."

"My mom and dad always talk about Cottonwood Manor," Stevie said. "What's it like? They never let me go."

Adri glanced at me. Did she know something? I fished out one with different shades of purple striped through it.

"What do you think of this one for Judy?" I asked.

Adri smiled. "Perfect."

"Who's Judy?" Stevie helped Adri stuff the scarves into her bag.

"A friend of mine," Adri said. "And she'll love it."

If she knew anything about Violet and Judy being the same person, I couldn't tell because of her downcast eyes. Of course, there were the photos on her bedside table, so she had to have figured it out. I'd thought of putting them away the last time I was there, but couldn't take away the special things that kept Judy's memories somewhere in the periphery.

"A sweet friend," I said. "Maybe I'll take you to meet her sometime."

"Hooray!" he said, his voice so sweet at the prospect of making a new friend. My heart swelled at his innocence.

"Oh, by the way," Adri said. "The public service messages Keith did for Cottonwood Manor were so good that their sister home over in Nashville asked him to do the same thing. What do you think? Would he do it?"

"Of course. I'm sure he will," I said. "He's so good at that kind of thing." And he had a new personal stake in it, now.

"They want you to do it with him this time. You know, a couple thing."

"Me? You do it. You're the queen."

"Oh, come on, Manda. You know that if you could ride a horse, you would have been a great queen yourself."

I shrugged. I wasn't sure what she said was true, never mind my fear of riding horses. Besides, the queen thing belonged to Judy. While it was nice that Peyton had tried to teach me to ride on our slowest, and oldest horse, I would leave the fancy barrel riding to Peyton. I was more than happy for the rodeo queen memories to be reserved for her mom.

I had to tell Peyton. It was no use waiting for Keith. He wanted us to wait until Peyton was ready, but I'd come to realize that what he was really trying to do was wait until he was ready.

"If I am in that commercial with Keith, can I dress up in something blingy? Or would that be inappropriate?"

"You can dress blingy. How can you not? You're a blingy girl."

"I am," I said. "Even though I don't feel blingy lately."

Stevie picked up a knitted scarf that had tiny threads of shiny red woven throughout and wrapped it around my belly. "That's blingy!"

He started laughing and pointed at my tummy. "Look, Adri. Now my Mommy's got a blingy baby bump."

She leaned over and picked up some shiny jewelry on the night stand and placed it in the center of the blingy baby bump scarf. "There, now it's really blingy."

"Mommy. Mommy!" Stevie pointed at my belly. "Look what Adri and I did."

He never called me Mandy anymore. Just plain Mommy.

"It's a little bigger than a bump," I said "But it is blingy!"

I gave him a hug and wished Peyton could think of me the same way. I didn't expect the poor girl to call me Mom, ever. That would just be too much; especially when Judy sat unawares at Cottonwood Manor, both of them unaware of each other, but it would be enough to just be thought of as some kind of mom by her.

Of course, I also wished she would turn sweet like frosting and that all my advice would stick as easy as sprinkles on a cupcake, and also that I could have a baby without gaining fifty pounds. Looking down at my blingy baby bump that was really more like a mountain, I was pretty sure that the granting of all the above wishes was doubtful.

Chapter Eighteen

KEITH'S IDEA TO have Judy come visit seemed like a good one at the time. I was feeling much better, but the closer I got to my due date, the more I looked for distractions to keep me from worrying about my little bundle. Having Judy come would definitely keep me occupied. There was a program that helped connect people with disabilities with horses, so we planned the trip in conjunction with that program. Judy was a perfect candidate, and so was the ranch.

Judy barely resembled the old Violet anymore, but there was little doubt that Peyton would recognize her. I was happy that Keith couldn't avoid the introduction anymore, and before Judy's trip to see us, we sat Peyton down.

"Honey," her dad said. "We found your mom."

Peyton's jaw dropped and she began to sob. Not exactly what I was expecting at all, but, soon enough, I realized the sobbing was just a release for all the emotion that must have been attached to the longing she'd felt since she was just a little girl.

Keith drew her into his arms and the picture of the two

of them was so much like my dad with me and Marta that I had to grab a tissue for myself, too.

She sniffled. "When can I see her?"

"Soon," Keith said.

That girl's face lit up with joy. She turned to me then. "You don't mind?"

"Of course I don't, sweetie." She threw her arms around my neck.

"Thank you, Mandy."

I smiled, but Keith needed to tell her the rest himself. I waited for him to say something, but his face was white. I knew right then that my big, tough cowboy wouldn't be able to find the words to break his daughter's heart.

I took a deep breath. This would probably not be as hard for me as when Daddy had to tell Marta and me about momma's suicide, but it would be close.

"Honey…" I began. "We have something really important you need to know about your mom."

Her face fell. "She's not—"

"No." I finished, grasping her hand. She didn't pull back, so I inched closer to her on the couch. "But it's not good news."

Hours later, after we'd gone through tears, hot chocolate, more tears, some ranting and yelling, and even a prayer, taking a cue from my own daddy, we tucked her in. It felt more like we were tucking in a tiny little girl than our blooming, teenaged Peyton as we turned off her light and shut her door.

"I hope she can handle this," Keith said.

I pulled him as close as my stomach would let me. "She can handle it. The question is, can my big, tough cowboy deal with it?"

"I'll be fine," he said.

And the baby picked that very moment to kick. We both giggled and went to bed. Our baby seemed to wake up right at bedtime most nights and this night was no different. As I lay there, rubbing the place where a little arm or leg jutted out, I thought about how Keith and Violet would have gone through all this before, not knowing about the future. I loved my own baby so much already, and I promised myself that I would make this visit for Violet and her babies as special as I could make it under the circumstances.

ON THE DAY Judy came to visit, Peyton spent extra time on her makeup and hair and then we spent the rest of the morning getting the house ready. Marta went with Keith to get Judy in Pillar Bluff while we made Violet's guest room just right.

"Why do you seem so nervous? I'll be fine." Peyton had just vacuumed the floor and was wrapping the cord around the handle.

The action reminded me of how far she had come since I first married her father. She was growing up.

"I mean," Peyton said, "That if Mom has a special condition, like you say, then she's not going to care about the house. We're just supposed to help her have fun, right?"

"Right," I said, not mentioning all the time she'd spent on her makeup. I laced my fingers across my belly. I flinched at an especially hard kick.

"Oh! Let me." Peyton hurried over and knelt down, resting her cheek on my belly. I moved one hand to the top of my stomach and rested the other on Peyton's head.

"Hi, baby," she said. "Come out soon. I want to meet you in person." She kissed my belly.

I loved how unabashed Peyton had become when it came to anything about the baby. Hours of her day were spent helping decorate the baby's room, making little things to give it when he or she was older, and my favorite, taking photographs of my belly. If her photography talents didn't take her any further than right there in Castle Orchard, we would at least have the most beautiful baby belly gallery anywhere.

She stood and we were face to face. It struck me that she was starting to look more and more like her mother in those young photos in her room, and on Judy's dresser. I touched her face, thinking she would flinch, brush me away, but instead she laid her hand over mine.

"I'm glad you're my stepmom," she whispered.

A shyness came over her, and then me. This was the kind of moment I had been longing for since I'd known Peyton, and suddenly I was speechless. She smiled, breaking the spell, but before she walked away, she kissed my cheek. Now wasn't I surprised as she walked off to her bedroom, my fingers lightly touching the moisture from her kiss?

"They're here," Stevie shouted.

I walked into the living room to see nothing but Stevie's Wrangler bottom sticking out of the curtains. The rest of him was resting inside the window, watching his father's truck pull in. My heart gave a flutter.

Peyton, hearing Stevie, hurried in. "I'm glad we're doing this," she said.

"Well..." I ventured. "If this visit works out okay for the whole family, maybe we'll do it every few months."

Peyton spun around. "That's a great idea."

I smiled, pretending for her that nothing was out of the ordinary, but I was nervous. How was Judy going to react when she saw Peyton? How would Peyton react? She had been so young when Violet left and Violet – or, Judy – had changed so much with her condition that I didn't think Peyton would see a resemblance at all.

"She's going to look a lot different, Peyton, and she'll be different, too. Like a little girl sometimes."

"I know," she said. "You already told me."

My heart swelled for her. Now it was final. I loved that girl.

Before I could answer the door, Stevie swung it open. Peyton stood beside Stevie, staring at her mother. Her mother's eyes glanced around the room, right over me, and to Stevie and Peyton. She smiled at Stevie, patted his head.

"Hi, little baby."

"Hey, I'm not a ba—"

I placed a finger over my lips to shush him. He clamped his mouth closed. We'd just told him our friend Judy was coming. Since he already thought of me as his mom, and he barely remembered his own, explaining it to him would be a series of small conversations and not a big announcement like for Peyton.

The caregiver who had come to help her, urged Judy forward. She took a few steps into the living room. Her eyes fell on her daughter, and, for a moment, I was sure I saw some kind of recognition in the way her eyes lingered, flashed, but then flattened.

"Hello, girl."

Peyton's face turned white. She was hurt. It was natural, I knew, but I longed to save her.

"Hi," Peyton said, her face filling with color again.

She was a cowgirl through and through, just like her dad always said. Tough, kind, and never one to shirk from a hard task. At first she was shy, but ever the young lady.

I stepped forward, took Judy's hand and ushered her into the living room where I sat her on the couch. She pulled her purple cardigan tightly around her, let her eyes roam across her surroundings. Did she recognize her old house? Was there anything about it that she still knew? Not for the first time, I regretted my campaign early in our marriage to strip

Violet's things from the house and make it my own, but I hadn't known. If I had, it might have been a different story. I think I would have saved everything if I had known she was not simply an ex-wife who abandoned her children, but a mother whose love couldn't allow them to see her turn into a stranger.

"Judy," I said, as the children perched on the couch around us. "How are you?"

"Fine," she said. "I'm fine. Cowboy Man is here to see me."

Her helper stood at the ready and I was grateful. "Thank you for coming with Judy," I said.

"It's a pleasure," she said.

I'd met her before. She was in her fifties and had a kind, but competent-looking face that made me feel confidence in her abilities to help us navigate if anything went wrong.

"Kids, this is Pamela." I turned back to her. "We have a room all ready for you right next to Judy's."

"Thank you," she said. She motioned to my stomach. "You're coming right along, aren't you?"

"The way he or she's been kicking, you'd think today."

"It's going to be a bronco rider," Keith called.

He was busy in the kitchen, preparing tea, just the way Judy liked it, something I was certain he had done on a daily basis when they were married. Was he sad? How surreal it must have been for him to have her back in the house, in the condition that she was in, along with his current wife. In fact, it was downright strange for me, too, no matter how it all came about. To be completely honest, it was one of the most awkward and difficult things I'd ever done in my life, but I just kept telling myself that what Keith and the kids had gone through had been much harder.

"And if it's a girl?" I asked.

"A barrel racer like her big sister," he said.

I smiled at an amused Pamela. "Anyway, we hope it comes after the prom, because I'm a chaperone. A junior boy named Estefan asked Peyton to be his date."

Peyton flushed crimson.

I left Judy with Keith and the kids while I showed Pamela to her room. I hoped she would like it. Caregivers have demanding jobs, and I wanted this to be a bit of a vacation for her, too, even though she still had to work.

"I will try to stay close, but out of the way," she promised. "That way everyone can get to know each other."

Leaving Pamela to get settled, I returned to the living room. Judy was fine, babbling on to the kids. Her eyes kept traveling to Keith, and in my heart of hearts, I could tell that she did know him on some level. I had a feeling she would be fine this weekend as long as Keith was near.

"That was a long drive, wasn't it?" Judy exclaimed, looking at me. "You were there. Cowboy Man drives too fast!"

The kids, who knew their dad's driving habits, started to giggle, which made her giggle, too. They were like three children. I turned to see what Keith thought of her comment, but he only smiled, stirring sugar into Judy's tea.

"That wasn't mommy in the car." Stevie tried to tell Judy. "It was Aunt Marta."

Judy just stared, not comprehending. The kids giggled again. Marta had left as soon as they got there, so there was no way for Judy to see that there were two of us. I would have to explain to Stevie later. Hopefully, he wouldn't cause Judy to get too confused. Right now, Judy was having a good moment, but I had been reminded by her brother over the phone about Judy's fits when he visited her. We had to tread carefully, not pushing her, and be ready to call the whole thing off if we had to.

Keith brought Judy's tea and set it on the coffee table in front of her.

"Just the way you like it, Judy." He offered her a smile, and she stared at him with adoration.

She sipped the tea carefully and set the cup in its saucer. "It's perfect, Cowboy Man."

Peyton's eyes never left Judy's face, except for when her eyes lingered on Judy's bracelet. Her eyes lit up.

"Your bracelet," she said, casting her surprised gaze at her dad and then back at Judy. "You still have it." And then I remembered the day Peyton had seemed upset that her dad had gotten me a bracelet. That was when it came together, seeing Judy at the rodeo, her having a bracelet resembling mine and Peyton's. It had been a mother-daughter thing for them, not me and Peyton.

Judy studied her wrist. "Oh yes," she said. "A man gave it to me. A special one." She frowned. "I can't remember who, but..." Her voice trailed off.

"I have one," Peyton said, holding out her wrist.

Judy smiled and studied it. I touched mine lightly and Judy noticed.

"You have one, too," she said. "Three beautiful bracelets."

I glanced at Keith. "I'll bet I know who gave it to you." I told Judy, not sure she'd understand. "He's standing right over there."

Judy snapped her head toward Keith. "From you?" she asked. "Three beautiful bracelets?"

"For three beautiful ladies," he said.

There was a time I would've been hurt to find out he'd given me something he'd given his ex, but not anymore. Now it seemed as if the bracelets, like the items in The Southern Pair, when found by the right customer, fit perfectly. We were now connected, the three women in Keith's life, and I knew right then that even if it stretched our hearts a little bit more than was comfortable, it would be a beautiful weekend.

JUDY'S ROOM WAS empty the next morning. I pulled the door shut and stood in the hallway, trying to catch my breath. Keith had gotten up an hour ago to take care of the horses. It was still very early in the morning. I hesitated in front of Pamela's door, then knocked. There was a squeak of the bed springs and a good deal of shuffling before the door cracked open and a sleepy-eyed Pamela peeked through, her pink and blue striped robe pulled tightly around her.

"Is everything okay?" Her eyes darted to Judy's door.

"She's not in her room."

Together, we checked the bathroom and everywhere in the house.

"Let me just put on some shoes," Pamela said.

I put on a pair of my western boots – I'd had to buy a bigger size to wear during my pregnancy. I thought of how funny they looked with my fuzzy jammy pants, but didn't have time to think long about it as I slipped on a jacket. Pamela followed behind me in a pair of floppy Ugg boots, still in her fuzzy robe.

It was still mostly dark and the cold hit my face as I stepped out. We usually had pretty mild autumn weather, but this early in the morning it was still cool. A chill seeped through my pajamas as we walked slowly, both of us still drowsy, around the yard looking for signs of Judy.

"I can't believe this," I said, trying not to panic. "I locked the outside door, I promise. Keith must have left it unlocked when he went out to the barn."

"It's not your fault. She remembers how to unlock a deadbolt." Pamela reminded me. "Speaking of the barn, maybe she went there."

We headed in that direction, Pamela making me hold

onto her arm even though I felt fine. It always amused me how everyone I knew offered their arm if I had to walk more than five steps, as if I didn't know how to walk myself. I suppose the waddling motion as I swayed from place to place threw people off.

Before we made it to the barn, we heard Judy laugh. Pamela and I hurried, following the happy giggling coming from the open door leading into the side of the barn. We were just stepping inside when we heard Keith's laughter joining Judy's, or in this case, Violet's.

"Shhh." We stopped short, both of us leaning far enough in to see down the row of stalls. The site of her fully dressed in a pair of boots, a western blouse, and jeans, complete with her lavender tiara wrapped hat, took my breath away. I had no idea she'd brought her outfits. My hand went to my mouth.

"Oh, Keith. How did you make this barn so big without my noticing?" Her laughter was contagious and Keith smiled.

"You'd be surprised at what I can put past you, Violet," he said.

He called her Violet. But, of course, she was Violet in that moment. I held my breath.

"And what you can't," she teased.

Even in the dim light, I saw the color in his cheeks. His smiled faded.

"Hey," he said gently, as if she might fade at any moment, and of course she could. Then she would just be Judy again, and his moment would be lost. I couldn't look away from his private moment. I had to hear it, too.

"Hey, cowboy." She reached for his hand. "What's up?"

I could see her eyes from my hiding place. They were completely clear. She even held herself differently than Judy. This had to be Violet.

"I'm sorry about everything I ever did to hurt you." His voice was strong, sincere.

Violet was now looking away from me, toward Keith, so I couldn't see what she comprehended. What did Keith mean, hurt her? Was he being all-encompassing? Talking about the things that all married couples do to hurt each other?

"Oh, that," she said. "It's okay. I forgave you a long time ago. What, did you forget?"

I sighed, relieved. Whatever it was couldn't have been a big deal or she would be angry, right?

His shoulders slumped.

She touched his face. "Cowboy, why are you so sad?"

He shook his head, put his hand on hers, the same way Peyton had mine the day before as we had waited for Keith to bring her mom home.

I could see his jaw working, the pain wracking his features, the crinkle he got in his forehead when he felt sad, the way it had just before he had cried on the day I found him visiting Violet at Cottonwood Manner.

He forced a smile and looked at Violet. She was starting to twist her foot, an action I recognized as Judy's. Pamela knew it, too, and she stepped forward to collect Judy and take her back to the house, but I placed my hand on her arm.

"Just a minute." She nodded, pausing, ready to step in if she needed to protect Judy, and really, Keith, too.

"Violet," he said. "Did I ever tell you how much I loved you?"

"Loved?" she said. "You silly thing. Don't you love me right now?"

"More than you know." He choked.

And Violet moved, not like Judy, but like a wife, and wrapped her arms around Keith. He didn't cry. I could see he wouldn't let himself do that to her. She wouldn't have understood, but he held her gently, his hand splayed on her back, his chin resting on top of her head as she pressed her cheek into his chest. In the center of my chest, a tightness twisted, part pain, part compassion, and, yes, even some resentment, I won't lie.

"I love you, Keith. I meant to tell you that. I love you like the country song, forever and ever, amen."

I saw him smile before he placed a kiss on the top of her head. I'd heard Peyton and Stevie say that to Keith. "I love you forever and ever, amen, Dad." So this was where the endearment had come from. Their mother.

I held my breath a little longer, wondering how long this moment could last, when I saw her foot twist again. Keith sensed it, stepped back, and placed his hands on her shoulders. He smiled at her, and he was smiling at Judy again.

"Cowboy Man?" she said, hesitantly.

"Yes?"

"I'm cold. I want to go to my room now."

"Sure, let's go," he said, taking his coat off and wrapping it around her shoulders.

"Do you think they're having eggs this morning? I like eggs, cowboy guy."

He caught my eye as they approached the barn door, and I saw a trio of sadness, relief, and apology competing in his gaze.

"I think they're having eggs, today, Judy. Is that right, Mandy?"

"That's right," I said.

Pamela held her hand out to Judy who took it like a child and the two walked together back to the house. Keith and I stood at the corral, watching the sun come over the tree-covered hills, casting the ranch and the sprawling timber and brick house in a yellow lens.

I thought I should say something, but nothing seemed right. I didn't want to spoil the moment for Keith. He wrapped an arm around me, pulled me close, but he didn't say anything, either.

One thing I was learning about being a cowboy's wife was that sometimes fewer words were best. Sometimes a plethora of feelings could be expressed by a simple gesture, such as a touch, an action, or a kiss, which was what Keith offered me as the sun rose higher, illuminating the ranch, so that the rooster crowed, yes we had one of those, and noises that signaled work, horses, and family filled the air around us. I felt revitalized by the morning's energy.

"Dad! Mom! Breakfast!" Stevie slammed the door as he ran back inside, and I tried not to think about his other mom, wondering if she had heard Stevie calling out to us and if it meant anything to her, or if Violet was gone to us again.

Chapter Nineteen

IF WE COULD have ended Judy's visit on the morning she became Violet in the barn, it would have been almost perfect, but, like regular life, ranch life isn't perfect, even though it is worth it. Cowboys and cowgirls, though dependable, can have a wild streak; and while Keith was a bronc rider and Stevie had been learning to rope cattle, the two real cowgirls on the ranch that weekend were barrel racers. Only Pamela and I were afraid of riding horses, but no matter. We had plenty else to do while everyone else rode.

"They're so gentle." Pamela commented as we prepared supper. She was looking out the bay window at everyone astride horses trotting off to the hills.

I had told her she didn't have to help cook. I knew it wasn't in her job description, but she said she liked cooking, and would enjoy it. I had to admit it was nice to have her company. Marta had opted to stay away for the weekend, saying we needed our privacy. I strongly suspected she was spending time with Quentin, and that made me happy, even though I missed her.

"They are," I said. "I might be afraid to ride them, but, in all honesty, I've never seen Keith's horses hurt anyone." I told her about how I was afraid.

"Do you think you'll ever ride one?"

I nodded, surprising myself. "Yes, I think I will someday, after this baby is born. It would really impress the kids. I'll make it a surprise when it happens. What about you?"

"I don't think I'll ever have a reason to ride," she said. "But I like to watch them. They're so beautiful, so free."

I nodded, knowing exactly what she was talking about. Seeing my family riding off in the sunset made me realize how free they all looked on the backs of horses, even Judy. We didn't have wild broncos for riding at the ranch, only riding horses. Keith had given Judy the horse he trusted the most and she had swung herself up on it without help. Apparently, riding horses was like remembering how to drink tea or unlock deadbolts. Some things were still inside her, like second nature.

We were almost finished with cooking supper, steaks from the small herd of cattle that Keith raised, along with roasted potatoes and string beans I found in the freezer leftover from the summer's garden.

"Look." Pamela pointed out the window. "They're back."

"They look happy," I said, noting their smiling faces.

"And it looks like Judy and your daughter have become good friends."

Pamela was referring to Peyton and Judy, laughing at something as they rode their horses into the corral.

"I'm going out for a second," I said. "Do you mind keeping things warm?"

"I'm okay. If Judy needs me, let me know. I'll be watching out the window."

"Thanks," I said, grabbing a light sweater and heading down the path.

"Did you have fun?" I asked Judy. I leaned forward against the fence.

She looked down at me from astride her horse. "Oh, hello, M—"

"Mandy." I reminded her.

"Look at this horse," she said. "Isn't it beautiful?"

"Gorgeous," I said. "Just like you."

She smiled at this, her vanity taking over, and I smiled myself. I could relate. We were both women who liked to look good. Judy still held herself prim and proper in the saddle, perhaps remembering on some level when she used to be a real rodeo queen.

"Alright," Keith called. "Peyton, help Judy off her horse, if she needs it."

Peyton, who had walked her horse into its stall while Judy and I talked, came toward us on foot.

"Stevie," she called. "Get down and take your horse inside."

Stevie turned his horse toward us. He was small, but no

stranger to horses. I had been surprised that he more or less knew how to do almost everything Peyton did with horses, although not as well.

He was a few feet away from Judy's horse when he hopped down from his, landing hard on the balls of his feet. The horses stood still, not at all fazed, until he screamed, the way kids do when they're really hurt.

"Oww!!"

"Stevie," I said.

His horse must have reeled, but I didn't see it as I somehow, even with my giant belly, managed to climb over the fence. I let myself gingerly to the ground, mindful of the baby, but also mindful of Stevie as I reached for him. At the same time, Judy reached down and took his hand and pulled him into her saddle, just as the front hooves of Stevie's horse hit the ground where he'd stood, and I felt the thunder of them, as sure as if they had trampled my own heart with their giant hooves.

I screamed. Out of the corner of my eye, I saw Keith rushing toward me, but before he got there, Peyton appeared. She ran forward, grabbed the reins of the horse and steadied it. By the time Keith reached us, Stevie was scared silent, sitting in front of Judy in her saddle, Peyton stood whispering to her horse, calmly patting the side of its head, and I—well, I was fine, but my pregnant body didn't know it. My legs began to buckle and I was about to sit down in the dirt, already bemoaning the stain it would leave on my pants, when Keith arrived at my side—just in time.

"Slow down, cowgirl," he said.

I tried to laugh as he lowered me to sit on his knee. I didn't know if I'd ever get used to the way my body had a mind of its own with this little munchkin inside of me.

"This baby is okay," Judy said. I touched my stomach before realizing a beat later that she meant Stevie. "I got him safe and sound."

Stevie, who seemed fine despite all his earlier hollering, started to correct Judy about his being a baby until he looked at his dad. Upon remembering, he mumbled a thank you to Judy.

"Thank you so much, Judy," I called up to her, remembering how big the horses hooves were as they were about to come down on top of Stevie.

"She saved your bacon," Keith told Stevie, who jutted his lip out.

"And what about the little cowgirl?" Judy asked, craning her neck.

Peyton walked toward us, having already put Stevie's horse away.

"I'm okay," she said, reaching up for Stevie, helping him down. Judy, seeming to have forgotten about the horse for a second, tried to climb off. Peyton set Stevie down and helped Judy. The two stared at each other, mirrors of the past and the present, of what might have been and what could never be.

"I want to go to my room now," she told Peyton.

"Okay," Peyton said, offering her mother her hand. They walked along the corral, out the gate, and toward the house—together.

"Do you think we're having eggs for dinner?" she asked of Peyton. "I like eggs. There was a man—he used to make eggs." She giggled.

"What's his name?" I heard Peyton ask.

"Um—Cowboy—I think. Cowboy Man, a man. Very nice."

Peyton walked Judy all the way to the house, but just before they got out of earshot, I heard Judy say, "He makes me fire tea. Every day. I like it fire."

"You like hot tea?" Peyton asked.

"Yes, hot."

"Me, too."

"Do you know where that man is?" Judy asked, her voice inquisitive. "He loves me, doesn't he?"

"What man?"

"Cowboy Man. He makes fire tea."

Still holding Judy's hand, Peyton turned, looked back at us. Keith was busy putting the horses away and must not have felt his daughter's eyes on his back as he walked the horse into the barn. Peyton turned then, following Judy inside, but I suspected Peyton's frustrations with her father might have evaporated in that moment. I don't know what she was really thinking. I never asked, but she was different after that, cloaked with a sort of maturity I hadn't ever expected of her so soon after learning about her mother. I'll always think of that moment as when Peyton stopped being a little girl, and a part of her became a young woman.

Chapter Twenty

PIA'S MOM, KIM, had seemed surprised when we invited her family over for dinner, but not Pia. It had been her idea, because naturally, Peyton had already told Pia that her mom's best friend, Violet, was really our friend Judy, from Cottonwood Manor. She miraculously had not told her mother, leaving that to me and Keith. I think in other circumstances she would have already told her mom, if Violet was not an Alzheimer patient, that is, but the truth was something Pia probably didn't know how to explain.

"Can I help you clean up?" Kim's smile was so genuine – too much so. How she had treated me at my wedding was still fresh in my mind, so I wondered if she was being fake.

"We can just save the dishes for Peyton," I said. "I'll clean up later."

"Nonsense," Kim said. "Let's give her the night off." She stood and started to gather empty plates, leaving me to feel as if Kim disapproved of me giving Peyton chores. Did Violet not have chores for Peyton?

I shook my head, placing my hand on my tummy. I was being ridiculous.

"In fact," Kim said. "You sit down. You have already done enough by having us for dinner. I wish I'd cooked myself so you wouldn't have had to."

"Keith did most of it," I said, easing myself onto a barstool.

"I'll bring in the dishes, too," Keith said, waving us away. I noticed Kim gave him a long look.

Out of earshot, Kim said, "You've trained him well."

"Oh, Keith isn't the kind of man who can be trained," I replied. "He just can't seem to stop helping when he's home, especially with me being pregnant."

She smiled. "Well, I never saw him help clear the table when he was, well, you know—in the past."

"When he was married to Violet?" I watched her face register surprise that I had mentioned Violet's name out loud, but I was over it now.

"Well, yes. He seems to be doing a lot of things for you that he never did for Violet."

"People change." I smiled.

After all, this was Judy's best friend I was talking to. I didn't know if I would have liked Violet or not, if I was altogether honest, but I cared about Judy.

"Indeed," Kim said. "It's sad, you know? I can't help but wonder, if he'd done some of those things for Violet—" She didn't finish, leaving me puzzling over her tone.

Was she upset? Or was she just confiding her thoughts in me? After all, it had been years since Violet left.

"It is sad," I said. "But I don't think the past matters. My husband is a good man."

"Of course, he is." She placated. "That's not what I meant, Manda." She sighed. "I was just meaning that, yes, he is different."

I thought about Keith's apology during that moment when Judy was Violet again in the barn, and bit my tongue. There was no reason to go off on Pia's mom, but I admit I was on the defensive for my husband at that moment. As my pregnancy progressed, my tolerance level had dropped a little bit more every day. I'd boldly told the man in line at the park water fountain to stop smoking in front of me because I was pregnant, I shook my fist at people who drove too fast through town, and the other day I regretfully told Ginger Sue at the post office to stop speculating, out loud, what was inside every package that I dropped off. Tonight, my body wasn't doing what I wanted it to. I felt big and bulky, so my tolerance level was especially low.

I took a deep breath. "Kim, I don't want to talk about the past. I invited you here for other reasons, one of which was because I wanted us to be friends for Pia and Peyton."

Kim's face flushed. She touched my hand, then pulled back, her eyes pooling. "It is hard," she said. "Sometimes, I just get so angry at you."

I gasped a little. "You know, Kim. I've never done anything that should keep us from being friends."

"You have," she said. "Sometimes, it seems like you

stepped in and took over Violet's life."

I kept my tone low. "I most certainly haven't done that." I wondered. Had I done that?

The images of Peyton fighting to keep Violet's things haunted me. How could I own The Southern Pair, see how important "things" were to people every day, and not have thought about poor Peyton and the only things left that connected her to her mom? And Kim. She obviously felt the way Peyton had, only what I had taken over in Kim's eyes must have been Violet's life.

"You know," I said, attempting to keep my voice kind. "Since my daughter and yours are best friends, maybe you and I can start over."

"*Your* daughter?"

Her tone hurt. I couldn't even think of what to say next, because her insinuation was right on target. Kim was right. I wasn't Peyton's mother, but I was doing everything I could to be a mom to her. To some people that would look like I was trying to erase her mother from her life, but they didn't know what I knew about her mother. I wanted to tell Kim about Violet right then, but she was on pins and needles around me.

"You want to be friends. See?" she said, shaking her finger "That's what I'm talking about." She slipped her hands between her knees. "Everyone wants to forget Violet ever existed."

A tear slipped down her cheek and my heart burst open a

little. Violet probably never realized just how hurt Kim would be by her sudden departure.

"Kim, that's not true." I reached out to touch her shoulder, but she moved away. I exhaled, wanting to deliver the news kindly. "The reason we invited you over tonight was because Keith…"

"Keith." She spat his name like it was rotten fruit. "Keith ran her off." As soon as she said it, she slapped her hand over her mouth, surprised, I guess, at her own vehemence.

I felt my own mouth drop open. Even without knowing the truth about Violet and why she really left, nobody could ever believe something so terrible about Keith. Could they? Was this what people thought?

"Ask him," she said.

I refolded a napkin in front of me, trying to forget about the exchange I had witnessed in the barn between Judy and Keith. He had apologized for hurting her in the past, but that did not change the real reason Violet left.

"Ask him about Adri's—"

"Adri is like his little sister." I was even disgusted that I'd ever been the teeniest bit wary of Adri.

"I'm talking about Adri's older sister," Kim said. "The one he had an affair with."

The glass I was holding crashed to the floor, just like you see in the movies. I even saw it drop in slow motion and, for the first time, I finally got it. When something like this happens, you're in such shock that time stops, so a glass would drop in slow motion. When it crashed, the shards shot out, also in slow motion, across the floor around us.

I stared at Kim, who actually had the decency to look regretful, but I didn't care.

That was exactly when Keith and Kim's husband, Brett, stepped into the kitchen.

A moment of silence passed between us, Kim's eyes regretful, begging me not to say anything in Keith and Brett's presence. I thought about the girls in the other room, even glanced over Kim's shoulders to make sure Peyton's door was shut. I admit it. I'm not perfect. I'm capable of meanness, and if Marta were here, she would have backed me up, but I didn't have back up. My husband was looking at me, concerned, but he was suddenly a stranger.

How could he have not told me about that? In one moment, Violet had become even more of a saint to me, and my husband the opposite.

"Is everything okay?"

"Everything's fine," Kim said, but I could see the men didn't buy it.

All three of these people had known each other longer than I had. They all had a history together and I figured the men probably knew enough about Kim to know things were not good at all.

"How about we go home?" Brett walked over and took Kim's arm.

She shrugged it away and I could see that all of her hurt

over Violet's vanishing was spilling out right here, right now.

I should tell her now. It was an awful thing she had endured, thinking her best friend had abandoned everyone, even her, but even if what Kim said was true, it was not anyone's fault. I let the words flood out before Keith could stop me, knowing he wanted to be the one.

"We asked you over here tonight because we found Violet. She's in a home in Pillar Bluff, and…"

"Whoa, whoa, whoa…" Keith rushed forward, trying to rein me in the same way Peyton reined in Stevie's horse when it almost trampled him.

He took my arm, but it was too late. Kim's eyes were wide. Since Keith had interrupted, she had only heard the first half of my speech, and it had the opposite effect. She was smiling.

Oh no. This is terrible. Why do I mess things up?

"Kim," I started, but Keith gave me a warning look. He waved everyone into his office, where trophy belt buckles and pictures of him riding broncos were blown up on the wall.

"Let's all have a seat. The girls don't need to hear this."

Brett broke in. "Why wouldn't the girls need to hear? I'd think it good for Peyton to know her mother is—"

Keith let the door click behind him as he walked to his desk, leaned against the front of it, facing us. He crossed his thick arms, looking more serious than I'd ever seen, except in the chute before a competition.

"What's going on? Where has she been?" Kim was still smiling.

I looked at the floor, sorry I had gotten her hopes up and despite my earlier anger, sorry for the turn things were about to take.

"Do you remember when we had Judy over for the weekend?" Keith asked.

"Oh yeah," Brett said. "The nice lady with Alzheimer's? Pia told us about that. So sad for a woman that young. I thought that was cool of y'all." He laid a hand across Kim's shoulders. "Kind of made me think that Kim and I need to do some kind of random act of kindness, too. Maybe not something like that, but still—"

"What," Kim interrupted, "does this Judy have to do with Violet still being alive?" Her eyes were wide and I thought maybe a part of her had just connected the dots.

As Keith explained, Kim's face fell, her shoulders slumped, and then she buried her face in Brett's shoulder. She couldn't speak, so Brett asked for her, "Can we see her? Do they allow visitors?"

"Of course," Keith said. "That's why we wanted the two of you to know."

"Peyton already knows? She didn't tell me," Kim found her voice again.

In an instant, confusion flooded her face. "Wait a minute. She was here all weekend and you didn't call me, Keith?"

"We told Peyton not to tell you," he said. "And I'm sorry."

Kim stifled a sob.

"Kim," Keith said gently. "She isn't the same as before. She even looks different."

"Then how do you know—"

"Trust me," he said. "I'd know my wife."

My heart swelled and broke a little. I'd made a choice to accept all of this. It didn't make it easier. I sat on a nearby sofa.

Kim looked sober, sad. She stood and I couldn't help but admire that woman. She was strong. Her prior anger at me had vanished. Poof! Just like that, I was no longer the enemy. I like a woman who is able to put her priorities in the right order when it comes right down to it.

Later, after I managed to stand back up without the help of a crane, we walked them out to the car. As the men talked, I handed Kim a card.

Violet Judith Black, Cottonwood Manor, 232 East Stockard St., Pillar Bluff, Tennessee.

"Thank you," she said. "And, Mandy, I'm so sorry for how I acted back there."

I waved my hand in the air. "All's forgotten."

"I hope so," she said. "I was wrong. All this time I've been blaming Keith and disliking you, and it turns out it was something totally different. It all makes me so sad." Her eyes glistened in the moonlight.

I touched her shoulder. She was small like Judy.

"We all say and do things we don't mean when we're under pressure. I'm probably the worst."

"And please," she whispered. "Forget what I said about Keith. I was just being mean."

"You mean it's not true?" I hoped she would say it was a big fat lie.

"I... I... No—it's not. Of course, it's not."

AFTER THEY WERE gone, leaving Pia to stay the night, I tucked Stevie into bed and asked the girls to keep an eye on him while Keith and I did some checking on the horses. Keith's eyes lit up, because going to the barn to check on horses used to mean something special, but tonight, he was in for a surprise.

I let him help me out to the barn. We entered a regular sized side door that led into a kind of office. Keith's barn wasn't like most barns. Where the barn at the orchard was filled with hay, and chickens, and a few milk cows, Keith's barn was sleek and fancy. It was kept immaculate, for a barn, and one could walk over concrete along the stalls on most days and not step in any horse poo. Even the smell wasn't too bad, but tonight we didn't walk around. I sat behind the makeshift desk in the little office and Keith leaned against the wall. I didn't waste any time.

"Why didn't you tell me about Adri's sister?"

His eyes widened, but after the shock wore off, his eyes narrowed.

"The girl I dated in high school?"

"The girl you cheated with."

"Is that what Kim was telling you in the kitchen?" He paced the tiny room a few times. "I could tell you were upset."

I tried to read his face. He'd always been my perfect cowboy, courageous and wild on a horse, and steady and true as my husband and the father of Peyton and Stephen.

"Is that true or not?" I asked. "Did you have an affair? Is that what you were apologizing to Violet for?"

His face turned white and his eyes filled with regret. That was all I needed to know.

"You cheated on Violet."

"Listen," he said, his voice hoarse. "I can explain." He shifted his weight to one booted foot, one hand shoved halfway into his jeans pocket. He stared around the room, working his jaw back and forth, trying to thinking of what to say. I ignored how strikingly handsome he looked when he was mad.

"So," I said. "Is all this taking care of Judy and being glad we found her, an act to redeem yourself?"

"No, of course not." His eyes welled. Not what I was expecting. "Okay," he said. "Maybe about the last part. I don't know."

"I guess the good thing for you is that Judy can't remember it anymore. That works out well for you, doesn't it?"

He crossed his arms, paced the room some more, pausing occasionally to speak. "First of all, Kim doesn't know as much as she thinks about my last marriage."

"She was her best friend."

"I was her husband."

I flinched.

"And second," he said. "What does my last marriage have to do with you?"

I shrugged. He had a point. What did it have to do with us? Except that if he cheated once, he might cheat again, like my last husband.

"I guess I just thought you would never do something like that to anyone. And it makes me feel like I don't know you." I paused, letting the truth form on my tongue. "Like maybe if you could do it to her, you could do it to me, too."

His face grew sad, but as I watched him pace the room, hoping he would say something to make me feel better, he suddenly turned and walked out, slamming the door behind him. I heard the truck start up, so I fished the flashlight out of one of the desk drawers and wobbled my way to the house. A part of me couldn't believe he let me walk back to the house alone. He was always overly protective. I guess that was how frustrated he was.

When I looked in on the girls, they were smiling and giggling over a new poster of their latest boy band group.

How many times had Marta and I done the same thing? If only we could go back to those days, but then when I thought about getting grounded, all those heartbreaks, and then losing Momma, I remembered that "those days" weren't always as great as we remembered. I only hoped Peyton's were better, and that finding Violet didn't bring more sadness than joy to her teenagerhood.

Once I had climbed into bed wearing my roomiest jammies, I grabbed my cell phone from the night stand. First I texted Marta that Keith and I were in an argument and he was still gone, knowing I would get sympathy from her, although I left out the part about Adri's big sister.

"Honey," Marta said when she called back. "I'm sure all will be well tomorrow. Just so you know, he's over here having a cup of coffee with Daddy. They're talking business."

"Really?"

"Really. He'll be home soon. Do you want to tell me what's wrong?

"Not right now," I said.

"Okay. I love you."

Next, I texted my husband.

"*I still love you.*"

I didn't receive a love you, too, but then again, we weren't in high school. It might not have meant anything at all.

Chapter Twenty-One

KEITH AND I went on as if nothing had happened. Prom was getting closer and in a small town like Castle Orchard, it was a big deal to the kids. Heck, it was a big deal to the grownups. People were already talking about which kids were going together and who was going stag. Since Peyton and Pia had both been invited by junior boys, they joined the prom committee. One evening, I found them both practicing their dance moves in the living room.

"This will be the best prom ever thanks to my dad," Peyton said. Keith had pulled a few strings in the rodeo community and helped them find a country act that was a perfect blend of Lady Antebellum and Florida Georgia Line. For the past week, Peyton and Pia had been practicing their country dance moves, even roping poor Estefan into practicing the two-step with them. They were all three pretty good, but I was especially surprised to find that Peyton could dance her little boots off, mastering not only the two-step, but also the waltz and the West Coast Swing. Estefan seemed impressed, too, I noted.

"Where did you learn to do all that?" I asked. "You're

really good."

"There's lots you don't know about me." But she said it with a smile.

"I am sure of that," I said.

It seemed that her mother's condition should have made her depressed, but Peyton seemed to be making lemonade from lemons. She'd hadn't stopped talking about her mom, sharing little memories she'd never told me about before, and I found I didn't want her to stop.

"Actually, we learned a lot on the Internet," Pia said. "There are how-to videos everywhere. I bet you could even learn how by next week."

"Just like with knitting," Peyton said. "All you need is a how-to-dance video."

I didn't tell her that I knew plenty of country dance moves from my partying days before I'd met Keith. Keith and I'd also done our share of two-stepping.

"If you're going to be a chaperone, you need to know."

I gave her a smile. "Honey, don't forget there's a good chance I'll have the baby by then, or be about to. I might have to have your Aunt Marta switch places with me as chaperone."

"Nothing she hasn't done before, I've heard." Peyton grinned. My escapades involving switching places with Marta were legendary.

"In case I don't go, how about I dance now? Come here, Estefan. Let's just practice a little. Show me some steps, girls."

"Are you sure you should be dancing?" Peyton asked.

"I have to stand up a little bit," I said. "And I just have to move slowly."

I stepped forward, smiling at the careful way Estefan placed his hand on my very round waistline.

"Don't worry, honey. You can't hurt the baby."

He blushed.

The last few months had passed with no incidents. My pregnancy was going great, and bed rest wasn't necessary. I was tired, which was to be expected so close to delivery, but sitting around was as bad as standing up. I couldn't get comfortable.

Next to us, Peyton and Pia partnered up and went through the basic two-step. Estefan and I followed at a more gingerly pace.

"Great job." Pia congratulated us. Peyton looked cynical.

"Now, try this." Peyton jumped right to the West Coast Swing.

This must be Peyton's competitive side.

"Okay," I said. "I'll give it a go."

"Take it easy on her, Estefan." Peyton crossed her arms over her chest. "Don't let her lose her balance."

I smiled at Estefan, gave him a wink. He grinned, quick to catch on, and we boogied like we had been dancing together for years, but very carefully and not exactly keeping time with the music. I probably looked like a mix between a giant toddler and a very, very old lady. Behind us, the girls squealed and clapped until pretty soon, Keith was standing behind them in the doorway, grinning like we were seeing each other for the first time. As Estefan and I twirled, Keith caught me up and gently spun me around. We danced slowly, like we used to, before we were married, when we met in the dance tent after the rodeo.

"You've still got it, cowgirl." But he noticed my panting for breath and gracefully lowered me to a couch to rest. Then he moved on to Peyton, spun her around for a few minutes at a much faster pace, and then passed her to Estefan while he moved on to dance with Pia. I waddled over and switched Peyton's music to a faster song and sat back down to watch.

Peyton, no time to be embarrassed with the pace of the music, matched Estefan's steps perfectly. Keith noticed, and instead of looking angry like a dad might do, he smiled. It was good to see Peyton having fun. That smile on her face was worth the discomfort of seeing her dancing with a boy. Besides, what harm could come with Estefan? I'd known his parents for years. He was a good boy.

THAT EVENING AFTER dinner, Keith and I climbed into bed, Keith stretching in his boxers, lean and beautiful. I touched my tummy, wondering what he was thinking when he looked at me.

"I love your body right now," he said, and I smiled. He always seemed to read my mind.

"Are you tired from all that dancing?" he asked.

"Yes." I was quiet for a moment. "What was I thinking? Dancing?"

He scooted closer. "Cowgirl, you weren't doing back flips, and I don't want to hurt your feelings, but you weren't doing all that much dancing, either."

"As if I could in this condition." I joked.

"I think the fact you felt like dancing and forgot to worry about the baby is proof that everything's okay. There isn't a rule that you have to be worried every minute of your pregnancy. When Peyton was born—"

"What happened when she was born?"

"Never mind," he said. "I'm sorry."

"Don't be sorry. She is your baby."

"Well, I'll tell you the story another time."

"Okay," I said. "So, when are we having Judy back, so that Peyton and Stevie can see her?"

"After the baby comes," he said, placing his hand over my stomach and rubbing softly back and forth.

"I just don't want to wait until Judy's memory worsens. Maybe if we won't wait too long, there might be a chance she will have a moment where she remembers Peyton. That would be good for Peyton, to have that affirmation."

"She might also break Peyton's heart, if she never recalls. What if she doesn't remember her at all? What if she launches into the kind of tirade she has when her brother visits? That kind of event would break her heart."

The thought of that happening to Peyton made me shudder, but I wondered if it had something to do with the truth about his first message. He felt guilty. We hadn't spoken about it since that night.

"Honey, are you afraid to see Judy again?" We hadn't talked about Kim's announcement about his affair since that night.

"I'm not afraid," he said.

He moved his hand up to my shoulder and pressed his lips for a moment against my cheek. We were both quiet and after a while I thought he was asleep, but then his voice, serious, broke into my thoughts.

"What Kim told you, is still bothering you, isn't it?"

"What makes you think that?" I snuggled against him.

"I can just tell." There he goes, reading my mind again.

"I'm sorry. Yes, I guess I have been insecure ever since that night."

He was silent for a while. "It's in the past," he said, his voice low. "And it didn't really happen the way Kim described it. She likes to act as if she knew Violet better than I did, but she didn't. She doesn't, and I didn't have an affair."

In the past, that was what my ex always said.

"Then what? If not an affair."

"Honey, it's in the past. It has nothing to do with us."

I truly hoped not, because there wasn't much worse in a marriage than being married to a cheater. That much, I knew for sure.

"Let's concentrate on our family," he said. "And on this baby."

He didn't add, "And making sure all is well with my previous wife who isn't in her right mind anymore." That would have been too weird, but it was in everything, in the walls of this house that she lived in, in her friendship with Pia's mom, and in this room. Not the bed, of course. I'd had that switched out, but lately I'd become very aware that Judy – no, Violet – had spent a lot of time in this very same room. And while I could never be jealous of Judy, sometimes I still got jealous at the thought of Violet. Call me shallow, or just call me pregnant, but it bothered me.

When Keith reached his chin in to nuzzle my neck, I pulled back.

"I want to sleep in a different room."

"What? Why?" He did nuzzle me then. "I like sleeping with you."

I giggled. I couldn't help it. All jealous fears aside, being married to Keith was like having my own cowboy character from a romance novel, so he always knew how to coerce forgiveness, if you know what I mean. Sometimes, I wondered if it was this side of Keith that made me so jealous of other women. Who wouldn't want to marry a cowboy?

"I don't mean separate rooms, silly. I mean us, together, in a different room."

I could see him smiling at me in the half-darkness as he reached out to smooth a curl behind my ear. "Okay," he said. "Let's do it."

My heart grew bigger for him because he understood what I was saying. What more could a woman ask for? A hot cowboy for a husband, and an understanding one, too.

"Right now," he said.

"Now?"

"Why not? It's our house. We can sleep where we want to."

He climbed out of bed, slipped his jeans on. That always amused me, Keith walking around shirtless in an old pair of jeans instead of sweats or pajamas. Then he scooped me up. I waited for him to groan. I'd always been curvy, but now I was much rounder.

"You shouldn't carry me. I'm pretty heavy now."

He snorted. "Cowgirl, I ride wild horses for a living. I think I can lift little itty-bitty you."

He had a point, and he called me itty-bitty. How could a girl not love that?

I reached down and grabbed one of the covers as we walked out, down the stairs, and into a room flooded with moonlight. I'd nicknamed it my garden room and filled it with all kinds of flowers and herbs. I pretended not to hear him grunt a little as he sat me on a wicker chair, disappeared, and came back lugging a futon mattress that I recognized from the den and a pillow underneath each arm.

"Just for tonight, will this room do?"

"That depends, is it, you know, Violet free?" It was a fair

question.

"This was a mud room before you came, sweetheart, and as you can see from all these smelly flowers, it has your fingerprints all over it now." He scooped me up again. "And no Violets. Now, come to bed."

He helped me onto the mattress like I was sleeping beauty, only suddenly I wasn't sleepy anymore. The dancing, it seemed, had not worn me out after all and a new sense of energy glowed through my limbs. I watched him undress, admiring his body in the moonlight, lean, scarred, and muscular from years of riding bucking broncos. Seeing him every day, I sometimes took for granted what a specimen of fitness he was. I scooted closer to his warmth as he settled himself beside me, kissing my shoulder, moving one hand in soft, slow circles along the curve of my belly. I let out a deep sigh when his hand circled over the thin silky fabric of my nightgown just below my breasts. Testing the waters, he passed one hand over each breast, circling from one to the other, finally resting on one, cupping gently until I moaned for more contact. He then leaned over, pressing his mouth on the fabric, his kisses hot, until I cried out.

In a flourish, the fabric agonizingly separating my skin from his was quickly discarded and in a warm rush, as if it had been years instead of only a few months, every smoldering ember between us was rekindled.

AFTERWARD, WE SNUGGLED close, nose to nose, and he

reached down to touch my stomach. Timing couldn't have been any better than at that moment, when a flutter swirled inside my belly.

"Oh!"

We'd felt it kick many times, but each instance made me long once more for this to be the time that I got to keep my baby here on earth.

Our baby fluttered again. Then kicked hard.

"Oh, thank you, God."

Every kick was a blessing, a promise that this pregnancy would be different than all my others. I might have whispered my prayer out loud, but Keith didn't say anything if he heard. For a long time, he just lay there, saying nothing, caressing my tummy, occasionally kissing my forehead. Just before I fell asleep, I reached up and touched my cowboy's cheek. It was damp.

Chapter Twenty-Two

"WHERE'S PEYTON? SHE said she would help with these tarts." Marta was busy lining a tray with peach pastries. We were planning a family dinner at Daddy's house.

"She left early this morning to help Estefan and Pia with some pastry deliveries." The website had been going crazy since Peyton had created it. Orders came in daily. "They have some prom committee errands, too."

"Really? I thought they delivered everything." She fished around in her bag. "Well, I can't find my list."

"Maybe they have the list."

"Maybe so. Probably. Well, you're here, so you'll have to do. Grab that bar stool if you feel tired."

"When do I not these days?" I sat. "This little one might just do me in."

"Don't say that," she said. "You're going to be fine."

Marta may be my wild and crazy twin, but when it came to me and babies, she was a bigger bag of nerves than I was. I hoped Peyton or Pia wouldn't mention the dancing to her. She would flip out.

"Here." Marta handed me a tray. "Arrange these tarts. Hopefully the kids will get all their prom stuff done in time for dinner. We should invite Peyton's boyfriend."

"Estefan is her boyfriend now?"

"Well, you're the mom. You should know."

"Yes," I said. "I guess he is, but she's not calling him that just yet."

Stevie burst through the door demanding another pitcher of lemonade. Quentin followed close behind.

"Hold on there, scout. Don't forget to say please."

"Oh, okay. Hey, we need more peach lemonade!"

"Please." Quentin reminded him.

"Please."

Marta and I giggled while I mixed up another batch for him. I noticed Quentin's wink at Marta as he helped Stevie on the way out.

I placed the back of my hand over my forehead and closed my eyes. "Oh, be still my heart." I teased.

She snapped me lightly with a tea towel. "Stop it."

"What? He's dreamy."

"He is that."

"You two are spending a lot of time together," I said, serious.

"We sure are. And he's definitely my boyfriend." We giggled.

"That's so sweet, sis! We both have cowboys."

"Well," she said. "I'm not getting my hopes up about

anything. I've had too many losers to count before Quentin."

"Honey, Quentin is no loser. I can assure you that. If he were, then Keith wouldn't have ever hired him. Plus, he has a little place at the ranch, you know." I was referring to the little cabin behind the barn where Quentin stayed when he didn't want to drive back to Pillar Bluff.

"I am aware," she said.

"So we could be neighbors."

"Well, don't mention it to Keith yet, but a little bird told me that Quentin bought a little piece of land right next to your ranch. And he's building his own house on it."

I grinned, dismissing Marta's words about not getting her hopes up. I knew all about the land. Keith and I had sold it to him.

"He told you about that?" I asked.

"Yes. He did."

I squealed, spinning on my bar stool.

"Be careful, girl!"

"I hear wedding bells!" I giggled.

She blushed.

"Did you just blush? You? Marta? Blushing?"

I walked to her, turned her around, and squeezed her hands.

"Now, it's your turn to be happy, honey," I said. "Just enjoy it. Don't borrow trouble."

She nodded.

"Besides," I said, "I saved one of my honeymoon bikinis

for you that I never wore." I patted my waist. "I certainly am not going to be wearing it again, not for a good long while."

"Is it the red one?"

"Of course!"

"With the little polka-dots?"

"That's the one."

She giggled. "How did you not wear it?"

"I took so many, just in case," I said.

"Well, you just hang onto it for a little longer."

"I wonder if we should text the girls to come on back," I said. "I think Daddy could use Estefan's help."

"Don't worry. I'm sure they'll be back any time."

"Hey, sis." I sat back down on my barstool and picked up a Sharpie. "If you found out something about Quentin, something not good that had happened before you knew him, would you be angry that he didn't tell you before you got married?"

"Well, I'm not even engaged yet, Mandy. And is there something about him I need to know?"

Daddy walked up behind us. "You're engaged, Marta? Now, Quentin didn't even ask my permission." Marta whirled around, ready to pounce, but when we both saw Daddy's face, we knew he was joking.

"Daddy. Stop eavesdropping." But of course we didn't mean it. We didn't keep many secrets from Daddy. We never could anyway, so we'd stopped trying long ago.

"It's not eavesdropping when you're in my kitchen." He

kissed each of us. "You never said I had to stay out, so what's your worry today?"

I smiled. Daddy always teased us about our worrying, but in our defense, our worries usually resulted in solutions, at least ultimately.

"Mandy's in a pickle about something Keith didn't tell her."

"Oh, well, I'm sure they'll work it out. See you girls later." He headed toward the door. I'd noticed that over the past few months he'd resisted giving opinions about my marriage. I appreciated the privacy, but I wanted his opinion.

"Daddy?"

"Yes?"

"If you found out Mom had done something that wasn't right before she married you, and she didn't tell you, would you have gotten mad?"

He placed his hand on the door and looked past us into the pantry where he still kept all of the embroidered kitchen towels she had made when they were first married. I knew that sometimes he went into the pantry and just stood there, to be with her things, and all the memories of her in the kitchen preparing meals and loving all of us with food, smiles, and hugs. That was one of the things that inspired The Southern Pair, the way Daddy reacted around the mementos he'd saved of our momma. Marta and I each had our own keepsakes of Momma's. Sometimes they were the only reminders of happier times.

"That would have depended on why she didn't tell me. I guess if it was to protect me, say, maybe from getting my feelings hurt, or worrying, I guess I would try to get over it." He shrugged, smiled sadly. "I've been thinking, since y'all found Judy, that maybe your momma would've understood Judy's decision to go away. Remember, she didn't tell me about the voices when they first started. She didn't want me to worry.

"Oh, Daddy." Marta turned to face the sink, but I walked over and kissed him on the cheek.

He patted me on the back, as if I was the one who needed to be consoled and not him.

"Thanks."

He walked down the porch steps toward the barn. Marta started filling another tray with food.

"So, what is this big secret, Mandy?"

"Like it's your business." I still hadn't told her about Kim's accusation about Keith, or that he said there was more to the story and for me not to worry.

"It's not, but you know you want to tell me."

I did. As meddling as my sister seemed to be, when it came down to real life, we were always there for each other.

"Well, a little bit ago when Kim and Brett came over… well, you remember the argument Keith and I got into? He came over to Daddy's for a bit?"

"Yes." She turned to place the tray on the table.

"Well, Kim told me something that shocked me about

Keith."

Marta pulled some apples out of the fridge and doused them with the sink's spray nozzle.

"What did Kim accuse him of?"

"Well…"

"Mandy?"

Keith. I wheeled around, caught in the act. He looked disappointed, but he should know by now—the whole twin thing. Still, it didn't keep me from feeling guilty.

"Can I talk to you?" he asked.

Quentin walked in behind him.

Marta gave me a sympathetic look. "I'll let you have her if Quentin will help me here in the kitchen."

"Now, what makes you think I can cook?" Quentin reached for an apron, choosing the frilliest among those hanging on a hook by the fridge.

"Lots of reasons," she said, just as Keith and I slipped out the back door.

"YOU FEEL LIKE a walk?" Keith asked.

"Yes," I said. "And then I'll feel like sitting down, and then another walk, and so on."

He smiled, despite the frustration I'd read on his face earlier and led me into the orchard. We walked hand in hand, not saying anything, until we got to the spot where we got married.

"Honey, I'm sorry," I said. "I have no right to tell Marta

your secrets, and she still doesn't know because you walked in right on time."

He shushed me, took me into his arms, and kissed me. His mouth was warm and sweet, his cologne wafting through me. When he let go, I literally had to catch my breath.

"What was that for?" I asked, having expected a much different scenario.

"To remind you of why I married you." He stared down at me from beneath his cowboy hat, reminding me of how I felt on our wedding day, after I had shed the offensive first slip and made my way back to my groom. I recalled how he'd looked at me with relief when I walked back up the aisle on Daddy's arm.

"Mmmm." I said, reaching up for another kiss now, but I only got a peck on the cheek that time.

"But we do need to talk."

"Okay." I turned. "Let's walk. I can't stand in one place for long." I pressed the bottom of my stomach with my palms. Keith caught up to me, offering me the crook of his arm. I leaned into it.

"Sure is pretty this time of year," Keith said.

"My favorite time," I said. Most of the apples had been harvested by this time, but a few still hung on the trees, their scent sweetening the air.

"Cowgirl, I know you're still mad at me about what Kim said. And I realized when you were about to spill out my most embarrassing secret to your sister…"

"I'm so sorry," I interrupted. "I shouldn't have even tried to tell her. I don't know what I was thinking."

"Yeah, about that. Do you two have to tell each other *every*thing?"

"Most things," I said. "But no, not everything."

"Good," he said. "Because I think married people should be allowed to have a few secrets."

"I agree."

"Great," he said. "Now that we have that settled, let me tell you what happened with me and Violet, so you can get it out of your mind."

For some reason, I didn't know if his telling me would get it out of my mind, but I did want to know.

"I'm tired of your being mad at me."

"I'm not mad, Keith. It's just that I feel like maybe I don't know the real you. To tell the truth, it scares me. I've been married to a cheater before, and I can't handle that again." I offered him an apologetic look. "I'm not saying you are going to cheat on me, but just that since you have, I know you are capable."

"Ouch," he said.

"I'm sorry."

"Stop apologizing. I deserve that, but can I explain?"

We had stopped at the end of the orchard and were facing each other.

"I've been waiting for weeks for you to do that."

He took each of my hands, laced his fingers through

mine. His eyes engulfed me and I prayed he was still the honorable man I thought him to be, because I could not live without this man.

"Mandy, I didn't want you to know that Violet and I didn't have a perfect marriage. That's why I didn't tell you."

"Nobody has a perfect marriage," I said. "Don't you know that by now?"

"But with you is as close as I'm ever going to get."

My eyes welled. I felt the same way, but I was so moved by his words, I couldn't say it out loud.

"I was always too busy with the ranch, but mostly I was off at the rodeo. She went with me the first few years, but eventually she had to stay home and I had to leave her to deal with the ranch and the house on her own."

"I thought she went to all the rodeos with you."

"No," he said. "That became impossible, but I had a living to make for us. It was her idea to stay home. She said she wanted to and she was more than capable of running the ranch. I thought she loved it. She never complained to me and I always bragged on her to people. One day I walked in while she was talking to Kim, the way I did just now to you and Marta, and she was spilling all her frustrations out to Kim."

"I see why you were upset back there in the kitchen."

"Not upset, but it reminded me of Violet and how I needed to communicate with you better than I did her. Make you feel more appreciated."

Well, Oprah would be proud. A man wanting to communicate.

"Anyway, she told me she was sick of it all." He didn't say what all was. "One day when I came home, she'd changed all the locks."

I couldn't picture sweet Judy doing that. I said as much to Keith.

Keith laughed. "Believe me. Judy – Violet – wasn't a wimpy girl. It's why I married her." He smiled. "It's not like we were headed out to get a divorce or anything. She'd just had it with my cavalier way of heading off to the rodeo without thinking of her, and wanted to show me she meant business, that I had to change, and she was right to do it."

"Wow," I said, shaking my head. "I mean, it's no concern of mine, I guess. I wasn't there, but it just seems so out of character for Judy."

By now we were walking toward one of Daddy's barns and Keith led me to an old, but sturdy, bench that I vaguely remembered sitting on with Marta and watching Daddy work. He gently sat me down and sat beside me. He was so tall, he looked like he was sitting on a little kid chair.

"Listen, Mandy. Judy is all the good that was in Violet, but Violet was a whole person, and people are not perfect. I'm not perfect." He winked at me. "Even though you are."

"Stop teasing me," I said, playfully slapping his arm. "I am the farthest thing from perfect."

"Not that far," he said, and his smile was gone and he

was serious. "Honey, there's something you need to know about Violet and me. We met very young when I was just starting to rodeo. We were both into it, her barrel racing, me saddle bronc riding. We really were the sweethearts of the rodeo back then."

Mental note—don't be jealous of a woman who is definitely unattainable now.

"We lived like young people do, before Violet decided to stay home on the ranch," Keith said. "Until then, the two of us were known to have a little too much fun in the dance tent. After the rodeos, we didn't go straight home, but partied and drank, having a great time. Sometimes we took it too far and paid for it the next day."

"At least you didn't have kids," I offered. "And you were with each other."

"That's true," he said. "But later, after Peyton was born, all that changed. We went back to church, settled down. I stopped drinking, and that's when Violet decided to stop racing. She'd stopped doing the queen thing before we got married, but I worried she'd regret leaving behind barrel racing. At that point, she thought she just wanted to be a mom. That left her home to take care of the kids while I was off at the rodeo, doing all the things we had always done together."

"You kept partying without her?"

"No, not those things. I mean real rodeo things."

"She got tired of it, didn't she? Your being gone so

much." I could picture it now. Her waiting, wishing he would come home sooner, receiving those calls that he was staying a little longer and not knowing why, just like I had.

"Yes, she did. And for a while we grew apart, but only for a short while."

"And that's when it happened?"

"Yes. I was stupid. Stupid, stupid, stupid." His eyes grew stormy and he shook his head.

I definitely couldn't imagine Keith doing something like that to Violet, not really, but the embarrassment in his eyes told me it was true even if he couldn't bring himself to say the words.

"You know what?" My previous patience and understanding were quickly evaporating and were replaced by the poison still in my heart from my previous husband, feelings I thought I'd dealt with, but once a heart is trampled that way, maybe you never really forget it.

Keith squeezed my hand. "What, cowgirl?"

"I think I've heard this speech before from my own ex. Let me guess, the next thing that happened was you were off on a trip – in your case, the rodeo – and you ran into your old friend. She was probably a former queen, like Kim and Violet, right? You got a little drunk. Then you got really drunk. And then we both know what happened. Violet found out about it, and *that's* when she changed all the locks."

He was red now, and I admit I hoped it was from the

shame, because he should be ashamed. I hated a cheater. But I didn't hate my husband. I sighed, not really sorry I'd said what I had, but feeling crummy nonetheless.

"That pretty much sums it up," he said, giving me a shrewd look. "You're pretty tough, cowgirl."

"Just experience," I said, dismissing it with a wave of my hand. "Was that the only time you did that to her, or was it just the only time you got caught?" What I really wanted to ask was, would he do the same to me?

He hung his head, low, hiding beneath the brim of his hat.

But I couldn't judge his past today. He was my husband.

"So, what they say about cowboys is true? They are rabble-rousers?"

"Not true," he said, regaining his spunk. "Listen, what I want you to know is that Violet and I loved each other. That was a horrible mistake, but what Kim didn't tell you is that Violet and I made up and we were happy until the day she disappeared. Incredibly happy."

I scooted closer to him.

"That," he said, gazing out into the apple trees, "is why I felt so much joy when God gave me that moment with her in the barn a few weeks ago." He smiled, released a breath, as if he had been holding it for a long, long time. "It felt so good to say that to her and when she said I was forgiven in that tiny window of that Violet moment, she set me free."

I remembered the look on Keith's face that day.

"I thought that was beautiful," I said. "And then Kim came along and made you feel guilty again."

"Kim means well," he said. "But she's wrong about a lot of things. One of them is I didn't change for you."

"You didn't?"

"No, because I was already a changed man before Violet left, and that's why it was so hard to understand when it looked like she up and left me."

"So, where does that leave you and me? Us?" I touched my stomach.

He shook his head, as if he hadn't just explained it already. "What do you mean, us?"

"How do I know you won't do stuff like that anymore? How can I be sure you won't make the same mistake again?"

"Well, for starters, I don't drink on the road anymore, but mainly, because I love you. I would never let anything like that happen again. I was lucky that Violet forgave and that we worked things out. I'd never expect another woman to go through what she did." He gave me a sad look. "And I know your ex already did that to you."

I shrugged. "So, Violet just dropped it?"

"Yes."

"Just like that?"

"Well, I wouldn't say just like that, but there did come a day when she was okay."

"How do you know?"

"I guess I didn't really," he admitted. "Until that day in

the barn." He pulled me closer. "I know I don't deserve for anyone to ever trust me again, Mandy. I can't tell you how it makes me feel that I introduced this into my life in the first place, and now into yours."

"Kim did that."

"No, Kim didn't do it. I did."

It surprised me more than a little that he admitted it. It was a gentle reminder that while this news was all new and horrible to me, he'd been dealing with it for years before he met me. Violet had, too, but had forgiven him, although not without making him suffer a little bit when she changed all the locks. The thought of it made me smile, just a little. I liked a woman who didn't wallow in self-pity.

"I promise, Mandy. I've never cheated on you, in case that's what you're worried about."

And those were the words I had really wanted him to say.

"Mandy, I made a mistake in my first marriage, yes, but I changed. It sure as heck has never happened since I've met you."

When he wrapped those muscled arms around me and pulled me into his chest, I melted into that moment like an ice cube.

The funny thing is, I don't even think Keith knows that I am putty in his hands, and maybe I'd better not tell him. I was really thinking about letting bygones be bygones and was just leaning in to kiss him back when his cell phone went off in his shirt pocket. The vibration made me jump back.

Frustrated, he glanced at the screen.

"It's Kim."

"Calling you?"

"Hello?"

"What does she want?"

"What? Are you sure?"

Silence.

"When did they leave? Uh-huh? Gotcha. We're on our way now."

He took my arm, leading me back to the house. "Keith, slow down."

He slowed his pace, taking my hand. "I'm sorry. We have to hurry. Peyton and Pia roped Estefan into running off with them."

"What? Running off where?"

"I don't know, but Carlos called your dad and said Estefan took the truck and they haven't seen them since early this morning."

"Peyton told me they were making deliveries."

"I don't think so," Keith said.

We hurried through the orchard. I was out of breath halfway there, so I had Keith go on ahead.

"Are you sure?"

"I'm fine," I said. "Go on. I'll be there in a few minutes."

When I walked into the kitchen, Marta took one look at me and sat me down in a corner rocking chair. I guess it was silly to have a rocking chair in the kitchen, but it had always been there. Daddy said our mom had rocked us in that chair when we were babies. Before she started showing signs of her illness. I always felt like it held a piece of her, a memory that was warm and soft and comforting.

"Do you want me to call the doctor, sis?"

"Oh, no. I'm fine. Just tired."

"Okay, but you just sit there for a while, okay?" She bustled around the kitchen, doing a bunch of nothing, it looked like to me, and so I knew she was worried.

"So what's going on with the kids?"

She whirled around. "I found that list, so I know they aren't making deliveries."

"Maybe they're just skipping out like kids do. Remember the time we skipped out and went rafting with our friends?"

"How could I forget? You fell out of the boat and our friend Randy had to fish you out of the water."

"Oh, yes. That's right." In my mind I saw Peyton rolling through the water, her little body limp, or something worse, and felt my heart rate quicken.

Marta sat down at the table, but her foot bounced up and down like she was tap dancing.

"I wish one of them would just answer their phone."

"I'm sure they're alright." My own foot started bouncing. "You think they're alright?"

Marta stood, forgetting she was supposed to be calming me. She paced the room. I longed to join her, but made myself sit in the chair and take deep breaths.

"They've been gone for two hours. Kim said neither Peyton nor Pia will answer their phones. Estefan's dad is angry, going to ground him into next week."

"Well I think they all need grounded further than next week."

She sat back down, tapped her fingernails on the table. I stood.

"I'm not sitting around and waiting," I said. Marta followed me out onto the porch. We both saw Dad at the same time and made a beeline for him.

"Now slow down," he said. "I've already talked to Keith. They're checking your house, Pia's, and Estefan's first. It's probably just kids being kids. You'll remember how that goes." He gave us each a pointed look.

I shook my finger. "If that's what they're doing, then Peyton's grounded until college. I hope that's what they're doing."

"It'll be okay."

"Let's check The Southern Pair."

Sure enough, they had been there.

"Wow, Mandy. That was a good hunch. How did you know?"

"Remember the time we snuck off with our friends Mitzie and Caroline? First we raided their mom's office. Remember how she had that extra fridge with all those drinks and snacks?"

Her eyebrows shot up. "Yes, but we didn't want those

kinds of beverages. We wanted the ones hidden down in the salad crisper."

"That doesn't mean they're as precocious as we were." Inside, sure enough, a six pack of 7-Up and Diet Coke I'd just bought was gone from the fridge, along with all the candy bars and a note that read, IOU – Peyton.

"Bingo."

"So which part of the river do you think they're at?"

"I don't know, but they are in big trouble for not asking permission."

We were thinking the river because that was where we would have gone when we were their age, but there were many other places they could be. My mind spun as I imagined what they could be up to. Hopefully, we'd find them sitting on the banks being normal, but they were still in big trouble.

"What if they're smoking cigarettes?"

"Or marijuana," Marta said.

"Oh, Lordy, help us."

"At least we know they aren't getting drunk with all that 7-Up and Diet Coke."

"True," I agreed. We were back in the car, driving along the river, looking for Estefan's truck. After a while, we turned around and headed back to Daddy's. We'd been texting Keith and Quentin, but nothing.

"Is there some other friend they might hang out with, besides Estefan?" I tried to remember who Pia had a crush on. It would have been more fun to be rebellious with another boy around.

"If there's another boy, then that can't be good."

"Oh, my word, Marta. What if they get pregnant?"

"What? No, I don't think Estefan would be like that. He's a gentleman, Mandy."

"He's a boy!"

"True, but not all boys are like that, especially with girls like Peyton and Pia."

I hoped Marta was right. Back at the orchard, we tumbled out of the car. Daddy was hanging the kitchen phone receiver in its cradle on the wall as we walked in. I forgot to even say hello before I plied him with questions.

"Now, calm down girls." He put an arm around each of us. "Just got off the phone with Keith and they found them. Sort of."

"Sort of?"

"Yes. They are in Pillar Bluff."

"What? Have they been gone that long?"

Marta forced me to sit in the rocker again. She leaned against the table, waiting for Daddy to explain.

"They are fine, but Keith got a call from Cottonwood Manor. Said some kids claiming to be relatives tried to get in to see Judy."

Marta, Daddy, and I exchanged glances.

I was angry, but grateful, and not at all surprised once I thought about it.

"Of course," I said. "Of course she wanted to see her mom. She didn't want to wait until after the baby is born. Who can blame her? We should've taken her days ago."

I looked at the others. "A girl needs her mother." They both nodded.

I sat back in the rocker to wait.

BRETT, KIM, AND Estefan's dad, Carlos, met at our house as Quentin drove up with the girls in his truck, and poor Estefan sat in the passenger side of his own truck, Keith in the driver seat.

Kim put a hand on my shoulder, but there wasn't much to say. The kids were safe. In trouble, of course, but safe. Estefan's dad approached as Keith got out of Estefan's truck. He was a short Hispanic man. Even I towered over him, but what he lacked in stature he made up for with confidence.

"I'm sorry about Estefan," he said. "I don't know what got into him."

"I do," Marta said, grasping Quentin's hand. "The love bug."

Carlos looked surprised and then amused as the truth donned on him. He nodded. He got into Estefan's pickup and started the truck, but before he could leave, the passenger door flew open. Estefan headed straight for Keith.

"Can I talk to Peyton before I go? Please?"

Keith gave him that look that every dad must look forward to giving a boy someday. Estefan didn't shrink though.

He stood up straighter.

"I already told you. I'm sorry, sir. For going along with this. I should've stopped her instead of…"

"Instead of driving her to Pillar Bluff without her parents' permission?" I asked. He gave me a regretful look.

"Yes, ma'am."

I took pity on him, feeling like he'd probably been terrified enough on the two hour drive with Keith.

"Only for a minute," I told him. "You can talk to her just a minute. Your dad looks ready to leave."

He looked frightened. "Yes ma'am. Thank you."

"And Estefan?"

"Yes, ma'am?"

"You might have a driver's license, but you can't just take the girls off two hours away and not check with their parents."

"Yes," he said. "Mr. Black said as much on the way back." I bet he'd said it over and over, too.

"Okay," I said. "Just for a minute." Estefan turned away, his shoulders sagging. Keith started to follow him to the truck where Peyton and Pia still sat, even though Quentin had gotten out. I grabbed his elbow, shook my head.

"What? You want me to let him talk to her alone, after what he just pulled?"

"Yes."

Keith looked doubtful, but walked to where my dad and Quentin stood.

I stood nearby with Kim and Marta. After a bit, Pia climbed out of the truck and shuffled nervously up to her mom. Kim gave me a look and ushered a brooding Pia to their truck where Brett was already waiting in the driver seat.

I snuck a glance at Peyton. She was crying. I paused, ready to swoop in and rescue her, but before I could, Estefan leaned through the window, and their lips touched, only for a split second, but they touched.

I stopped in my tracks, turned around, placing my hands over my mouth. Did all moms feel this way about their daughter's first kiss? Worry? Pride? Even a bit of joy, not that I wanted her kissing boys, but the kiss had obviously been innocent, right in front of their parents! But when I glanced at Estefan's dad, he was busy on his cell phone, Keith and Brett were deep in conversation, and my dad was suspiciously studying a shrub at the edge of the driveway. Only Marta and I had seen. We shared a little smile.

Chapter Twenty-Three

THE NEXT DAY we drove to Pillar Bluff. I suppose I could've gone into labor on the way there, but it was where I'd be having the baby anyway, so I wasn't really being risky by traveling. Peyton was grounded for a few days, but we weren't monsters. We'd obviously underestimated her desire to see her mom. Even though she was happy, if it were me, when it was me, I'd visit my mom every day, and definitely if my dad wouldn't have taken us, Marta and I would've taken ourselves.

"I'm kind of scared," Peyton told her dad as we stood at the front desk.

When Peyton had driven there with her friends, they weren't allowed in. It wouldn't have been a good idea, not knowing how Violet would have been without Keith and I there, too.

"Don't be afraid," Keith told her. "Nothing to worry about."

I watched as Peyton wrote her name on the registry. She turned around and faced the rest of us.

"Yes, but seeing her here is not like her being at our

house. This is such a sad place. It feels weird."

"It'll be fine. Your dad will be right beside you, and I'll be here if you need me. Just come get me."

"Okay. Here goes nothing."

I smiled, proud and worried. She followed her dad around the corner and I took a seat on a stiff couch in the lobby. No matter how many times Keith and I'd been there to see Judy, I would never get used to it. I was just settling my purse beside me when I heard the sobs. You know the kind where the person can hardly even catch their breath because their grief is just so deep and wide?

I hurried toward those sounds, right past the nice lady at the sign in desk. Peyton came around the corner the same time I got there. My heart tearing, I reached for her. She brushed them away, stopped and turned in a circle.

"Honey," I said, stepping closer. "What is it?"

"It's so different than hanging out with her at home, Mandy. It is like a hospital." Her words were a flood of pain and surprise. "There is metal everywhere and it's like a prison." She wailed. "And it smells. How could my dad let her stay in this place?" She melted in a puddle on the floor, and she looked more like a toddler than a girl almost fifteen.

I caught her up, big as she was, big as I was, and held her tight, whispering to her that it was okay. She would be fine. I would be there for her. I'd been there before, a girl nearly her age having to see her mother in such a sterile, cold place.

The lady behind the desk approached us, handed Peyton

a tissue.

"Now, darling. My name's Nancy. You just come sit in here until you're ready." She walked us into a little waiting room. "Now, your Daddy is in there with Judy, Peyton. He's gonna stay there, and if you decide to come in, you can. If you want to wait until another day, you can. No pressure." She looked at me and said under her breath. "Bless that poor baby's heart."

Peyton nodded, and I wished I'd had a Nancy when I was a girl visiting my mom.

"Thank you." I said. We each drank a cold Pepsi Nancy brought us before Peyton finally stood. She held her breath a minute and then spoke.

"Mandy. Will you go with me?" She had found her voice again. "I know it's silly since I've met her before, but I feel so nervous."

"Of course, baby." I held my hand out and she slipped hers inside. "I won't let you go without me this time."

We walked down that hall together until we got to Judy's room.

She looked at me, her uncertainty reminding me of the moment when I put my wedding veiled hat on her pretty head at my wedding. I wished I had that thing with me, because she needed something to protect her, but all she had today was her dad, and me.

"You ready?" I asked. "Once you are inside the room, you'll notice other things besides all the hospital stuff. It's really a happy room, once you look around. She's comfortable, I promise."

"Really?"

"Yes. It's okay," I said. "You're the strongest person I've ever met, Peyton. You can do this, and you'll be glad you did."

She smiled, still unsure, but stepped across the threshold.

INSIDE, JUDY, DRESSED in one of her fringe-trimmed rodeo queen outfits, was sitting on her bed. Keith was seated at the little table in the corner drinking water from a purple tea cup. It made Peyton smile, albeit a bit wobbly. Her eyes were glued to Keith's, afraid to look at her mother sitting on the edge of the hospital-looking bed.

"Girl. You came!" Judy exclaimed.

Peyton's eyes grew wide.

"Sweet girl," Judy said. "And there's baby."

Peyton turned, her mother wasn't looking at her, but at the picture of Peyton and Stevie on the desk.

Peyton whispered to me. "Did you give her that?"

"No. She had it already when we found her here. When your dad found her."

That made Peyton smile a little more, but it quickly faded. Her lips trembled. This was not the mother she'd dreamed would come back someday, and it would take some getting used to, definitely more than two visits. I wanted to help, but I followed Keith's lead and went to sit down beside him.

"That little girl in that picture, she's my girl," Judy said.

Peyton stared at her in the way that a kid might stare agape at a stranger, only I didn't chastise her. She stood, her little body shaking, and I was sure that girl's knees were going to buckle.

"My girl, my cowgirl, used to cry when she was tired, but you know what I told her?" She looked at Peyton then.

Peyton gave a slight shake of her head.

"Cowgirls don't cry," Judy said.

But they do.

Peyton didn't cry, though. She smiled.

"My mom, I mean you, used to say that to me, too," she said, her voice shaky.

I glanced at Keith. He nodded.

Peyton stepped close to the bed. Judy was looking at her in that way where she cocked her head sideways like a child. Peyton was looking at her the same way, and then I saw the resemblance in Judy. That mouth, the perfect nose, the olive skin. Judy's eyes widened for just a moment, and Peyton's did, too. I wondered what was going on in both of their confused minds. Judy continued to look at Peyton, her eyes wide, but Peyton regained her composure and gently sat down beside her mother. Her mother rested her hands on either side of her and I knew she wasn't there right now. Her mind did that, wandered off into places we had no idea about. It was probably just as well, because that was when

Peyton reached up and awkwardly wrapped her arms gently around her mother, rested her head on her mother's shoulder and stayed there. After a while, a long while it seemed, Judy raised one hand and began to pat Peyton's hand. Her eyes were far, far away, but Peyton's were looking in the dresser mirror at the image of herself with her mother. It was sad, but also precious.

When Peyton glanced at Keith and then at me, I held up my cell phone, a question in my eyes. She nodded, and I snapped a picture of those two. At the exact same time, Judy turned to stare at her daughter. I don't know if she recognized Peyton or not, but when we looked at the picture later on, there was a slight smile on Judy's face.

"I WANT TO call her Judy," Peyton said.

We were back home and I was busy cleaning the house and obsessively checking my hospital bag. It would be any time now. I would not be able to chaperone Peyton's dance that was for certain.

"That's what she calls herself," Peyton said. "So I'll call her that. She won't understand why I'd call her mom."

"I think that's a good idea," I said, proud of her sudden maturity.

Over the last couple days, she opened up about how she felt, and she found little ways to deal with what was obviously a complex and difficult truth about Judy. Sometimes, she jokingly called her dad, "Cowboy Man," which made us all laugh, mostly because it made her laugh. Once she walked into the kitchen in one of her mother's old rodeo outfits when Kim came to pick her up for another visit to Cottonwood Manor. We had all stopped talking, stunned. It was almost as if Judy, as Violet, had walked in, so striking was the resemblance to Judy's younger, healthier self. Keith had told her she looked beautiful and Kim had given her a gentle hug.

Over the past week, she seemed to be at peace with Judy's situation, although we couldn't be sure. It was still pretty early, but it appeared that she wanted to see the silver lining of it all.

"Let's go comb the horses," I said when she was having a really good day.

"Are you sure you feel up to it?" Peyton looked doubtful.

"I'm sure. As long as we don't have to ride them."

Peyton giggled. "Luckily you have a good excuse not to continue our lessons, but after that baby is here, we're going to try again." I nodded my agreement, although inside I wasn't sure I would ever be any good at riding horses.

"Honey, I'm so sorry I can't come to your dance tomorrow night. I really wanted to boogie with you kids."

She laughed. "Trust me, it's okay if you don't come."

I chuckled at her meaning. "So you don't need me to send Aunt Marta in my place?"

"Please, no," she said. "I am a big girl. I'm almost fifteen."

"You've been saying that for the past nine months, sweetheart."

She giggled. "I know, but soon it will be true."

Out in the barn, we ran the large round brushes along the horses' sides and backs. There was even a special brush for combing their manes, which always made me think of Marta and combing the manes of our Barbie horses when we were kids.

"Peyton, there's something I want to share with you."

"Uh-oh. Is it bad?"

"No. Well, yes. It is not good, but it's not bad anymore. It doesn't have anything to do with you, Stevie, or your dad, but I just think that if we're a family, you should know some things about me that I don't usually share with many people."

"Sure," she said, rubbing the comb over the horse's mane. I tried to relish this moment, knowing that not every moment with Peyton was going to have this oneness we were currently feeling, but I wished the subject matter wasn't so difficult to talk about.

"Well, to start with, this isn't the first time I've been pregnant." Her eyes widened as I told her all about my other babies, and especially about the baby I held for a little while. She was crying by the time I finished and I hated to break her little innocent heart, but I felt it was the right thing, to tell her.

"Sarah," she whispered. "Baby Sarah. It's like I almost

had a sister."

I smiled.

"I love that name." She hiccupped.

I did too. I named her after the nurse who sat silently outside the door of my room as I said goodbye to my baby. Nurse Sarah was older, probably close to retiring, and had been there through it all beginning to end. I'll never forget how when it was over, she had touched my shoulder, assured me that God was still in his heaven and that Sarah was with him.

"So," Peyton said, blinking back tears, looking at me over the back of Lizzie. "Is the reason you're telling me this because you might lose your baby, the way you lost Sarah?"

"Oh no, baby girl, that's not why." I ran the comb over the pretty paint horse's back. "Well, maybe, but I have a good feeling about it. It's different than all the other times before."

Wow, I sounded like my dad. I guess all his preaching had gotten to me, but now, as I thought about Peyton or Stevie, or the baby I was carrying going through life with no faith, I could see why Daddy never gave up on me and my shaken faith. He had always been bound and determined to pray me back to it. And besides, I wanted Sarah to have a heaven.

"How do you know this baby will be okay?"

I patiently explained all the things that had happened, even the medical details. She took it all like a mature person, which also amazed me. While I believed kids needed to be protected, I was seeing with Peyton that we didn't need to treat her like a child. She really was growing up.

"I'm going to pray for your baby," she said.

Ah, so Daddy had been teaching her, too. I smiled.

"Did Grandpa Marshall tell you that sometimes prayers are answered in ways we don't understand? Like when I prayed for my momma to get well and she didn't."

Peyton stared. "Pia's mom said your mom was sick and that's why she died. That's so sad." Her eyes held compassion.

"What did Kim say was wrong with her?"

"Schizophrenia." Peyton gave me a sympathetic look. "That's as sad as Alzheimer's."

"Yes. It is."

"Our mothers were so young. Is it true that your mom, you know…?"

"Took her life?"

She nodded.

"I don't know. Daddy said she didn't know what she was doing. Maybe she did it to get away from the voices in her head."

"Maybe it was like my mom leaving us. Maybe she did it because she thought it was the right thing."

"Maybe. I'll never know."

"If she knew about her disease, do you think it was the right thing for her to do?" Peyton asked.

I shrugged. How many times had I asked myself that same question?

"I don't know, honey. What do you think?"

"No," she said. "I don't think it was the right thing to do. You would have been better off with your mother in your life, even if she was sick and in a home."

I smiled. "The same as you?"

"Yes. I don't agree with what my mom did." Her eyes glistened, but she didn't cry.

"Peyton," I said. "You amaze me, honey. You know, you don't have to be strong all the time. It's okay to cry."

"As they say, cowgirls don't cry."

"Peyton, about that."

She giggled. "It's just something that my mom and dad always said, but I know it's okay to cry. Right now, I'm just fresh out of tears."

I stared at her as she combed and loved on Lizzie.

"That's okay," I said, rubbing the back of my flannel sleeve across my eyes. "Being pregnant with this baby makes me an emotional wreck. I have enough tears for both of us."

She laughed, looking all the world like her father at that moment.

"You know what I think?" Peyton said.

"What's that?"

"I think God brought you and me together because we'd understand what each other was going through. I mean, think about it. What are the chances that my mom would have early-onset Alzheimer's and yours had schizophrenia, and they both decided to leave us—and both in this small town?"

"But you found yours," I said.

"*You* and Dad found her," she said.

The horse before me nickered.

"Mandy, do you think the same thing will happen to us?"

I stared at her. She was utterly beautiful in that moment and while I wanted to believe that it wouldn't happen to her, I wasn't sure. I prayed that it wouldn't. I opened my mouth in answer, not sure what would come out.

"I don't think I want to know," she said. "Is that okay?"

I smiled, nodded. She went back to combing her horse, her eyes still bright with hope, despite the toppling of her childish fantasies. I wanted her to stay that way forever, to protect her from any harm that befell her, tear down every wall that stood in her way, and shield her from any pain that threatened her happiness. I didn't care if she was my stepdaughter in the eyes of the world. In my heart, she was my daughter.

So, this was the feeling of parental love that Momma felt for me. This was how Keith felt about his children, and how Daddy felt for Marta and me. I thought I had known before, but in that moment, I finally understood, and I wondered if on some level it was *this* feeling that made Momma leave Marta and me, to protect us from the pain of seeing her succumb to her disease. I wished for a long moment that I could call her back, tell her I would have survived, just like Peyton was doing.

"I love you, Peyton." I let it slip out. It was just a spontaneous thing that I couldn't have helped if I'd tried.

"I love you, too," she said.

Now, I hadn't been expecting that.

Chapter Twenty-Four

ON THE NIGHT of the prom, we sent Peyton off with Estefan. I was too tired to chaperone just as I'd predicted. Peyton seemed to understand, but I was careful to put extra time into everything she'd need to get ready. I wanted it to be dreamy for her. She spun in a circle, draped in a short, flowing lavender dress that I made – and yes, that was a nod to Judy.

Keith pulled me aside. "You didn't tell me her dress was so short."

"Oh, stop it," I teased. "It is not too short."

Keith looked doubtful, but I could tell he'd handle it. He stepped between her and Estefan as they walked outside. We took lots of pictures, Stevie cried because Peyton would not take him with her, and I cried a little bit when Estefan helped Peyton into the passenger side of the truck like a true gentleman. When Keith called Estefan over before he could escape, Peyton leaned out the window and shot me a worried look. I don't know what Keith said to him, but Estefan's tanned face turned white, even in the fading light. I wanted to save him, but I stayed back. This was a father thing, I guessed. It was exactly what my own daddy had done before every single dance.

"What did you say to him?" I asked.

"Something fatherly," he said.

"Something mean," I said.

He just chuckled and walked in.

I waved them out the driveway and hobbled toward the house behind him and Stevie with plans of taking a nice long bath, but I never made it to the steps.

"Keith?" He turned, his smile faded and he ran to me.

"Are you okay?"

"I am, but…" I glanced down at the ground where a tiny puddle had gathered at my feet. The contractions hit me hard. I had been feeling twinges all day long, but hadn't said anything because they were sporadic. The next one to hit was strong.

He rushed to open the car door. I got in. Slipping into the driver's seat he started the car and backed out of the drive away."

"Keith?"

"Huh?"

"Stephen?" Stevie had already skipped into the house, no idea what was happening.

"Oh yeah." He flung the door open.

"Keith?"

He popped his head into the window.

"While you're getting Stevie, grab my leopard suitcase

beside the bed, and call the doctor before you come back out."

"Okay," he turned and ran.

Even with all that pain, I had to chuckle. For a man who had two children, he was acting like he'd never been through this before, and with all his rodeo trips, I realized he might not have. On the way to the hospital, I called Marta. I knew she would call Daddy.

"Should we call Peyton?" Keith asked.

I looked at him like he was crazy. "Are you nuts? No! Don't ruin her first prom. The baby probably won't even be here before she gets home. Call her in two hours."

"Um, okay." He said.

"What does that mean, um, okay?"

He chuckled.

"What?" I demanded.

"It just means you're going to be one of *those* women when you have the baby."

"What are you talking about?"

"A bossy one."

"I am not, and I order you to stop saying stuff like that. It's ticking me off."

He obeyed, but I saw him grinning ear to ear.

I moaned. "You think this is funny?"

He grew serious. "No, not at all. I'm sorry.

He put his hand on my knee.

"Don't. Touch. Me."

"Daddy? Is Mommy okay?"

"She's fine, honey. She's just having a baby."

In the back seat, Stevie clapped his hands happily. "A baby. A baby. A baby. A baby. A baby."

By the time we reached the hospital in Pillar Bluff, I was more than ready to have that baby, and I think the baby knew. Because it didn't waste any time in coming. I barely remember, it happened so fast after I got there, but besides how quickly the baby came into the world all shiny and new, everything was normal. Marta and our dad didn't even make it in time, so they swung by to pick up Peyton, regardless of what I'd told Keith, and the first time she held her new baby brother, she was still wearing her prom dress.

All my grumpiness gone, I had Marta take a picture of Peyton, Stevie, and little Judson. Peyton, beautiful in her dress, sat in the middle, the baby nestled in her arms, while Stevie leaned in with the kind of grin only a five-year-old could have. Marta snapped the picture and leaned back to admire her niece and nephews.

Peyton smiled down at Judson, looked at me, and said, "He's perfect. Just perfect."

"I'm sorry we ruined your prom," I said.

"Oh, Mandy." She waved it away. "It's my baby brother. No prom is worth missing this."

Keith and I shared a look that said, *our little cowgirl's growing up*.

"A few more days and he would've been born on your

birthday," I said.

"It's okay," she said, staring into his sweet, little face. "He deserves his own little day."

"So do you," I said, still tired and longing for sleep. I guessed I'd be feeling like that for quite a while. "We'll still celebrate your birthday."

She smiled. "Can I invite my mom?"

"Yes," I said. "Invite everyone."

And she did invite everyone. Thank goodness we'd delayed the party a couple of weeks to let me and Judson get adjusted. But Peyton is a smart girl, and when the party came around and the fifteen candles were blown out, she let me know her demands for having a delayed birthday party.

"For my birthday," she told the small crowd of teenagers. "All I want is my Mom, Mandy, to let me teach her to ride. I'll give her a few months to prepare, but she's going to ride with me."

I must have looked shocked because the room broke out in laughter, but at that moment, I was so overwhelmed with the fact she'd called me mom. I would've agreed with anything. Even getting on the back of a large beast that could trample me in a heartbeat.

Chapter Twenty-Five

I DON'T KNOW why I always underestimate God. He really came through for me this time. Motherhood suits me, and I'm not just talking about the baby, either. I'm talking about Stevie and Peyton. I love them so much, and I have banished every Disney DVD with an evil stepmother from our library of home movies.

My kids have an unconventional family, I admit it, but who doesn't? Think about it. Most families don't fit that conventional bill, and whether it is Grandpa living in the guest room or a single mom working double shifts while Grandma babysits, what's important is that the kids know their parents love them. As I watched little Judson wrapped in the blanket I knitted him and saw the way his big brother and sister doted on him, I realized more and more that I no longer cared about what people thought about my divorce, or Judy, or the fact that Stevie called me Mommy and Peyton didn't, even though she did take me and Judson to the mother-daughter banquet at her school a week after he was born. I wanted to do for my kids what my dad did for me, let them know they are loved, loved, loved.

Keith's last ride happened the next year in Tucson. I sat with Peyton behind the chutes, all cowgirl even if I do say so myself. I felt like I finally fit into this crowd just a little bit. I turned back to the chutes, smiling. This time, I had Peyton's camera and Peyton beside me. She squealed. It had been a last minute decision, but Keith and I had surprised her when we checked her out of school on a Wednesday afternoon to head off to the rodeo.

"I can't ride my last time without you," he said.

She had shrieked and hopped up in the truck. "But who's going to help Grandpa and Marta with the kids?"

"They can handle it," I said. "Grandpa has raised two kids already."

She grinned. "But I need my boots, and my suitcase."

"I got everything you need, honey."

She smiled. "Everything?"

I nodded, innocently. "And a few new things, as well, for the special occasion."

"Oh no. Does that mean you're going to make me wear something pink and blingy?"

"Pink? Of course not. Blingy? Well…"

"I saw it," Keith said. "You're going to need sunglasses when you put that shirt on."

In the end, she loved it. It was turquoise blue and was the same as mine. It was blingy, but it had her dad's name emblazoned on the front, so she didn't care.

There was a tent for the families of the cowboys and

cowgirls, but I wanted Peyton and I to be right behind the chutes.

"I guess my mom used to do this a lot." She commented.

"Yes, she did," I said. "Do you remember her barrel racing?"

"No. I guess I was there a few times, but I don't really remember."

"That's okay," I said. "Maybe you'll be next."

"Maybe," she said. She was pretty talented, having made a name for herself at the more local rodeos.

When the time finally came for Keith's ride, Peyton's face filled with excitement, and so did mine.

"Go, Dad!"

The crowd whistled and called out as the chutes clanged and rocked. Keith was up. The announcer made a real big deal over it being Keith's last ride. I wished he'd hush, in case he made Keith nervous, but when I saw Keith's face, I knew he wasn't listening.

"Ladies and gentleman, let's hear it for Keith Black, at his age, he's one of the grandfathers of saddle bronc riding! If that sounds rude, ladies and gentleman, in saddle bronc riding where the competition are all young men, it's a compliment to be called one of the grandpas of the sport." I hoped Keith felt the same way.

I watched as the pickup men took their places and Keith adjusted his hand on the hack rein. He pulled his hat down low, rock music blared over the speaker, and time stood still for just a moment. I shivered, could hear Peyton breathing beside me, the fans around us hummed with excitement, and then the chute gate swung open and there he went on the back of a beautiful black horse that seemed to me appropriate for his last ride.

"Go, Dad!!"

I was torn between photographing him and watching him. I finally decided to hold the button down and just watch. We would see what pictures turned out, but I wasn't missing this firsthand. I had seen Keith ride enough to know that this was his best, maybe ever. The announcer was about to spin off his rocker with excitement as Keith maintained his form, losing his hat halfway through, holding on until that horn sounded at eight seconds and the pickup man plucked Keith from that horse. I thought I was going to pass out.

What a beautiful ride.

Peyton and I screamed, hugged, screamed again.

"Oh, Peyton. I'm so glad you came."

"Me, too," She squealed. "My dad is a superstar."

"He sure is."

She turned around and yelled the same thing to the audience and then we hugged again.

Keith sauntered across the dirt arena, picked his hat up out of the dirt and waved it to the audience. Finding Peyton and I, he waved at us, dropped to his knee, and held his hat over his heart.

"I love you, Dad!" Peyton's voice carried over the crowd.

"I love you." I mouthed.

Before he left, he obliged the announcer and the audience by walking out to the middle of the arena one last time. The last time ever, turning in a circle, saluting the fans, forever grateful, I knew. He held his hat over his heart again to show it and tossed the hat up in the air.

There would be interviews later and parties to go to. Everyone wanted to know what he would do now, the next generation of cowboys wanted to congratulate him, and pictures, boy, did he get tired of the pictures, but the whole time, he just smiled and thanked everyone. I was so proud of that man. Just so proud. It was bittersweet for him, and that night, I think I fell in love with that cowboy all over again, and his daughter, too.

Chapter Twenty-Six

"**A**RE YOU SURE?"

It was the Christmas season and Keith and I sat drinking our coffee. Judson kicked in his high chair. Stevie was still asleep. It was a Saturday morning and he was exhausted from a busy week of first grade.

"I'm sure," I said. And I was. I'd been thinking about this for months now.

One look at his face told me how grateful he was. His relationship with Judy was complex, hard to understand for anyone outside of the family, but nobody else needed to understand. Keith didn't choose this situation, and neither did Judy. Sure, she set it up this way, right or wrong, but she didn't choose the disease. And let's be honest. What is the right thing to do in a situation like this? She was trying to make a plan for Keith and the kids, so they would have a better future. She didn't know they might have had a better future with her still in their lives. She didn't know that Keith wouldn't have divorced her. She only wanted him to be free to find a new wife, a new mother, for their kids. And he had. I was indebted to her for that.

Believe me, I'd gone through all the what-ifs in my mind. What if she hadn't done this and he'd dedicated himself to taking care of Judy. What if we'd never gone out on a date because he wouldn't have been dating? What if it was wrong for us to be married? What if Judy actually wasn't in her right mind when she drew up divorce papers and disappeared, all for the love of her family?

The answer was, there was no answer, but what was I supposed to do? Keith and I had never even discussed it. We weren't getting divorced. We hadn't known any better before, and we loved each other still. No, not still, but even more, after having gone through this.

And what about the kids? The kids definitely didn't ask for this. And this solution? It would be best for them, because right now, what really mattered was the kids and Judy. For the short time she might have left, they deserved to be part of that.

"STOP DROPPING THE presents, Stevie." Peyton stooped to pluck a few brightly wrapped gifts out of the snow.

"Sorry," Stevie said. "I didn't mean to."

"I know," Peyton said, patting him on his head. She was just nervous. It was so obvious. Ever since she found out we were going to see Judy for Christmas, she hadn't been able to concentrate. We hadn't spent Christmas with Judy last year because the weather had prevented us from going all the way to Pillar Bluff."

That morning we had let the kids open their presents, met Marta, Quentin, and Daddy over at the farm for breakfast, and then announced we were all headed over to see Judy.

"On Christmas morning?" Peyton said, disbelieving. "It's snowing outside. I thought you said we were going tomorrow when the weather was better."

Keith shrugged. "I have a truck."

"I know," she said, "But…"

Daddy piped in. "So you don't want to go, Peyton? That's probably good, because I need someone to help me clean up all these dishes."

"Of course, I want to go, Grandpa." She ran to the door and grabbed her coat off the hook.

On cue, we all stood and grabbed our coats, too.

"What about the dishes?" she asked.

"Oh, the dishes." Daddy paused, like he'd forgotten. "We can do them when we get back."

"They'll be gross." She warned. "And why is everyone going?"

We all made various silly excuses, carried the presents for Judy out to the car, Stevie dropping them in the snow, and we all piled into our different vehicles.

Peyton shook her head. "Whatever." Then she rolled her window down. "But hey, wait. There's Pia! And her parents! What are they doing here?" Her cell buzzed. "Hmmm. Pia said they're going to see Judy, too. They're going to follow us. That's nice, isn't it?"

"That's very nice," I said. "I'm glad Brett brought their truck."

"Me, too," Peyton said. "What a long drive in the snow. It's really coming down. Are you sure it's okay to go, Dad?"

"Are you trying to tell me how to drive, cowgirl?" he said, pulling out of the driveway. The snow crunched under the weight of his truck, even sliding a little, which I was sure Keith made happen on purpose. I hid a smile.

We drove for a while, a caravan behind us that Peyton kept turning to look at, but didn't say anything more about it. I guessed she'd accepted that grownups were weird and was glad that Pia was coming along.

"Can we stop somewhere, so I can get in with Pia?"

"Of course," Keith said, even though, unbeknownst to Peyton, there would be no need to stop at all.

"Awesome." She looked down, obviously to text Pia and let her know. She didn't look up as we drove across Castle Orchard and turned up a road just right outside of town. When, just a little bit later, we found a parking spot at our real destination, Peyton looked up.

"What are we doing here?"

She looked out the window. We didn't say anything. We just got out of the truck, Keith unbuckling baby Judson and handing him over to me. Stevie hopped out.

"Come on, Peyton!" He took her hand.

"Everyone else parked near us and walked across the

parking lot towards the entrance. Peyton just stood there.

"I thought we were going to see my mom."

I placed my arm around her. "We are, honey. We're here."

It all hit her then, the sign that said Lodgepole Manor, the presents, everyone together.

"This is a lovely place," I said.

"She's *here*?" Peyton asked.

Keith grinned. "We arranged with your uncle to have her moved here to this home, so she could be closer to us. Now she'll almost be living just down the road from you."

Peyton smiled ear to ear. I loved when she smiled like that. Then she jumped up and down like a giddy kindergartener. Keith reached out to steady her in case she slipped in the snow.

"Oh, my gosh! Dad! Thank you so much! Thank you." Happy tears ran down her cheeks and I decided once and for all that the saying everyone in this family always quoted was a big joke.

Cowgirls do cry.

JUDY WAS WAITING for her visitors, mostly Cowboy Man, in the lobby. She was dressed in her best white rodeo outfit. The manor had fixed it up to be cozier than usual with poinsettias, Christmas trees, and tinsel. Christmas-themed country music was playing on the speaker and the TV set was tuned into *It's a Wonderful Life*. I had avoided Lodgepole

Manor since Momma had been there, even though Keith and I were supporters, just as we were for Magnolia Manor. Some things were just too hard, but I was over that now. Stronger, tougher, maybe even a little bit wiser. I did whatever I needed to do for my husband and family. Judy was now my family.

Judy's face lit up when she saw us all walking in her direction.

"Oh!" She cried. "Oh! Oh! Oh!"

For a minute we were all worried. She looked like she was going to cry. I thought of the fits she used to have when her brother showed up to see her.

Kim broke away from the group. "Hi, honey." She sat down in front of Judy, who was now looking away into space, seemingly suddenly lost who knew where in a memory from who knew when.

Kim squeezed Judy's hand. "We all came to see you. It's Christmas."

Judy smiled, and then she frowned. She did that a lot. We usually just sat beside her, hoping that somewhere inside, she knew we were there, or that our presence maybe reminded her of some moment of love from people she used to know. There just wasn't really any way of knowing. I didn't know if any of us would ever get used to it, who could? But it was how things were. We made the most of it.

Peyton sat on her other side, held her hand, chatting about what she got for Christmas. Stevie, still too young to know that his funny friend Judy was his mother, sang her Christmas carols he had learned at church in his Sunday school class.

After a while, Judy stood up and walked away. She sometimes did this, too, so we waited until finally Kim went to her room and brought her back.

When she walked back into the lobby, her face lit up, her eyes landed on Keith.

"Hey there, Cowboy Man." She glided toward him, her back straight and her neck long like a rodeo queen. He greeted her with a hug. I knew he'd been hoping for that greeting, because it meant there was some sort of recognition there, even if it was very blurry.

"Judy, I got you a present."

She sat down and pulled the paper back from the gift he handed her. Peyton was smiling. Judy held the old, but still glossy, magazine in front of her. Scrawled across the picture of Violet and Keith from their rodeos was Keith's signature in black Sharpie. We'd forgotten about it, but when we were packing her things up to move her to Castle Orchard, we found it and were reminded of her innocent request for Keith Black to sign her magazine. She ran her fingers over the glossy cover.

"Keith Black signed my magazine?"

"He did," Keith said.

"How'd you get him to do that?" She gazed at him with a wondrous look.

Keith grinned. "Well, I had to pull a few strings, but I managed to get him to do that for you."

"For me?"

"Yes. But only for you, is what he said."

Her eyes lit up and she smiled. "Thank you, Cowboy Man. This is a lovely present." Then she frowned. We waited for her to be lost again, but she looked at Keith and said sadly, "I don't have a present for Cowboy Man. I'm sorry."

He chuckled. "Cowboy Man doesn't need a present. You're a good enough present."

She giggled. "Well, I have no idea what that means."

We all laughed and she looked around, as if seeing us all for the first time, and in her mind I guess she was. She greeted us all again, paying this time, special attention to Peyton.

"I used to know a little girl who looks like you."

"Yes." She said, not letting an ounce of sadness show on her face. "And guess what, Judy. I have a present for you, too."

It was one of those pictures with two holes. I'd helped Peyton choose the rustic western hand carved frame from the shelves of The Southern Pair. I hadn't even done anything to refurbish it because it was beautiful just the way it was. On one side was a picture of Peyton herself on a horse, and the other was of Violet, also on a horse. Violet was very young in her portrait, not much older than Peyton, really.

Judy brightened. "Twins!" Somehow she'd never caught

on that Marta and I were different people, but she thought she and Peyton were twins.

Peyton laughed and agreed, and I wondered again at the grace she exhibited. It was difficult to know how she'd work through this all in the future, after her mom was gone. Maybe she would need counseling, which sometimes I think I could use myself concerning my own momma, but no matter what, the two of us would be there for each other, because like she'd told me, we understood each other's situations.

I watched as after a while, Judy's eyes landed on Judson who was now playing on Keith's lap.

"A baby!" she called.

Keith sat the baby in Peyton's lap as Judy cooed and sweetly made over the baby.

Marta, Kim, and I unpacked some snacks we'd brought for everyone. It wouldn't be Christmas without cookies, now would it? We even shared them with others in the lobby and it warmed my heart, knowing that some of them probably never had visitors, but waited in the lobby all day for their loved ones to come. I always wondered, were their loved ones gone from this earth? Living thousands of miles away, or was it just too painful for them to face a place like Lodgepole Manor? Of all people, I could understand that. I hoped for these people who waited all day every day for them to come, that their loved ones would be able to get over whatever their reasons were and come for a visit.

Marta nudged me with her shoulder as she passed me with a plate of cookies.

"See? This isn't so hard, is it?"

I thought of Mom in this place, and how my heart no longer seized with panic when I came here.

"No, not as hard as I once thought."

"That's my sis." She smiled, hurrying toward a group of older ladies.

"I won!" Stevie, who was playing a game with Brett and Quentin, sat with his hands up in the air, victorious.

I noted that Judy paused to study him curiously before turning back to the baby. I stood back, watching, happy that Judy was having such a good day. When Judson's eyes drooped, Keith took him in his arms and rocked him. This made Judy break into a smile.

My eyes rested on Peyton dressed in a pair of jeans and her new boots next to her mother all decked out in her own boots and fringe, something she'd worn in another era when she was still whole. Her mother was confused, but she held on tightly to Peyton's hand, hanging on the best she could. I thought about how easily Judy had scooped Stephen up, saving him from heavy horse's hooves, perhaps a motherly instinct that had, in a split second, inexplicably risen up out of her disease.

Peyton and Judy looked up at the same time, and anyone could see that they were mother and daughter, and yet, Peyton was my daughter, too. Her and Stevie, gifts given to me, and I realized in one breathless moment that I loved them as much as the little bundle cradled in my husband's arms.

Chapter Twenty-Seven

"OKAY, MANDY. IT'S time for your lesson."

"She stood in the doorway holding a stick with the leather strap hanging from the end. She was dressed in jeans and boots. She was holding a dirty pair of boots in her other hand. I noticed they had spurs.

"But those boots are ugly," I said. She just smiled.

"Come on, Mandy."

"Fine," I said, offering Judson to Marta, who had come over to spend the day with us. My daddy reached out and took him instead, which made Marta pout and me smile.

"At my birthday party, you told everyone you'd let me teach you how to ride a horse," Peyton said.

It was true. In front of twenty people, I'd told her it would be her birthday present.

"But that was ages ago! I think you've had another birthday since then, Peyton. That promise expired."

"Just because you hoped I'd forget doesn't mean I did." She teased.

"You can't go back on your word," Daddy said, cradling Judson in his arms.

"You can't do it, sis." Marta clapped her hands.

"A promise is a promise," Keith said.

"You are enjoying this, aren't you?" I asked.

Keith grinned ear to ear. I was already wearing jeans, so I sat down and pulled on those dirty boots. I spun the spurs. They were a lot smaller than I thought they would be.

Out in the round pen, I worked Lizzie the way I had before, back when I'd ultimately fallen from the horse before it could even take off. Daddy stood back from the pen with Judson while Peyton, Estefan, Aunt Marta, and Stevie all sat on the fence watching.

"You have to let her know you are the boss," Peyton said.

"That shouldn't be too hard for her," Keith called.

I glanced over at him, leaning nonchalantly on the other side of the fence. Oh, that cowboy. He still ignited sparks in me.

"Now, pay attention." Peyton gently chided.

I tried to recall the instructions from last time, before Judson came along. The stick wasn't for whipping, but for guiding her as I directed her to walk in wide circles around the pen. Occasionally, I was to gently let it fall on her flank, but not to hurt her. Boy howdy, was I glad to learn I didn't have to whip her.

"You've seen too many movies," Peyton said. "Okay, now put that down and get on her."

"What?"

Keith hopped over the fence like it was nothing and

walked toward Lizzie and me. He took her bridle while I climbed up, instructed me on how to get my feet in the stirrups, and handed the reins up to me.

"When you want to go right, pull the reins to the right, putting the pressure of this strap on the left side of her neck. When you want to go left, the same." He went through instructions on how to get her to trot, gallop, and stop.

"I'm never going to remember all that," I said.

"We'll instruct you from the fence." He walked away. "Hey, you're leaving me?"

He smiled as he climbed up the fence.

"Okay," Peyton said. "Let's go."

"Okay," I said, pressing my heels into her sides. Peyton assured me the spurs did not hurt her at all.

"She's a big horse. She can't feel it."

"Okay." I tried it again and she took off. There I was walking, eventually galloping around the pen.

"Whoohoo!" Stevie clapped from his place on the fence.

"Whoa, Lizzie. Easy, girl." I walked her for a while, before trotting, galloping, and walking again.

I even walked her in figure eights, but, of course, it was all because of Peyton's excellent training of Lizzie that she did what I said, but I felt in control. I never imagined how no longer being afraid of a horse would make me feel. I didn't fall, the horse didn't run away from me, and I didn't die. I'd say I was pretty successful and free.

I guided her into a trot, and as I moved through the air,

my hair blowing behind me, I listened to the clop of Lizzie's hooves hitting the ground firmly, and I couldn't stop the smile that spread over my face as my heart flew its doors wide open.

"How do you feel?" Peyton called.

"Like a cowgirl," I called back.

"That's because you are, cowgirl," Keith called out.

On a whim, I held my hat over my chest and then held it out to the pretend audience, and then I threw it high in the air.

And the crowd went wild.

The End

Dear Reader,

Love and family are complicated. This novel about those kinds of complexities has been inspired by two things that I feel deserve more attention: Stepfamilies and Alzheimer's Disease, especially Younger/Early-Onset Alzheimer's.

Several years ago I was shocked to see a story in the news about a very young person who was diagnosed with Alzheimer's Disease and it made me wonder what life would be like for that person as they lived their last "good" years. How would their spouse and family feel? What kinds of complications would this add to their relationship? I couldn't stop thinking about it, so what resulted was this novel.

Before I saw that news story, I thought Alzheimer's only happened to elderly people, but according to the Alzheimer's Association's website, five percent of the Alzheimer's population has Younger Early-Onset Alzheimer's in which they are diagnosed young. It can affect people in their 30s, 40s, and 50s.

I am not an expert on Alzheimer's, but I endeavored to be correct as possible to tell the story of Manda, Keith, Violet, and their children. If I have erred in judgment, I did not intend to, but strove to tell a family's story that might entertain, inspire, and hopefully bring attention to this type of Alzheimer's Disease that affects patients much younger than the normal Alzheimer's age. For more information about Alzheimer's, visit http://www.

alz.org/

As for stepfamilies, I have been married to my husband for eleven years and we share three teenaged children, so writing about the love stepparents can have for their children and the complexities dealt with by the children and entire family in this book were not difficult for me to write about. All stepfamilies are different, but it is easier when you have support. I didn't know about it when our stepfamily was first born, but an excellent resource is http://www.stepfamilies.info/

Love and friendship transcend things like the complexities of Alzheimer's and being a stepfamily, both of which, I daresay, aren't situations we dream of when we are looking for a soul mate. My wish for readers is that after reading this novel, you will have a deeper understanding, or at least another reminder, of how true love has no boundaries.

Sincerely,
Tina Ann Forkner

Book Club Discussion Questions

1. Manda doesn't think she will fit into Keith's rodeo lifestyle very well, based on the fact that she is not a real cowgirl and hates riding horses. Keith definitely disagrees. What do you think Keith sees in Manda that she can't see in herself?
2. Keith has two children that Manda is happy to take on as her own. Were you surprised at the love she felt for her stepchildren? What things from her past might have prepared her for motherhood? What things might stand in her way?
3. The novel is set in a small fictional town in Tennessee. In what ways, negative or positive, does the size of the town contribute to the story of Manda and Keith? If you have read Forkner's other novel, *Waking Up Joy*, how does *The Real Thing's* Castle Orchard compare to Spavinaw Junction? Do you have a favorite?
4. Manda has a strong extended family that includes her twin sister and her dad, while Keith's parents are never around. How might this contribute to how they each deal with marriage? Why do you think Manda still goes to Marta for affirmation and advice, instead of to Keith?

5. Manda's relationship with stepdaughter Peyton changes throughout the story. What key scenes contribute to her reconciliation with her stepmother?
6. When ex-wife Violet's truth is finally revealed, did the way you felt about her character at the beginning of the story change? Did you agree or disagree with the decision Violet made about her future without Keith and the kids?
7. Nobody seems more shocked about the truth than Keith. Do you think he bears any responsibility for the decision his ex-wife made?
8. Manda and Keith reach a crossroads in their marriage after they find out the dark truth of why Violet left Keith. How do you feel about how they handle the impossible choice? Would you have made the same, or a different, decision?
9. Manda wants so badly to be the real thing, as is suggested in the novel's title. What are the key events that finally define what the real thing is for Manda?
10. What is the most memorable "thing" or impression that readers might take from this novel?

More by Tina Ann Forkner

Waking Up Joy

Behind every lost dream lies a second chance...

When adored town spinster Joy Talley ends up in a coma after a peculiar accident, she is surprised and incensed to hear what is being said in her hospital room, including plans for her funeral. When she finally wakes, her well-meaning, but bossy, brothers and sisters dismiss her claims, thinking her accident has knocked her off her rocker, but Joy has never felt better, and is determined to set the past right.

Now Joy must face her darkest secret and risk reopening wounds caused by an old flame who rejected her more than twenty years ago. But taking risks brings change, as well as a new, younger man into Joy's life, making her feel like a teenager again. Suddenly Joy's once humdrum life is anything but boring and routine and the future beckons, exhilarating and bright.

Available at your favorite retail store and online everywhere

About the Author

Tina Ann Forkner is a substitute teacher and author of four women's fiction novels including *The Real Thing*, *Waking Up Joy*, *Rose House*, and *Ruby Among Us*. Tina's novel *Waking Up Joy* from Tule Publishing is a Virginia Romance Writers 2015 HOLT Medallion Award of Merit Recipient – Romantic Elements. She grew up in rural Colcord, Oklahoma and currently lives in Cheyenne, Wyoming with her husband and their three teenagers.

Learn more: www.tinaannforkner.com

Thank you for reading

The Real Thing

If you enjoyed this book, you can find more from all our great authors at TulePublishing.com, or from your favorite online retailer.